FOREVER
SILENCED

FOREVER
SILENCED

RICHARD S. COHEN

FOREVER SILENCED

Copyright © 2021 Richard S. Cohen

ARCO EDUCATIONAL SERVICES, LLC

155 Main Street, # 635

Peapack, New Jersey 07977

ArcoEducational@yahoo.com

ISBN 978-1-7375266-1-2 (paperback)

ISBN 978-1-7375266-0-5 (ebook)

Cover and Interior Design by We Got You Covered Book Design

WWW.WEGOTYOUCOVEREDBOOKDESIGN.COM

FOR MY FAMILY AND FRIENDS

ONE

A LOUD THUD echoed as a body hit the ground. An ear-piercing siren followed and guards came sprinting from every direction.

Curious, Dr. Willem Gerhardt hopped off his cot and rushed to the front of his jail cell. As he peered out between the steel bars, he used his hand as a visor to shield his eyes from the blinding strobe lights illuminating the entire west wing. In the distance, rival gang combatants were separated and quickly escorted toward, "Dark Cubicles," an area long designated for those requiring solitary confinement.

After several minutes, all guards had returned to their assigned stations—except for one, who remained seated in the hallway, reading a newspaper he held high above of him. Whistling between his teeth, he nonchalantly flipped through crinkled pages of **The Houston Post** as the plastic wrapper, from his freshly eaten muffin, crackled as it unraveled beneath him.

Squinting, Dr. Gerhardt managed to read the front page headline.

DOCTOR WILLEM GERHARDT OFFICIALLY CHARGED

He stepped back for a moment, mumbling a few curse words,

before biting down on his knuckles. After releasing his clenched jaw, he examined teeth imprints left behind. As he sat back down on the cot, images of his River Oaks home entered his mind. He recalled times in his backyard when he would recline on a soft cushioned lounge chair, puffing away on an aromatic pipe packed with cherry-vanilla tobacco and a pinch of black licorice—his very favorite concoction. He closed his eyes for a moment and slowly sucked in air from his pursed lips, pretending to take a drag. Exhaling, he envisioned himself sitting poolside, clouds of smoke rings around him. He could practically hear the sound of bubbling water from the Jacuzzi. Images of beautiful hibiscus and breathtaking bluebonnets flashed before him— as did the large display of colorful stones that he, together with friends, had stacked around the State of Texas-shaped fountain bordering the pool.

"Home-sweet-home," he muttered before reopening his eyes.

A media feeding frenzy swarmed on the outer part of the penitentiary courtyards as dozens of police officers stood beside their idling cars by an area that had been roped off for reporting purposes. As helicopters circled the skies, news correspondents flooded the street, placing microphones beneath chins of shocked bystanders who spoke personally of Dr. Gerhardt—a renowned psychologist and longtime resident of River Oaks. Most pointed out his distinguished family lineage—he being the son of Elizabeth Gerhardt—daughter and sole-heiress of the late billionaire oil tycoon, Alvin Gerhardt.

While much of his early childhood had been defined by loss and transition, nothing had prepared Dr. Gerhardt for sudden confinement. He lifted his forehead from the base of his sweaty palms and swallowed hard, grappling with the reality of his new home, at least for now—East Texas State Penitentiary. This was not the way he had envisioned his life at the age of forty-five. He lay back upon his unforgiving stiff cot and reflected back in time.

TWO

THIRTY-SEVEN YEARS PRIOR

THE SOUND OF a bullhorn reverberated. At least, in her less than vigilant state, she thought the ring emanating from the phone was a bullhorn. Her head snapped up from the pillow. But beyond her trembling shadow, she could not see a thing. Regaining partial cognizance, she felt relieved to have awakened before the tsunami crashed upon her as she surfed in shark-infested rivers along the edge of the moon. Unnerved by the endless ringing, she wondered who could be calling at such an early hour. She jerked herself upright, tossed the quilt aside and tugged several times on the beaded cable until the lamp lit up. Through blurry eyes, she looked toward the clock. Gasping, she nervously acknowledged the time, 6:33.

Who is it? she wondered. Goose bumps formed on her arms as her curiosity rapidly escalated into a state of panic. Clawing toward the phone, she opened her mouth wide, trying to catch her lost breath. She froze for a moment, recalling the last time the phone rang at such an early hour and the ever so dreaded reason. That was four years ago, on October 26th, 1976 to be exact. Not quite this early, but now more than ever, playing heavy on her mind. She recalled the robust voice of the officer who had called to provide specifics of the fog-related car accident on Interstate 10 that had taken the lives of her parents.

She placed the pillow behind her, using it as a cushion to separate her stiffening back from the rock-hard bedpost. Indecisive, conflicting thoughts vacillated between the pros and cons associated with lifting the receiver. Squinting, she gazed toward the clock. Twisted numbers, italicized in neon green, glared back, 6:34. She snatched up the phone and pressed it firmly to her ear. Without saying a word, she just listened as if she were a young child capturing ocean sounds from a seashell.

"Hello?" a female voice, unfamiliar to her, echoed from afar. "Can you hear me?"

"Yes," she whispered back. "May I help you?"

"I am looking to speak with Ms. Elizabeth Gerhardt."

"This is Beth," she said, swallowing with a gulp.

"I am sorry to call so early this morning. My name is Cara."

C-a-r-a? Ms. Gerhardt repeated under her breath, wincing in confusion. Thoughts raced in quick succession in her mind about her parents, police, friends, neighbors and distant relatives. Her throat narrowed as she struggled to swallow thickened saliva. Once again, she glanced in the direction of the clock.

"Ms. Gerhardt?"

"Yes, Cara? What is it?"

"I've got some wonderful news for you," Cara said with excitement. Ms. Gerhardt exhaled during a moment of relief.

"I am here at The Texas Adoption Resource Center. We have your son. He's here with us, now. I'm sorry for calling this early. It's a long story for another time, perhaps."

"Thank you," Ms. Gerhardt said in her distinct southern twang. As her eyes filled with tears, she eased her grip on the phone and reached for a tissue.

"I do apologize for calling so early and on such short notice. Unfortunately, I am not able to go into detail. We do need for you to pick your son up today."

"Today," Ms. Gerhardt repeated, rejoicing. "Today..."

THREE

MS. GERHARDT ENTERED the blue-painted room and walked over to the bed where she rolled her palms along silky sheets before reflexively patting down both satin pillows, one at a time. A slinky box and Stretch Armstrong action figure were set by the foot of the bed, both unopened, original tags attached. Smiling, Ms. Gerhardt cupped her hands to her waist and inhaled deeply, feeling so ready to replace meaningless years of emptiness with a lifetime of love. Her own family was about to begin.

Lightheaded, Ms. Gerhardt held onto the banister as she side-stepped down the stairway. In the foyer, she plucked lint from her sweater and sprayed a zesty lemon-scented perfume onto her forearms before rubbing her wrists together. Once in her driveway, she hopped into her Mercedes and positioned herself in a comfortable driving position while turning the knob on the radio dial. Through static, she heard a Frank Sinatra song. After turning the dial a notch further, she stopped at the Bee Gees, "Too Much Heaven." A smile graced her lips, listening to the song she adored.

On her way, she sang along while tapping her fingers on the steering wheel in a drum-like manner. As her eyes drifted from the roadway, she saw colorful trees, bluebonnets and caught a glimpse of three rabbits—two larger sized and one much smaller. *Perhaps parents and their precious baby,* she thought, her smile widening.

THIRTY MINUTES LATER

Ms. Gerhardt pulled up to the guardhouse at the entrance of The Texas Adoption Resource Center where she was greeted by an officer whose head hung out from a glass partition.

"Identification, please," he shouted, waving a clipboard toward her car before stepping out and approaching her open window.

"Of course," Ms. Gerhardt said, closely examining the plastic photo badge dangling beneath his wrinkled shirt pocket. She reached toward the passenger seat for her purse.

"How can I help you this fine morning?" he asked, studying her driver's license through thick reading glasses. "You do know we are closed, now."

Nervously, Ms. Gerhardt said, "Please let Cara know I am here." Then more confidently said, "She is expecting me."

"Elizabeth Gerhardt," he muttered, bringing the license closer to his widened eyes. Above his ovals, he looked back toward her. "You certainly are a young looking thirty-seven."

"Why, thank you," she said, feeling uneasy, but at the same time flattered. *Kind of creepy,* she decided.

"And, you said you're looking for Cara?" he rhetorically asked, handing back her license. After a few awkward silent moments, he pressed a green circular button to open the gate.

"You smell very nice, by the way," he said, winking. "You remind me of my barefoot days in Argentina breathing in the joys of life beneath the heavens of lemon trees."

"Oh," Ms. Gerhardt said, nodding. As the gate lifted, she breathed a sigh of relief and followed the narrow driveway set between grass fields and a stream. After pulling up to the tall administration building, she parked in-between an unoccupied security car and a bright red van covered in emblems shaped in the form of Texas. She applied another coat of lipstick and puckered her lips in the mirror before dropping a tissue with an imprint onto the center console. Shaking with excitement, she hopped out of her car and then nodded up toward the sky, acknowledging her faith.

"It's time," she muttered. "It's time."

The administration building was six-floors high. Originally built in the 1930s, it had previously been a hotel, centrally located on the well-manicured estate of bright green grass surrounded by trees. Two separate walking paths encircled the property and joined together near the rear at a lily pad-covered duck pond, a haven for frogs.

Ms. Gerhardt strutted across the parking lot toward the front of the building and made her way up the stone steps that led to the entrance door. Midway, she stopped for a moment and looked up, noticing the only lit room on the third floor. Arching her neck, she stared more attentively at a third story window where a young boy looked out through small circles he had created with his hands cupped together in the shape of binoculars. Pretending not to notice, she looked away and continued along the looping steps.

Upon arriving at the entrance, she opened an old wooden door to the sound of a loud creak and stepped into the poorly lit lobby. Hesitant, yet excited, she looked around the musty-smelling, dark room as the door slammed shut behind her. Startled, a maintenance worker jumped up from an old desk, holding a dripping cup of coffee in one hand and a large walkie-talkie in the other.

"Hello," he called out. "Can I help you?" He cleared his throat as he spoke. His next words were garbled due to loud static resonating from his walkie-talkie.

"Yes, I am looking for Cara—"

"She will be right with you," he interrupted, turning down the volume. "Are you Ms. Gerhardt?"

"I am…I am," she said, breaking into a smile.

"And, you're looking for Cara?" he said beneath his breath.

"Yes, sir," Ms. Gerhardt said, rising up on her heels. She softly repeated, "I am."

Loud thumping footsteps from the stairwell brought their conversation to an immediate halt. Ms. Gerhardt heard voices, though unable to make out the content. The maintenance worker smiled and took a deep breath, bracing himself for a very special life moment.

"Voilà," he shouted out, pointing toward the bottom of the stairs. Ms. Gerhardt panned to the corner of the room and placed her hand upon her chest. Her blue eyes bulged as her mouth opened wide.

"Ms. Gerhardt, I am Cara," the woman said, "and this is your son, Willem." Smiling, she flipped her wrist and slowly rolled out her palm.

Willem was eight-years-old. He had very fine hair and a slender build. He was wearing a bumblebee T-shirt with matching black shorts and white socks stretched high, just below his kneecaps. A deep, looping centipede-shaped scar curled below his left eye.

Willem leaned his head against Cara's hip. As he peeked out, he gazed in the direction of Ms. Gerhardt.

"It's okay," Cara said, leaning over. "Remember what I told you before." She bent down and whispered into his ear.

"Really," he said, his eyes widening, "Forever??"

"Yes," Cara said, "Forever and ever." She put her hand between his shoulder blades and nudged him forward.

"Mom," Willem called out, "Oh, Mom."

Elated to be referred to as *mom* for the first time, Ms. Gerhardt dropped to her knees. "Willem," she said, reaching out her arms, realizing this moment would be captured and cinematically recorded

9

in her memory for the rest of her life.

Willem sprinted and wrapped his thin arms around her waist as tears of joy evaporated into the warmth of her cashmere sweater.

"You don't have any pets, Ms. Gerhardt, do you?" Cara asked.

"I do not," Ms. Gerhardt said, shaking her head. "Not at this time." She wondered about the nature of the question.

"OK, good," Cara said. "Please reach out if I can be of any help or if you have additional questions." Cara smiled as she made her way back up the stairway.

Ms. Gerhardt stared for a moment at the looping horizontal scar beneath Willem's left eye before pressing her cheek against the top of his forehead. After caressing his face, she rocked him back and forth while wrapping her arms around him. She could not help but to think of her late parents, Alvin and Ellen. All they had ever wanted was for her to be happy and have a family of her own. She was ecstatic, but, at the same time, wished they could be part of this moment. For her, it was as if she had just given natural birth.

"Oh, mom," Willem said, lifting his head up from her stomach. He rubbed his face deep into the smooth texture of her sweater. "O-h-h-h, mom," he whispered.

"My son," she said, kissing his forehead.

Willem cocked his head and looked straight up. "Forever," he said, arching back, squinting.

"Forever!" Ms. Gerhardt repeated in jubilation, squeezing him tighter.

FOUR

MS. GERHARDT TIPTOED across the hallway and pushed the door open. As she peeked into the blue room, she saw Willem snuggled in the blanket, clutching onto his teddy bear that had a deep indentation around its belly where it had been squeezed. An uncoiled slinky was wound around the upper part of the pillow.

She stepped in and made her way toward the side wall. In a swift motion, she yanked the curtains to the side and lifted the window halfway.

"Somebody is tired," she said with a smile, looking back toward him. She leaned to the side for a moment to clap away the window sill soot on her hands.

"Mom," he said before opening his eyes. "I'm only a little tired." His voice was hoarse.

"Good morning, Willem. Rise and shine." Ms. Gerhardt patted her hands on the backside of her Guess jeans, trying to remove the stubborn window sill stains. As she sat on the middle of the bed, she wiggled her fingers through his fine hair.

"You're not wiping window dirt on me," Willem said, leaning away. "Or, are you?"

"Of course not," she said in a purposeful sarcastic tone.

"I'm kidding, mom," he said, giggling.

Ms. Gerhardt broke into a wide smile before leaning down and kissing his forehead.

"Oh, wait," she said, softly. "There just may be a few particles in your hair."

"You're just kidding," he said. "Aren't you?"

"Well, let me have a look, here." She squinted as she raked her fingers through his hair before dropping her eyeballs close to his scalp.

Uncertain, Willem glanced up through the corner of his eyes.

"Yes, I'm kidding," Ms. Gerhardt said. She then asked, "Do you wish?"

"Wish what?"

Ms. Gerhardt stood, and after clearing her throat, she sang, "When You Wish Upon a Star." Her voice was high pitched, though gentle and soothing to the ear. Singing was her form of expression and catharsis, something she hoped to share with Willem. She expressed her emotions best in the songs she sang, many of which she had written herself.

"Wow. Your voice relaxes me," Willem said, tilting his head. His chest expanded as he took a deep breath.

Ms. Gerhardt smiled, serenading him with lyrics as the sun from the half open window lit up her blue eyes. She ended the song in her own way, dramatically producing vibrations from her vocal cords with a falsetto, *Because, I love you-u-u-u.*

Willem looked away, blushing. He loved her voice and, even more, loved the attention upon him. Yawning, he stretched his arms over his head.

"I'm so happy," he said, speaking through a yawn. "And, thank you for the toys." He rolled over and fingered the uncoiled slinky at the head of the bed.

"You're most welcome," said Ms. Gerhardt after finishing the last *u* note. "What kinds of toys do you like?" She asked in a curious tone.

"I like the ones you got me," Willem said, pulling her arm closer. He paused for a moment. "And I also like video games."

"Let me guess. You like Pac Man," she said, smiling, "or, Space Invaders." She chuckled, awaiting his reaction.

"Neither," he said, crinkling his nose.

"Well, whatever it is that you want, just ask," she said, patting him on his upper shoulder.

"Thank you." He planted his puckered lips against her arm.

"Okay—get up," Ms. Gerhardt said. She clapped her hands three times as she stood. "Get yourself up, get dressed and brush those teeth. I'll be downstairs fixing some breakfast."

Willem propped up on his elbow. He rubbed his eyes with the back of his hand, using his pinky nail to dig out crust lodged in the corner of his lid.

"Fine," he said, yawning again. He stretched his arms to the side and then up toward the ceiling.

After making her way down the stairs, Ms. Gerhardt stepped into the kitchen where she flipped on the light switch before grabbing bacon and eggs from the refrigerator. She cracked four eggs above a frying pan and more carefully placed six pieces of bacon on to another. Shaking both pans, she checked the time as the food sizzled above the dimly lit flames.

The fresh aroma of bacon, reminded her of Sunday mornings back when she was a young girl, eating breakfast with her family. The faces of her parents flashed before her eyes. In her mind, she heard their voices and recalled special moments once shared.

I wish they could be here now, she thought, reflecting back. She reminisced about the past and what she looked back upon as, *the good ole days.*

"Is breakfast ready?" Willem asked, standing at the top of the stairs.

Startled, Ms. Gerhardt snapped back to the present.

"Yes, please come on down." Sighing in deep thought, she pulled the stool out from beneath the counter.

Willem ran across the kitchen and jumped up on the wooden stool. "Cool," he said, spinning around.

"Do you like to read?" Ms. Gerhardt asked as she made her way back to the stove.

"Sometimes," Willem said, shrugging. He leaned forward and lifted the newspaper from the marble countertop.

"Comics?" she asked.

With a sourpuss expression, he stuck out his tongue and shook his head, *no*.

Ms. Gerhardt stepped toward the counter, a pan in one hand and a glass in the other. "So what do you like?"

"Dunno," he said, burying his head deeper into the Obituary section of **The Houston Chronicle**.

Alarmed, yet acting calm, Ms. Gerhardt looked over his shoulder. "Are you reading anything interesting?" She asked, trying her best to remain nonchalant.

"Not really," he said, flattening the page creases, "just the dead people part." As he scooted up on the edge of the stool, he closely examined the photos above each write-up.

"Have your breakfast with more cheerful thoughts," she said, pushing the Comics toward him. "Humor is the best way to start the day."

"This is kind of interesting, though," he explained, pushing the Comics to the side. He turned to the next Obituary page and focused on more photos.

Ms. Gerhardt stopped in her tracks and looked down. "And what is it that you find just s-o-o interesting?" Her eyes widened, awaiting his response.

"Well, ya know—" he said.

"I know what?" She asked, interrupting as she leaned forward.

"Just about people who die," he said, sounding fascinated. "They always die in alphabetical order."

"Oh, no," she chuckled. "Honey, it's—"

"I know, I know," Willem said, cackling. "I was kidding, mom." He bounced on the stool, tickled by his own sense of humor.

Ms. Gerhardt loosened her lips and forced a grin of her own. "You are truly something," she said, using a spatula to slide a pair of sunny-side-up eggs onto his plate. In deep thought, she poured cranberry juice into a tall glass.

"Aren't you going to eat, too?" He asked, hoping she'd join him.

Ms. Gerhardt walked over to the stove, thinking about *Obituaries*, before returning to the counter with two plates in hand.

"Of course, I am going to eat with you," she said, exuding enthusiasm. "Do you really think I would ever let you eat alone?" She smiled while elbowing him gently on the shoulder in a comforting way while aligning the plates on placemats.

"Good. I don't like to eat alone," he said, sighing. "But, I guess I'm used to it."

Her wide smile suddenly dimmed as she poured orange juice into another glass that had, River Oaks, written on it. *How unfortunate*, she thought, her lower lip curling over her upper.

During times like these, she only wished she had been given more information about his background. There was so much she did not know. So many questions raced in her mind, though she continued to bite her tongue.

"Well, you won't be eating alone, anymore." After a moment of silence, she began to sing, "Let It Be."

"The Beatles," Willem shouted out, giggling. "Let's rock with some Van Halen." He drummed with his index fingers and playfully bobbed his head in an exaggerated way.

Ms. Gerhardt had a pleasant look of surprise, realizing that Willem had not been overly sheltered in his previous life. In a dramatic way, she sang out lyrics from the song, "Romeo Delight," to which he sang along with her.

As they ate breakfast, Willem hummed. Ms. Gerhardt remained pensive, taking small bites of food, thinking, *I wish I knew more.* After gulping down her last sip of juice, she turned her stool toward him.

"Are you okay, mom?" Willem asked, appearing puzzled.

"Yes, honey," she said. "How is your breakfast?"

"Yummy," Willem said. He rubbed his stomach and took a sip from his glass.

"So, tell me what happened to your eye?" Ms. Gerhardt blurted out. She examined the scar and rolled her index finger along his upper left cheekbone.

Willem swallowed hard before dropping his head.

"I dunno," he whispered, hoping she would change the topic.

"You know what," she said, pleading, "I really want to know more about you."

Willem set his glass down. "What do you mean?" He asked, staring back at her.

Ms. Gerhardt turned the other way while clearing her throat.

"Well, you know," she said. "What you like? What you don't like? What makes you happy? What makes you sad? You know—stuff like that."

Willem chomped off another piece of bacon with his front teeth and stretched his legs out from the stool as if he were pedaling on a stationary bicycle.

"I want to get to know more about you, too," Willem said, smiling with a closed mouth. "What you like. Or, don't like. If you are happy or if you're sad." He giggled before swallowing.

Ms. Gerhardt pinched his cheek and stood from the stool. She then wiggled her finger on the inside of his ear.

Smiling, Willem leaned away. As he turned back, he said, "Stop it."

In this instance, she sensed that *stop* meant *tickle me more*. After all, he was ticklish and loved attention upon him. She tickled him by his waist. As he tried to tickle back, Ms. Gerhardt brushed away a small crumb from his lower lip and gave him a hug. She pushed her stool to the side and walked to the other side of the kitchen where she stood over the sink as hot water filled to the brim. She slipped her hands into large yellow rubber gloves and squeezed several drops of green liquid from a plastic soap dispenser. A loud stream of water poured down from the faucet as they engaged in small chat. Willem walked over to the sink and dropped his egg-stained plate into the bubbling soapsuds. He then returned to the stool and rested his cheek flat against the counter.

Concerned, Ms. Gerhardt pressed the faucet lever downward, putting an immediate stop to the running water.

"What's wrong, Willem?" Her voice dropped to a whisper. She removed her rubber gloves, one at a time, and then pressed the lever tighter to stop the wasteful drip.

Willem turned his head and put his other cheek down upon the counter. As he covered his eyes, he let out a sniffle. Ms. Gerhardt walked over to take a closer look at him. At first, she thought he may be joking. But when she tried to tickle him, Willem jerked his body to the side and let out a grunt.

"Stop," he said. His stoic demeanor and brisk tone suggested annoyance. "Parents," Willem shouted out. His arms flopped to the side in a deadweight manner.

"But, I am your parent, Willem," Ms. Gerhardt said in a reassuring way. "I am your mom." She pulled the top of his head toward her. "What's the matter?" She rested her face on the side of his forehead.

"Your parents," he said, snapping up.

"What about my parents?" She asked, shrugging her shoulders up high. "Please, tell me," she begged him.

"They died," he said, then more softly said, "in a car accident." He slammed his hand down on his knee and cried.

As Ms. Gerhardt gasped, her mouth opened wide. Frozen for a moment, she was unable to think. As blood rushed to her head, she braced herself between the stool and the counter.

"Oh, no, they were not supposed to say anything to you." Ms. Gerhardt shook her head in utter disgust. "What exactly did they say? And, what else did they tell you?" She clutched on to the stool with both hands, speaking as fast as she possibly could.

"Nothing," he murmured, using the cuff of his sleeve to wipe away tears. He stopped crying for a moment and glanced back toward her.

Ms. Gerhardt dropped her fist down on the table and let out a deep, prolonged grunt. She reached for the phone and turned the rotary dial.

"Willem," she said, "please go on upstairs." Exhaling, she said, "I'm calling Cara to find out what this is all about."

Willem hopped off the stool and walked briskly across the hallway. He marched up the stairs, turning back every other step, eavesdropping on the phone conversation. After dragging himself up the full flight of steps, he stood at the top where he rested his chin on the uppermost banister.

"Yes. I need to speak to Cara." Ms. Gerhardt spoke in a loud, demanding tone. She paced in circles around the kitchen, maneuvering around the tangled phone cord as an operator said, "please hold." The water made a gurgling sound as Ms. Gerhardt delivered more dishes into the sink. Upstairs, Willem leaned over the banister with his hand cupped around his ear.

"Cara! It's Ms. Gerhardt, Willem's mother."

"Oh, yes, what can I do—?"

"Well, I am extremely concerned," Ms. Gerhardt said, interrupting.

"What's going on?" Cara asked. Her intonation sounded just as concerned.

"Well, I was astonished to find out that Willem was privy to a lot of personal information about me and my family."

"Pardon me? I'm not sure what you mean."

Ms. Gerhardt twirled the dangling phone cord for a third time around her forearm. She walked over to the sliding glass door where she moved the blinds to the side before looking out to the backyard.

"When I completed the paperwork years ago," Ms. Gerhardt said, "I was under the impression that the information would be kept confidential and used only for the adoption process." She tugged the wooden handle and slid the door open.

"That is correct," Cara acknowledged.

After a moment of silence, Ms. Gerhardt said, "Well, Willem knows everything."

"Everything?" Cara repeated, sounding perplexed. After a moment, she said, "Just what do you mean?"

"Well, he knows all about my background." Realizing he may be nearby, listening, Ms. Gerhardt paused mid-sentence and stepped outside. After swiping away sweat from her forehead, she then continued, "He knows about my parents and about the car accident."

"I'm not sure what to tell you, Ms. Gerhardt. All I can say is that his file has never left my hands."

Dissatisfied, Ms. Gerhardt stepped back inside and slammed the sliding glass door behind her.

"Okay, thank you," Ms. Gerhardt said, ending the phone call in a rushed, yet polite manner. She hurried toward the staircase, maintaining a frenetic pace as the wooden floors creaked beneath her. From the bottom of the staircase, she looked up and saw Willem sprint toward his bedroom where he slammed the door behind him. He then pushed the door forward a bit, leaving it open just a crack.

Ms. Gerhardt shuffled her way up the stairs and walked in a no-nonsense manner across the hallway. She ignored Willem's curious eyes, peering out through the narrow slit by the door hinge. After opening the hallway closet door, she looked down at two large boxes filled with important documents, photographs and detailed write-ups surrounding the tragic car accident. She bent down and examined each box, one at a time, both of which were still sealed with tape, no signs of tampering.

"Did you go into the closet, Willem?" She asked, her voice projecting toward his bedroom.

Willem opened the bedroom door, an inch at a time.

"No, mom," he said, stuttering, "I did not." He walked with small steps toward her, his head dipped downward.

Baffled, Ms. Gerhardt shook her head and sighed. "You really didn't go into the closet?"

In a soft voice, he said, "No".

Ms. Gerhardt turned away for a moment and then looked back toward him through the corner of her eyes.

Willem shook his head several times and emphatically said, "No-o-o."

Ms. Gerhardt felt a nervous sensation in the pit of her stomach. A long held *Gerhardt value* was trust. And she felt as though it was already being tested. Although accustomed to giving others *the benefit of the doubt*, something did not sit well within her. She had to choose who to believe, Cara or Willem?

Perhaps both were dishonest? She considered. *Perhaps both were stating truths?* She rationalized.

Ms. Gerhardt knelt down and lifted his tucked chin. She caressed his damp cheeks beneath his fear-stricken eyes before pulling his face toward hers.

"Honey," she said, blinking fast. "I am very concerned." She tilted her head to the side and repeated, "I am very concerned."

FIVE

YAWNING, DR. GERHARDT lifted his head and opened his eyes a crack. He leaped off his cot and stretched every bit of his 6'3" frame. His long narrow bare feet, well-manicured, absorbed the coldness resonating from the depths of the concrete.

It's freezing in here, he mumbled, rubbing his forearm where red blotches had formed. Examining his surroundings, he stepped toward the miniscule steel sink, honing in on the residue of fingerprints and smudge marks of scum left behind. He squatted, trying to balance himself on his long tippy-toes while holding onto his stomach. Feeling nauseous, he tried to distract himself by focusing on zigzag designs on the surface beneath him.

Why? he wondered, shaking his head in silence. He tried to make sense how his status had shifted from psychologist and lecturer to someone who sits dormant, focusing on cracks embedded on a prison floor.

On the other side of the hallway, several workers wore gloves, boots and masks while cleaning an area of contamination where feces had been flung. Dr. Gerhardt turned around and retreated back to his cot where he clutched onto the top of his head and again, reflected back upon his childhood.

SIX

MISS JONES SAT with perfect posture behind her desk. Her long strawberry-blonde hair draped below the middle part of her back.

Some students were in their seats. Others paced in circles, chanting the number of days remaining in the school year. Miss Jones helped remind her third graders the exact number of days left until summer break, using a countdown system of her own on a cat-themed calendar taped on the classroom door.

On this gorgeous day, the sky reflected an infinite bright tint of blue. The glare reflected off the beige linoleum floor as the brightness of the sun eased its way into the room. A fast moving breeze left the curtains stirring at the mercy of a gust, unraveling and then tightly coiling up like a ballerina spiraling into a pirouette.

"I would like for you all to be seated," Miss Jones said, looking above her reading glasses. "Summer vacation has not yet started."

All students returned to their seats, except for Barry, who approached Miss Jones at her desk. His untied shoelaces dragged behind him as he walked. Miss Jones shut an instruction booklet with force and shuffled herself to an upright position. She leaned forward, emphatically finger-wagging Barry back to his seat.

"You just don't understand," Barry said, whining. He dropped his hands into the deep pockets of his grey hooded sweatshirt. "You just don't." Moaning, he backpedaled toward his desk.

"Thank you," Miss Jones said, nodding hard.

At his desk, Barry looked back in disappointment. "Someone took my crayons," he said, looking down to the floor. "And my special giraffe pencil." He removed his hands from his pockets and clenched them into a fist before stomping his feet.

Miss Jones closed her eyes and shook her head. She then once again motioned with her finger in the direction of his seat.

"Oh, Miss Jones," Willem called out, bouncing up from his seat. "Miss Jones," he repeated with his arm stretched up high.

Sighing, her eyes widened. "Willem!" Miss Jones said, surprised, yet not surprised. "Is Willem actually speaking," she said sarcastically before clearing her throat.

"Yes," Willem said. "Yes, I am."

Miss Jones made a *shhh* sound while placing her finger in a vertical position over her lip.

Willem pinched his lips before plopping back down on his seat. He had a dark green collared shirt, which was, as usual, buttoned to the very top of his neck. Seated in a hunched position, his arms were folded with his chin resting on the top of his clenched hands. His loose-fitting sneakers dangled from his feet just above the floor as his legs swayed back and forth like a pendulum, rapid and constant, as if someone had wound him up.

"Barry's crayons—" Willem said. Pausing for a moment, he looked up toward the ceiling and took a deep breath. "It's just that—"

"Please stop. I will handle this," Miss Jones said, putting her hand up, interrupting.

"They may be at the top of a shelf. Or near bunches of coats," Willem said, hurrying his words.

"Excuse me?" Miss Jones said, sounding offended.

Willem closed his eyes and raised his hand. "They are beneath some green folders," he said, stuttering, "or near an old box."

"Excuse me!" she shouted, "Or, shall I say excuse you?" Her voice echoed. "So just what are you talking about?" Annoyed, she chuckled to herself and walked away, shaking her head.

"Well, it was just a thought I had," said Willem, forcing his eyes open.

Miss Jones darted toward the side of the classroom. The heels of her open toe shoes clicked with each stride. As she stood in front of the coatrack, she shoved donated coats of various sizes to the side.

"Oh my," she said, reaching forward before lifting a box of green folders. She pushed her way through the colorful rack of coats and examined a very old, rusted tin candy box. "Someone has some explaining to do," she said, noticing crayons next to a tall giraffe-shaped pencil.

Miss Jones put the green folders down before scooping up the crayons and pencil. She let out a grunt before making her way back to the main classroom area, maneuvering her way in between seats as she reentered.

"Here you go, Barry," she said, extending her arm out with the crayon box and giraffe pencil in hand.

Barry stood up from his seat and rapidly approached Willem.

"Why hide my things?" Barry shouted, swiping at Willem's eyeglasses.

"I didn't do anything. It was a thought I had," Willem said, reaching down to retrieve the lenses that had separated from his loosened frames.

"And where are my marbles?" Barry shouted.

"You need to go to the Principal's office, Willem," Miss Jones said. "Right now!" She pointed toward the door. "And, Barry," she said, turning, "you need to sit down."

"But, Miss Jones," Willem responded in a cry, "I didn't do a thing…Just trying to help."

"Now!" She demanded, holding the door open.

Frustrated, Willem stomped his way out of the room. Miss Jones used the intercom system to inform Mrs. Perlman. Without providing details, Miss Jones explained that Willem would be arriving at her office shortly. She let out a sigh before releasing the call button.

With sheepish eyes, Willem stood outside the Principal's office. Seated, Mrs. Perlman looked out from behind an old wooden desk, shaking her head in disbelief. Her full head of grey hair was feathered back, her thick arms crossed under her chest.

"W-i-l-l-e-m," she called out in a prolonged way. Her voice was stern, yet raspy. "How many times must we go through this?" She motioned for him into enter her office.

Hesitant, he walked with slow strides and stutter steps to the chair directly in front of her desk where he plopped himself down, leaned back and clasped his hands together on the top of his head.

"Did you call my mother?" He asked in a soft voice, avoiding eye contact.

Rolling her eyes, Mrs. Perlman shot back a sarcastic grin and grunted. "Why of course I did. Why would today be different from any other day?" She put the back of her fist up to her mouth before clearing her throat. "Your mother should be here any moment now." She exhaled, looking down at her wristwatch.

Willem did not respond. After an awkward moment of silence, he silently nodded his head in acknowledgment.

"Is there anything you would like to say for yourself?" Mrs. Perlman asked, tapping her knuckles against the desk.

Willem mouthed, *no*.

"Why do you take things from others?" She asked, letting out a sigh. "And, it was just last week," she said, "when you were calling out strange things in class."

Willem stared at the smudging of her lipstick. He then took a double-look at a thin hair growing out from a mole on the middle of her cheek. As he leaned forward, he squinted, wondering if the hair follicle was just beginning to bloom or if it was once much longer, but recently trimmed.

"Can you respond," she said, sighing. "For once and for all, say something."

Willem shrugged as he looked back toward her.

"Do you smoke?" Willem asked, his eyebrows arching high. He panned the office, awaiting her response.

"Now that is none of your concern," she seethed, shaking her head in anger. She exhaled loudly, then said, "How DARE you?"

"I was being serious," he said, nodding. "I am curious."

"I'm being serious too, Willem," she said.

Willem looked toward the corner of the room at a picture enclosed within a metal frame shaped in the form of a heart. The photo was that of a man, standing alone, wearing a dark blue suit, silver rimmed glasses and a Hawaiian floral design tie. After staring for a moment, he frantically pointed at the picture.

"What," Mrs. Perlman blurted, flapping her wrist up from the desk.

"Frank would not be happy you smoke."

The picture had been placed in the far corner of the room since the start of the school year, a month after she had lost her husband.

"What are you talking about, Willem?" Her voice lost its rasp, in favor of an embellished pitchy-tone. "I don't smoke."

"Well, not often," Willem said, correcting her.

"Excuse me?"

"Nothing," he said, his voice dropping to a whisper. He pulled his legs up toward him and placed his chin on his bent knees.

"Are you kidding me? How disrespectful," Mrs. Perlman said, exhaling. "Would you mind taking your feet off the chair."

Willem dropped his legs to the floor, crossed his arms and let out a grunt. He twirled his thumbs and hummed while glancing over at the wall clock.

Mrs. Perlman sighed. "You know," she said, "you are a very disrespectful young man." She then glanced over at the time machine, a large cuckoo clock shaped like a cathedral, which hung just above the opening of the office door. "Well, your mother should be here shortly." Squinting, she peeked down at her gold nugget bracelet watch, double-checking the time.

"Mrs. Perlman?"

"STOP," Mrs. Perlman adamantly stated. "Enough." She shook her head in disgust. At this point, she had grown tired of listening to him and no longer wanted to hear a peep come out from his mouth. She looked down and tapped her fingers gently upon her desk. Annoyed, yet at the same time curious, she then asked, "So, how do you know about Frank?"

"Well I—"

"Well nothing," Mrs. Perlman said, interrupting. She shook her head and stood up with force. Her sudden upward movement catapulted her chair backwards on its rollers. "Take a seat outside my office," she said, pointing beyond the door.

"Frank died from smoking," Willem said, stepping out.

SEVEN

NEATLY DRESSED, MS. Gerhardt arrived, wearing a white ruffle V-Neck blouse, complimented by a long red skirt. Her freshly manicured toes peeked out from her open-toe imperial red sandals as she stepped into the office.

"Please come in," Mrs. Perlman said, sounding exhausted, yet relieved to see her. "Willem, you can stay right there."

Mrs. Perlman straightened the wooden chair by the front of her desk. Ms. Gerhardt sat and flattened the pleats on her finely pressed skirt.

"Well, Ms. Gerhardt," Mrs. Perlman said, returning to her chair. "What can I tell you? We are extremely concerned."

"I understand," Ms. Gerhardt said, looking down for a moment.

Mrs. Perlman let out a sigh as she leaned back in her chair. "I really don't know what to say at this point." She sounded more apologetic than frustrated.

There was a sudden knock on the office door. Mrs. Perlman looked up, surprised, checking her watch. A few more rapid taps followed.

"Please, hold my calls," Mrs. Perlman said. "I'm in a meeting."

"Mrs. Perlman," a woman's voice echoed from beyond the closed door.

"I'm so sorry," Mrs. Perlman said before standing up. "Excuse me for just three seconds."

"That's fine," Ms. Gerhardt said, squeezing her eyes shut.

Mrs. Perlman marched over to the door while looking back toward Ms. Gerhardt. She mouthed, *I'm so sorry*, as she opened the door a crack to peer out. Her voice then resonated with excitement. "It's Mrs. Tettleham. Our school nurse." She pushed the door all the way open and welcomed her.

"Thank you," Mrs. Tettleham said, stepping into the office. "I received an intercom call from Miss Jones. If it's okay, I thought I'd join your meeting."

"Absolutely," Mrs. Perlman said.

Mrs. Tettleham was dressed in her usual white uniform, a white nurse cap and white Nurse Mate shoes. Her dark beige stockings showed visible signs of wear above her ankles.

"I'm the school nurse," Mrs. Tettleham said, introducing herself before taking a seat. "I am glad to be part of your meeting."

Mrs. Perlman dragged her chair out from behind her desk toward the center of the office. She enthusiastically twirled her finger, motioning for Ms. Gerhardt and Mrs. Tettleham to turn their chairs to face her, appearing eager to resume the meeting at a closer distance.

"Willem has been creating many classroom disruptions and he often says the most random things," Mrs. Perlman said. "And, he has been sent to the nurse's office countless times this year." Agreeing with a hard nod, Mrs. Tettleham had a look of concern.

Mrs. Perlman inched up on the edge of her chair. "Do you happen to have any background on Willem before you had adopted him?" She asked.

"No," Ms. Gerhardt replied, blinking excessively while forcing her lower torso back in her chair.

"So, you don't know if his parents had mental illness or took drugs."

Inside, Ms. Gerhardt was fuming. Adoption orientations had informed parents of the many stereotypes about adopted children. First hand, she was starting to see this come to fruition. *How dare you?* She thought.

Stoic, Ms. Gerhardt said, "I beg your pardon?" She arched her back while placing her hand upon her chest.

"Well," Mrs. Perlman said, reaching out to embrace the top part of Ms. Gerhardt's hand, "Please don't take my questions personally." Nodding, she said, "We are all just so very concerned about Willem. He does things. He says things. He knows things."

With an exaggerated nod of her own, Mrs. Tettleham acknowledged she was in agreement. She blurted out, "He is a little different."

"Okay," Ms. Gerhardt mouthed, bowing her head several times. She straightened her posture, crossed her legs and put her hands up to her flushed cheeks. "The records are all sealed. I don't know about his parents, siblings or anything about what he endured."

"He also tends to talk to himself," Mrs. Tettleham said. "Have you noticed?"

"I've noticed," said Ms. Gerhardt, who was uncomfortable, yet wanting to remain honest. "Yes, I've noticed." She repeated, sounding robotic.

Mrs. Tettleham looked up, then asked, "When did you adopt Willem?"

"Why?"

"No, I asked when—"

"Oh," Ms. Gerhardt said, pretending she misunderstood, "this past year."

Mrs. Tettleham shrugged before nodding in a pensive manner.

"We noticed he has a scar beneath his left eye," Mrs. Perlman said, looking up to the ceiling. "I'm assuming he had it before he came to you."

Ms. Gerhardt felt interrogated as if she were on the stand before a courtroom. She took a deep breath, trying her best to remain calm.

"Yes, he did," said Ms. Gerhardt, sounding annoyed. "I had nothing to do with whatever happened to his eye."

"Oh, Ms. Gerhardt, I was not making any such insinuation," Mrs. Perlman said, rolling her eyes in the direction of Mrs. Tettleham.

"Well," Ms. Gerhardt said, crossing her legs while looking the other way, "I really don't know what happened to his eye."

Mrs. Tettleham said, "Have you ever asked him?"

"Of course, I have," Ms. Gerhardt said, leaning back in her chair. "I have asked him about many things, actually." She stretched out her legs and reached for a tissue, then blew her nose twice.

Twirling her index finger in a circular manner, awaiting an answer, Mrs. Tettleham said, "And what?"

"And—he says he does not know. He does not seem to know about whole lot of things," Ms. Gerhardt said, patting the bottom of her nostrils with the folded tissue.

Mrs. Perlman joined in on the conversation. "Well, he either does not remember because he has blocked it out. Or he remembers, but it may be too painful for him to revisit." She nodded her head slowly in a compassionate way, then said, "Perhaps he has been silenced."

"Silenced?" Ms. Gerhardt repeated. After placing the crumpled tissue into her purse, she said, "Just what do you mean?"

"Well, have you ever taken him to a psychologist? Mrs. Tettleham asked.

No, Ms. Gerhardt mouthed.

"Has he ever been evaluated by a psychiatrist?"

No, Ms. Gerhardt said, shaking her head.

"How about a neurologist?"

Growing annoyed, Ms. Gerhardt said in a definitive, loud voice, "No!"

Mrs. Perlman tapped her clenched fist against her knee and then seized the opportunity to ask, "Just how is he with animals?"

"Excuse me," Ms. Gerhardt said, then repeated, "Animals?" She crossed her legs and let out a sigh. "We don't have any pets." She stuttered as her voice cracked. "Just why is it that you ask?"

"No particular reason. But keep an eye on how he interacts with, or should I say, how he treats animals." Mrs. Perlman was blunt in her response.

"Oh, Okay," Ms. Gerhardt said in a sarcastic way, maintaining eye contact through the corner of her eyes.

"Unfortunately, we must suspend Willem at this time," Mrs. Perlman explained.

"Well, why—" Ms. Gerhardt cried out.

"I know...I know," Mrs. Perlman interrupted. She embraced Ms. Gerhardt's hand. "This is very difficult for all of us," she said, patting the top of her wrist. "But we need Willem to be evaluated."

Mrs. Tettleham reached for Ms. Gerhardt's other hand, then reiterated, "More than a punishment, we are hoping the time is utilized to further assess and get Willem the help he desperately needs."

As Ms. Gerhardt stood up and walked toward the office door, she overheard one of them whispering, *Money can't buy everything.*

EIGHT

A SLENDER WOMAN wearing a navy colored top with exact color matching pants stepped out from the back. Her identification card dangled from a thick shoelace-type string as she poked her head out into the large waiting room area.

"Willem…" the woman called out, then more softly said, "Willem Gerhardt?"

"Yes, he is here," Ms. Gerhardt said, responding on his behalf before tossing *Prevention Magazine* back down upon the long, rectangular glass coffee table.

"I'm the office nurse," the woman said, tucking her clipboard close to her side. "Please," she said, turning back to the side door, "Follow me."

Both walked at a close distance behind the nurse in a follow-the-leader type manner down the hallway until they reached the very last examination room. The nurse flipped on a wall switch that illuminated fluorescent ceiling tube lights, one at a time. "Please have a seat," she said, pointing in the direction of two chairs.

As Ms. Gerhardt settled into the chair closest to the door, Willem hopped upon the examination table covered with crinkling paper. Willem balanced himself on his elbows while kicking out his legs in a pendulum-like manner, humming happily.

"The doctor will be right with you," the nurse said with a gentle smile. She pushed a vase containing an assortment of artificial flowers to the side before placing his chart on the top of the filing cabinet. She backpedaled and bowed before slowly closing the door behind her.

After several minutes, the door creaked opened.

"Good Afternoon," a deep voice resonated. "I'm Dr. Weinman." His voice was loud, exuding enthusiasm. After he sat down next to Ms. Gerhardt, he quickly scooted his chair backwards, respecting her personal space.

Hello, Ms. Gerhardt mouthed, nodding.

Dr. Weinman greeted her with a big smile while stretching his arm out for a firm hand shake. He turned to face the examination table. "I assume you are Willem?"

"Yes," Willem said, extending his limp arm.

"Come on," Dr. Weinman challenged. "Are you offering me a floppy-dead-fish?

Willem looked out from the corner of his eyes and tightened his loose grip.

"Ouch," Dr. Weinman said, chuckling. He grabbed the chart and retrieved his reading glasses from the pocket of his dark blue scrubs. After opening the folder, he scrolled through pages with his long fingers. "You were referred by the school, I see," he said, looking up for a moment above his glasses.

Ms. Gerhardt rolled her eyes and mouthed, *yes*. She reached down for her purse and placed a stick of Trident into her mouth before crossing her legs.

"First of all, what happened to your eye?" Dr. Weinman asked, leaning forward to examine his left eye.

Willem looked away as if he did not hear the question. Not wanting to press the issue, Dr. Weinman scooted back in his chair and continued to fumble through more pages.

"So, what brings you here today?" He asked in a hurried manner, his eyes widening as he looked across the room.

"Well," Ms. Gerhardt said, breaking the silence, "The school feels that Willem hears voices." She then crumpled up the gum wrapper before stuffing it into her purse. "So," she said, pausing for a moment while snapping her purse shut, "That's why we are here." Exhaling, again, she shook her head in frustration.

Dr. Weinman browsed through the chart while making small illegible notations with a pencil. "So Willem," he said, tapping the pencil down on its eraser. "Is it true that you sometimes hear voices?"

"I don't hear voices," Willem snapped back. After letting out a prolonged groan, he repeatedly clicked his tongue against the roof of his mouth.

"So, Ms. Gerhardt," Dr. Weinman begged, "Please help me out here." Appearing puzzled, he moved his chair closer toward her. "What is it that is going on?"

Ms. Gerhardt lifted her hands from the armrest of the chair and cupped her knees. "Well, Willem tells his teachers that he has thoughts that randomly come to his mind," she said, burying her head into her open palms. She then spoke thru the spaces between her fingers. "He seems to know things others do not," she explained, reaching for a tissue.

"Now is this a problem just in school?" Dr. Weinman asked, "Or do you notice similar type things in the home, as well?"

"Oh no," she said, fluttering her eyes. "Don't get me wrong. It's happening in our home, too."

"Please stop clicking your tongue," Dr. Weinman said, sounding annoyed. "Ok, do we know of any significant family history of mental illness?"

"Not that I know of," Ms. Gerhardt said, dabbing her eyes. She lifted a tissue to her face. "Willem was adopted," she said before blowing her nose.

"Oh, adopted." Dr. Weinman said, sounding surprised. Nodding his head in slow motion, he then asked, "How old was he when you adopted him?"

"I only adopted him this past year."

"Oh, this year," he mumbled, jotting additional notes in the chart. "Have you noticed anything unusual with attachment or inability to bond with you?"

"With me?" She asked.

"Well, with you, or in general, attaching to others. Sometimes children who are adopted have difficulty connecting or attaching to others and managing their emotions."

"Are you trying to say that his behaviors may be normal?" She asked. Perplexed, she tilted her head to the side.

"Well," Dr. Weinman said in a deep voice, "Please don't misconstrue what I am saying. I'm not suggesting these behavioral presentations are normal." His eyes peeped out over his reading glasses. He then touched his lower lip, trying to carefully collect his thoughts before he explained further. "What I am trying to say is that his behaviors may be common for a child who has been adopted."

"Oh," Ms. Gerhardt said softly. Her eyebrows wiggled over her squinted eyes. "But, he does not have problems with attachment," she explained, sounding perplexed.

"Well, we don't know that for sure," Dr. Weinman interrupted, putting a hand up. "Only time will tell."

Ms. Gerhardt shrugged and exhaled loudly. "He has random thoughts that come to his mind," she said as she crossed her legs. "Is that common with adopted children, too?"

"He may be trying to compensate for a lack of consistent social relationships," Dr. Weinman explained. Once again, he looked over toward the examination table. "Do you just hear voices, Willem?" He asked, peeking down at his watch, "Or, do you sometimes also see things?"

"NEITHER!" Willem shouted, annoyed by the line of questioning.

"Okay," Dr. Weinman said, unfastening the clip attached to a folder labeled, *Clinical Assessments*. "Let's go down a checklist."

Ms. Gerhardt mouthed, *fine*.

"Does he experience depression?" Dr. Weinman asked.

"Not that I know of…"

"Any symptoms related to anxiety?"

"I don't think so…"

"Any outbursts of anger, rage or violence?"

"Oh, no…" Ms. Gerhardt said, shaking her head, "Heavens, no." Squinting, she asked, "Do adopted children have that?"

Dr. Weinman ignored her inquiry and continued down the list of questions. "How about stealing?"

"Never."

Dr. Weinman turned the page over. "Any playing around with matches or fire setting?"

"I don't smoke," she said, "so, no."

"Do you see any signs of paranoia?"

"Meaning what?" Ms. Gerhardt asked, wincing.

Dr. Weinman paused for a moment and twirled his pencil. "Well, does he distrust others? Become overly suspicious or think people are out to harm him? Does he hear voices?"

"I don't hear voices," Willem said, chiming in.

Dr. Weinman nodded in deep thought.

"But you admit that you sometimes have thoughts that come to your mind?"

"Yes," Willem said, rolling his eyes. Sighing, Willem touted, "I said that already."

"Willem, please be patient," Dr. Weinman encouraged. "Do you sometimes feel people are watching you? Or, do you ever feel as though people are talking about you?"

"Yes," Willem said, "for sure."

"Tell me more."

"Well, my mom," Willem said, pausing for a moment.

"Oh," said Dr. Weinman. "That's not quite what I meant."

"Then, who?" Willem responded in an angry tone, appearing confused.

"Okay," Dr. Weinman replied, looking back toward Willem. "What type thoughts come to your mind?" He curiously asked, clearing his throat.

"I don't know," Willem said. "Messages, answers, ideas, thoughts, letters..."

Nodding in silence, Dr. Weinman made notations.

"Are we almost done, mom?" Willem looked down in frustration. He pulled his knees up to his chin, crinkling the examination table paper some more.

Grimacing, Dr. Weinman blew out some air. He looked toward Ms. Gerhardt and stood while reviewing the open chart through reading glasses set high upon the bridge of his nose. "I'm not sure what to say. I have been in the field for close to twenty-six years," Dr. Weinman said, scratching the top of his head, "and I have never heard a response quite like that."

"Oh, no," Ms. Gerhardt said, cupping her hand over her mouth. "What can we do?"

"Information about his biological parents may paint a more accurate picture," Dr. Weinman said, tapping his foot. "There seems to be more to the story."

Ms. Gerhardt nodded slowly in deep thought.

"How is he with animals?" Dr. Weinman asked.

"Animals," she repeated. *Here we go again with the animal question,* she thought. "Please, tell me," Ms. Gerhardt said, leaning back in her chair and scooting backwards, "Why do people ask about animals?"

"Oh, someone else has asked?" Dr. Weinman said.

"Well, y-e-a-a-a," she said in a prolonged, annoyed tone.

Dr. Weinman leaned forward, "And, what was your response? How is he with animals?"

"He is not around animals...So, what can I say?"

"Ok, so Willem," Dr. Weinman said, pausing. "Do you like animals?"

Willem perked up, making loud kissing sounds with his lips.

"Who doesn't," he blurted out. He twiddled his thumbs before looking the other way. "Well, most animals," he said, looking back.

"What do you mean by most?" Dr. Weinman asked in a concerned manner.

"Well, I like birds, horses and..."

"And—And, what?" Dr. Weinman said, bobbing his head.

"Drum roll please," Willem said, "And...Dogs." He then slapped a fist down to his knee, giggling

"Well," Dr. Weinman said, rubbing his forehead as he looked up to the ceiling. "Why don't we start by doing an MRI." He tugged at his chin beneath his open mouth, appearing in deep thought.

"What exactly is an M-M-I doctor?" Ms. Gerhardt inquired. Her voice was soft, southern accent even more pronounced.

"It is MRI, Ms. Gerhardt."

"Okay, MRI," Ms. Gerhardt snapped, rolling her eyes and shuffling restlessly in her chair. Agitated, she glanced with squinted eyes across the room, examining the various display of diplomas hanging on the side wall. "So, what is it, anyway?" She asked, folding her tissue and blowing her nose once again.

"It is called magnetic resonance imaging...A newer tool...A

powerful magnetic field that aligns the magnetization of atoms in the body," Dr. Weinman explained. He squeezed his hands together proudly and again, looked up toward the ceiling. "It allows us to examine radio frequencies and systematical alignments."

"Excuse me," she blurted out. "I don't think that is necessary, doctor." Frustrated, she said, "He is not a robot."

Ms. Gerhardt wanted to let the doctor know that she was on top of things and keeping close tabs on what was going on. Turning Willem into a science project was the last thing she would ever let happen.

"Did you attend University of Southern California?" She asked.

"Yes, I went to USC," Dr. Weinman acknowledged, glancing along with her at his displayed diploma.

"And you are," she asked, pausing for a moment, "a psychiatrist?"

"I'm a general practitioner, Ms. Gerhardt. Willem will likely need to see a neurologist in the near-term," he said, then continued, "or a psychiatrist perhaps, as well as a specialist in the area of adoption."

"Excuse me. Willem is not a guinea pig," she said with an exaggerated short nod.

Her lips vibrated as she exhaled.

Smirking, Dr. Weinman shook his head hard and shot her a sarcastic look from above.

"Ms. Gerhardt, please," he said, offended by her insinuation. "There are no guinea pigs, here. This will allow us to take a closer look at his brain." He confidently tapped the chart against the palm of his open hand. "It is because of the wonderful invention of Dr. Raymond Damadian that we can now use the MRI, an innovative and most informative imaging instrument."

"Excuse me," she said standing up. "Who is he?" She asked. "And why, by the end of the day, are doctors caring about brain *frequencies* and *alignments*, or whatever it is that you just said."

"You'll be hearing the name Dr. Damadian for years to come and the MRI…"

"Pardon me. Can I speak for a moment?" She said, holding her hand up high.

To her surprise, Dr. Weinman stopped talking.

"How does this all apply to Willem?" She said softly, flapping her arms to the side. "I hope that you are not using my son for experimental purposes."

"It is a start," Dr. Weinman said, snapping the chart shut. "Willem's presentations are rather unusual. I can prescribe medication. Or, I can refer him to a neurologist or a psychiatrist. I'd like to begin with an MRI to get a better grasp as to what may be going on." Nodding with confidence, he placed his large open hand on Willem's shoulder.

In deep thought, she stared down at the floor. *Wonderful, a game of musical doctors and trying out a new machine,* she thought. *This sounds like a bunch of stinky baloney.*

Dr. Weinman patted Willem on the back. "This test will allow us to rule out certain things." He sounded enthusiastic in his explanation.

"Rule out?" Ms. Gerhardt said. She rolled her eyes and looked up to the ceiling.

"Yes. What I mean is the test will allow us to rule out tumors, further delineate atypical brain activity and other potential brain anomalies." He spoke with poise in a deep resounding voice.

"I don't know what to tell you," Ms. Gerhardt said, feeling uncertain. She then snapped, "Alright, we'll do it."

"It is going to be just fine," Dr. Weinman promised, smiling. He removed his reading glasses and escorted them toward the front of the office. "You can go upstairs," he said, pointing out towards the hallway. "Dr. Hanson and his team will be happy to assist you. Go on up and schedule an appointment."

NINE

AFTER A DAY and a half of rain, different shades of bright blue lit up the sky without a cloud in sight. Weather conditions continued to reach excessive levels of heat and humidity as race fan enthusiasts filed through entrance gates in droves.

Thousands were scattered across the entire complex surrounding the dirt horse track. Some stood by the finish line holding umbrellas to shield away the hot sun while others were seated on bleachers inside the exclusive clubhouse in the comfort of air conditioning.

Together, Willem and Ms. Gerhardt walked hand-in-hand along the crooked pathway that led into the complex. Ms. Gerhardt wore a dress that had a plunging neckline that tightly hugged her narrow, yet shapely, waist. Willem was dressed in casual attire, a T-shirt and baggy shorts. At the magazine stand, they purchased, *The Daily Racing Form.*

In the distance, a sound of a bugle resonated as a bugler, dressed in a bright red vest and tight fitting black pants, marched to the high pitched tune. Ten horses, baring a wide variety of colorful checkered and striped displays, followed one another at a close distance in a single file type manner.

After releasing his hand from her grip, Willem darted over to the outer bounds of the track where he leaned upon the railing.

"Mom," he said, turning back. "What's that smell?" Coughing, he rubbed his nose with the back of his hand.

Ms. Gerhardt pretended not to notice the harsh odor even though her nose involuntarily twitched for a moment. After several seconds, she could not help but to use her hand to fan her face.

"Stand back here," she said.

Retreating, Willem did the moonwalk back toward her. As he stood beside Ms. Gerhardt, he hugged her around the waist.

"Much better here," he said, then for a split second, chuckled to himself.

"Let's take a look at the list of horses running in the next race," Ms. Gerhardt said, opening the glossy covered booklet.

"Race five," Willem said, standing on his tippy-toes while taking a quick glance.

"Yes, there are ten horses in the race," Ms. Gerhardt explained, scrolling her finger down the page. "You can choose a horse to come in first, second or third place." She counted with her fingers as she explained.

"Which do you like?" Ms. Gerhardt asked, tilting the page toward him.

"To win," he said, placing his finger up to his dimpled chin. His eyes panned the entire list of horses, again. "Don't know yet," he said, "I'll be right back." He returned to the railing where he examined each horse, individually, especially a grey horse with a white mane. Willem was fascinated by the color of the horse and by the color of the cloth draped around it. The jockey was wearing green striped silks and a pair of thick goggles.

Willem turned around to face Ms. Gerhardt. "How can they see out of those goggles, mom?"

"I am not sure," she said, "but I sure hope the jockey on my horse can see out of his." She chuckled while looking around at others standing nearby.

"Are those the same goggles I use for swimming?"

"I sure hope not," Ms. Gerhardt said, laughing, "which reminds me you need a new pair."

"Well, I like horse-five," Willem said matter-of-factly.

Ms. Gerhardt glanced down at the booklet, realizing that the horse set to begin at post position five had a perfect lifetime record. *The Daily Racing Form* indicated that the horse had won all seven of its previous races, all on this track.

Golden Warrior, Ms. Gerhardt said under her breath. She continued to read the commentary about the jockey and trainer written in bold print further below.

"Yup, horse number five," Willem reiterated.

"*Golden Warrior* is one of the favorites," she explained.

Willem nodded with confidence. "Mom, it is my favorite horse too," he said, grinning. He enthusiastically jumped up and down holding five fingers up high.

Ms. Gerhardt walked over to the main betting window located beneath the awning. After a few patient minutes, she reached the front of the betting line.

"Race five, horse-five, to win," she said, rapidly opening, then closing her hand twice, showing all five fingers. After receiving the waging ticket, she hurried back to the trackside to watch the start of the race.

It-s-s-s-'s post time, an announcer conveyed over the static-filled loudspeaker. All horses lined up at the starting gate. As a loud vibrating bell rang out, the starting gate opened and the horses were off.

Slow, but steady, a field of ten horses left the gate together in a pack. Upon reaching the half-mile point, it was apparent the sprint had come down to just a two-horse race. *Golden Warrior* had the outside position on *King Me*. The jockey on the five-horse put the final whip taps on *Golden Warrior* at the three-quarter pole, taking full command turning down the stretch.

Standing beside Willem at the finish line, Ms. Gerhardt bounced up and down on the balls of her feet as *Golden Warrior* easily galloped alone, extending his lead to eight full lengths before crossing the finish line. In a trail of dust, *King Me* held on for second place.

"Come here," Ms. Gerhardt said, gleaming, "We won!" She twirled Willem around and repeated, "We won!" She made her way to the cash-out window and then put up a fist full of bills upon collecting the winnings.

Ms. Gerhardt returned to the track where she slipped a twenty dollar bill into Willem's pocket. "Save it for later," she said, smiling, "use it wisely."

After jumping into the air, Willem skipped around holding the bill up high.

"We are up to the sixth race," Ms. Gerhardt said, licking the tip of her finger before reopening, *The Daily Racing Form*.

Willem placed the bill back into his pocket and stood beside her. Peering into the thin booklet, he studied the names of the thoroughbreds listed for the upcoming sixth race. He then sprinted down toward the rail to get a closer look at the field of horses.

The electronic display board showed ten minutes left until post time with the betting odds listed for each in the 12 horse field. *Herby* was the heavy favorite, at least according to the morning line odds-makers. He was also a favorite amongst bettors as well—with real time odds listing *Herby* as an overwhelming 1-5 favorite from post position six. *Deluxe Character* was also listed and touted as a co-favorite, positioned to leave the starting gate from post position two.

Willem leaned against the rail, examining all of the horses.

"It's almost post time," Ms. Gerhardt called out before approaching him. "So, who do you like in this race?" She asked. But before he had a chance to respond, Ms. Gerhardt said, *How about Herby, horse-six?* She then confidently shut the race booklet.

"No," Willem said, obstinately. "Horse-nine!"

"Horse-nine," Ms. Gerhardt said, her voice reaching a higher pitch.

"Yes, mom."

"But, Willem," she said, reopening the booklet, *Horse nine is Paraguay Amore.*

"Perfect," he said, clapping.

"A 17 to 1 longshot?" Ms. Gerhardt gasped. She cupped her hand to her waist and shook her head slowly. "Are you sure?" She shoved the booklet in front of him and emphatically pointed at *Paraguay Amore.* "17 to 1 longshot," she said again, "and from an outside post."

"That's right," Willem confirmed, nodding.

"Ok," she said in a prolonged, hesitant way. "Shall we?"

Still nodding, Willem raised both hands and held nine fingers erect, chanting *nine* several times in a row. He then pointed with his chin toward the betting window.

As Ms. Gerhardt walked away, an older man wearing a tall hat approached Willem. His charcoal cowboy boots closely matched his sombrero. His face was wrinkled, his back humped. Unstable on his feet, the man tried to balance himself with a cane.

"First timer, kid?"

"Huh?" Willem said.

"Is this your first time at the track?" The man asked, tipping his hat.

"Yes. And, it's my birthday, today," Willem said.

"Oh, Lordy, I've spent many birthdays of mine here, too. Not to mention Thanksgivings, Christmases." After pausing for a moment, he then said, "and, New Years'." He then nodded in silence and sighed.

"Oh, wow," Willem said, letting out a nervous chuckle.

"How old are you, son?" The man asked as he reached into his shirt pocket to retrieve his pipe.

"Who me?"

"Yes, you," the man said, bluntly. He then let out a deep hearty laugh before saying in a joking way, "Who else?"

"I am nine," Willem said. "No, sorry...I'm ten now."

The old man's knees buckled. "Ten-years-old," he muttered, looking down. Shaking his head slowly, he appeared lost in memories. "To be ten-years-old, again," he said, pulling out a lighter from his jeans.

"So, it's not fun to be old?" Willem said.

"What do you mean, son?"

Willem squinted. "Well, you said you want to be ten?"

"Well, not exactly. It gets better," the old man said, puffing hard on the tip of his ram-shaped pipe. "I saw you checking out them horses. Who do you like, young man?" He asked, grasping onto the top of his cane with both hands.

Self-conscious, Willem looked around and shrugged.

The old man opened his mouth and chuckled, revealing dark brown, smoke-stained front teeth. Winking, he took another prolonged puff from his pipe.

"Well, I really dunno," Willem mumbled.

The man blew out a steady stream of smoke above him. "Come on. I won't hold you to it. I believe in a little beginner's luck or maybe even some birthday luck."

Willem pinched his nose for a moment in response to the man's breath odor. He looked up at the man's wrinkled plaid shirt and stared at a large dark brown, oily stain by his collar.

"What are you looking at?" The man asked, tucking his chin and squinting downward before swiping at his collar.

"I'm going to look for my mom," Willem said, stepping toward the green awning.

With a pipe dangling from the corner of his mouth, the man

tipped his hat and, at the same time, bowed. He removed the pipe from his lips.

"Hey, kid!" He shouted out.

"Yea?" Willem said, stopping in his tracks and swiveling his head around.

"Just shoot me a number," the man urged.

"Fine," Willem said, confidently, "why not just go with number nine."

The man's eyes widened. "The nine-horse?" he repeated, thinking he may have misheard. Confused, he muttered, *Paraguay Amore?*

"Well, it's really up to you," Willem said. "It ain't gonna be easy and it ain't gonna be fun."

"What do you mean, son?"

"Oh, never mind," Willem said, flapping his hand.

"It's never easy, kid—but sometimes fun." He chuckled, once again, revealing his discolored teeth, heavily stained beneath his upper gums.

Willem shrugged. "It's really up to you."

"Why the nine-horse, young man? You just like the name?"

"I guess," said Willem.

The man stepped forward and whispered into Willem's ear.

"What kind?" Willem asked, snapping his head up.

The man leaned over and whispered, again. "And, always remember that young man."

Intrigued, Willem forced a smile through the corner of his mouth.

"Okay…I better go," Willem said.

"Happy Birthday, kid," The man shouted, waving with his cane before thrusting it back down to the ground to rebalance himself. Crouched over, he hobbled his way over to the wagering window where he reached into his pocket and handed the clerk a stack of bills held together by a rubber band that was double wound.

"All of it," the man said, "on the 9-horse... to win."

"All?" The clerk repeated, sounding surprised while counting all of the bills.

The old man looked in the direction of Willem and closed one eye for several seconds in the form of an exaggerated wink.

"All of it," he repeated to the clerk, nodding confidently.

Willem walked hand-in-hand with Ms. Gerhardt back toward the track. His face was pale, lacking any form of expression. He appeared to be lost in thought, unaware of his immediate surroundings. Within minutes, his mood had shifted from jubilant to flat. No longer interested in horses, he focused on the people seated on bleachers and birds flying in the distance. Squinting, he blankly stared straight up to the sky. Muddled in fear, he trembled as he looked across the track.

"Who was that man?" Ms. Gerhardt asked before clearing her throat.

"Well, I really don't know."

"Just what did he say?"

"Nothing really."

"What do you mean by, *nothing really?*" Concerned, Ms. Gerhardt stared back at him and said, "Well, I picked the number nine horse for you."

"Oh, mom," said Willem, clutching onto her open hand with a tight squeeze.

"What's wrong?" Her voice cracked as she spoke.

"Mom, we need to leave, now."

Ms. Gerhardt bent down and caressed his cheeks with both hands. As she looked him straight back in the eye, her voice dropped to a nervous whisper.

"Willem," she said, anxiously, "tell me what's wrong!"

His green eyes narrowed in on her worried blue eyes.

"Let's go, mom. We must leave."

The announcer tapped his microphone. Once again, static resonated throughout the track loudspeakers.

Jockeys and horses...It's-s-s post time, he broadcasted.

Track personnel helped load several of the more stubborn horses with pushes to their rears. Finally, all horses were lined up in their starting positions.

"All horses ready," a voice echoed before the gate lifted.

The start of the sixth race was underway. To no one's surprise, *Herby* had taken the early lead ahead of the rest of the field, who were lined up in single file positioning along the rail. Known for his sprint-like style, many cheered for the favorite whose graceful gallops were superior to his challengers as he hit the half-mile mark.

It's Herby, out front, in the clear, the announcer touted.

Herby started to slow at the three-quarter of a mile marker. His fast start, on this hot day, started to take a toll on him. The only horse within reasonable distance was *Deluxe Character,* whose jockey more rapidly applied the whip to its rear. *Deluxe Character* hit his best stride, propelling him around several horses, tiring down the final 100 yard stretch.

Herby at the top, but his lead is narrowing fast, the announcer called out with excitement.

Willem tugged on Ms. Gerhardt's shoulder and turned to face the exit.

"We need to go," he said, yanking at her purse. "Please, we must go."

"Willem, we will leave soon. The race is almost over. There's still a chance your horse could win." Her tone lacked confidence. "Go *Paraguay Amore,*" she said, cheering.

"Let's leave, now. Winning is not everything," he moaned, repeating her words of wisdom as he jerked her arm harder.

It's a two-horse race...Down the stretch, the announcer declared, as *Deluxe Character* caught up and ran alongside the leader and heavy favorite, *Herby.*

"Don't look. Let's leave," he said, covering up his eyes.

Ms. Gerhardt knelt down and put her hand on the small of his back.

It's Deluxe Character, taking the lead on the outside. Herby is in the mix as well, making a final bid on the rail, the announcer touted. His voice was loud, filled with the utmost of excitement.

...Ladies and gentlemen, it is nose-to-nose to the wire...

Deluxe Character and Herby...Herby and Deluxe Character, neck and neck...

And Paraguay Amore----now pulling out all the stops, in full gear on the far outside---five lengths from the lead...

The crowd roared as *Deluxe Character* and *Herby* galloped down the final stretch. Suddenly, cheers of exuberance turned into screams of terror. *Deluxe Character*, in full gear on the outside, started to slow before his graceful strides of beauty had abruptly turned into chaotic bull-like kicks of panic. The jockey was immediately ejected onto the racing field where he curled up in a ball and covered his head to avoid being trampled by the remaining field of horses.

Spooked by the fallen jockey, *Herby* veered off toward the railing, sending him off stride, limping. *Paraguay Amore* took full advantage of the situation, passing both injured horses and crossing the finish line first. *Herby* galloped gingerly on wobbly legs to hold on for a close second, before collapsing just beyond the finish line.

"Willem," Ms. Gerhardt cried out.

Mom, he mouthed, grasping her wrist with all his might.

"Are you okay?" She asked, dabbing his sobbing eyes with her thin blue scarf that she removed from around her neck.

At a loss for words, Willem tried to catch his breath.

All attention was focused on *Deluxe Character* who was on the track, beside the fallen jockey, kicking in agony.

The emergency squad quickly arrived in an oversized van. Several personnel helped place the fallen jockey onto a portable stretcher.

"Can we leave, NOW?" Willem said.

Ms. Gerhardt grabbed Willem by the hand and jetted toward the exit. Many other spectators, especially those with young children, also hurried to make a quick departure. Some remained close to the railing, curiously watching track veterinarians attend to the fallen horses.

"Let's go," Ms. Gerhardt said, dragging Willem forward by his arm. Together, they rushed out of the complex. In the distance, the old man stood smiling while waving his winning ticket in the air.

The announcement over the loud speaker declared the winner of the race, *Horse 9, Paraguay Amore, by a length and a half, over Herby.*

Race fans were also informed that there would be an hour and a half break before the start of the next race, suggesting that attendees look away, as *Deluxe Character* was euthanized. Track officials helped remove the fallen horse while other specialists attended to the needs of *Herby*, who was struggling to stand on his wobbly rear legs.

In the parking lot, Ms. Gerhardt opened the rear door and helped Willem buckle up before situating herself in the front seat. After turning on the ignition, she swiveled her body around toward the backseat to face him.

Breathing hard, she said, "What did that man say to you?"

"Nothing, mom," Willem said. "Just go."

"Are you sure?" She sounded worried.

"Fine," Willem said, tucking his head down. "He said I have a gift."

"A gift," she said and then asked, "Did he give you something?"

"No, mom. He just whispered that I have a gift."

"You have to be careful who you talk to," she said, "And, you know to never take anything from a stranger...Even if it's a gift."

"I know, mom," Willem said, sounding sad.

"What happened? How did you know we should leave?"

Willem stared back at her blankly, his face pale as ghost.

"I don't know." His voice lost its luster. "I really just don't know."

"A gift," Ms. Gerhardt muttered, tilting her head to the side. She put the car into gear and drove away while sustaining eye contact with him in the rearview mirror.

"Willem," she said, trembling.

Appearing in a fog, he looked every which way but back toward her.

"Please, just answer me," she said. She snapped her head around and slammed on the brakes. Growing more concerned, she shouted, "Willem!"

"Yes, mom," he finally responded.

"Do we need to go back to the doctor?"

"Maybe," he said, trying to catch his breath.

TEN

"IS THAT A Coffin?" Ms. Gerhardt said, fuming. Unwilling to wait for an answer, she stood and shouted, "I refuse to put my son in a coffin!" Her voice was firm, filled with passion and loud enough for all around to hear. She folded her arms tight to her chest while tapping her shoe loudly against the floor. With piercing eyes, she stared at what she thought resembled a coffin.

"Oh, Ms. Gerhardt," Dr. Hanson said, chuckling in a nervous way. "This here is not a coffin." He cupped his hand over his mouth, hiding a smile. He shook his head before turning to the side.

"Then what the —" she said.

"An MRI," he explained, escorting her toward the long, narrow tubular structure.

Ms. Gerhardt took several steps forward before coming to a complete stop. She tapped her foot against the floor, again.

Willem leaned over and took a peek into the circular tunnel. His backside was bare for a moment until Ms. Gerhardt tugged the back of his shirt downward.

"Oh, cool," Willem said, tilting his head. "We have one of these crawling tunnels on the playground at school."

"A crawling tunnel," Dr. Hanson repeated.

"Willem, stand over here," Ms. Gerhardt said. She grabbed his arm and pulled him back toward her. "It's not a crawling tunnel, honey."

"We will need you to go outside in the waiting room," Dr. Hanson said, speaking in a firm tone to Ms. Gerhardt.

"I'd prefer to stay here," Ms. Gerhardt said, "if I may."

Dr. Hanson exhaled, looking out through the corner of his eyes.

"We are going to take many scans and the machine is extremely noisy…The fewer distractions, the better."

"What do you mean," Ms. Gerhardt said, then repeated, "extremely noisy?"

"Well, when we slide Willem into the center, he will be enclosed for a good period of time. The machine will cast off various sounds."

"Oh, okay," she said, softly. "So he should expect to hear a lot of beeping. Is that what you are trying to say?"

"Beeping? You can say that," Dr. Hanson said, "for sure."

Ms. Gerhardt cocked her head. "More than beeps?" She asked, her tone suggested concern.

"Well, Ms. Gerhardt," Dr. Hanson said, "most would liken the sound of an MRI to that of a jackhammer and a constant beat that resonates like a nonstop blasting staple gun."

"Are you kidding me?" She snapped her head back with squinted eyes. *These doctors are all the same,* she thought.

"He'll be just fine, Ms. Gerhardt. We'll give him some ear plugs and the technician will remain in contact from the control room."

"Well, just so you know," she said, her pitch heightening to a very southern accent, "he likes animals."

"Excuse me?" Dr. Hanson said, wincing in confusion.

"Never mind," Ms. Gerhardt said, walking with rigidity toward the side door.

The MRI was the closed-type, preferred by most doctors because of its ability to take accurate images. Dr. Hanson nodded once, motioning for the technician to begin preparation for the MRI examination.

A male technician in his thirties entered the room wearing light green scrubs and plain white sneakers. He placed a hand on the top of Willem's shoulder, then turned him around and pointed toward the side window.

"Your mother is standing just outside the room," he said, showing Willem the window. "You can't see her, but she can see you."

Willem looked over toward the window, but could only see a reflection. Confused, he held his arm up and waved.

Reading word for word from pamphlets, the technician explained the MRI procedure and reminded Willem about the loud clanking and rattling noises. He reiterated the importance of remaining still throughout the entire procedure.

Willem was more interested in the *tunnel* than listening to protocol. As he lay flat on the table with his earplugs secured, he looked behind him, further into the structure. The patient table was similar to a body board or a mini-stretcher, designed specifically for MRI testing. An outside lever maneuvered the table in and out of the machine.

"Are you claustrophobic?" The technician asked.

"What's that mean?" Willem said, perking his head up.

"Are you afraid of tight spaces?"

"Don't think so." Willem shrugged.

"You see it's a narrow tube. Are you going to be alright?"

Willem puckered his lips and nodded. "I have no problem with this crawling tunnel."

"Okay, I am going to slide you inside the machine, now." The technician lifted his palm to the lever. "If you have any problem whatsoever, or if you get nervous, just press the red checkered box." The technician handed him a square shaped device that he referred to as a *call button*. "We'll be in contact at all times."

Willem grabbed the device, closed his eyes and exhaled.

"Do you have any questions before we slide you to the center?"

"No," Willem said. "I'm prepared for take-off."

The technician pressed the lever. The patient table made a humming noise as it slowly rolled Willem to the center of the machine. After assuring Willem felt comfortable, the technician scampered to the control room and proceeded with the scanning process.

In the waiting room, Dr. Hanson engaged Ms. Gerhardt in conversation. Both looked through the window during the MRI procedure.

"Who referred you?" Dr. Hanson asked.

Ms. Gerhardt stared at the MRI through the glass. Using her hand as a visor to block the reflecting light, she could only see Willem's legs dangling out from the machine.

"Dr. Weinman," she said, looking up.

"Any particular reason?"

"Good question," she said, blowing out air. "I guess we'll find out, soon." She then pressed her nose up to the glass window.

Thirty minutes later, the MRI scanning procedure concluded. The technician stepped out from the control room and walked over to the machine where he pressed the lever to slide Willem out from the center.

"Where's my mom?" Willem asked. Confused, his eyes panned around the room.

The technician helped Willem step down from the table. Groggy, Willem stood erect and put his arms out like an airplane, dipping from one side to the other. He vibrated his lips, producing sounds similar to a propeller.

From behind, the technician put a hand on Willem's upper back and guided him toward the waiting room where Ms. Gerhardt stood chatting with Dr. Hanson.

"Are you okay, honey?" Ms. Gerhardt asked before greeting him with open arms. "It's going to be fine," she said, kissing his forehead.

"We'll have the results ready by next week," Dr. Hanson said in a deep voice. "We will be in contact with you." Smiling, he handed Ms. Gerhardt a business card.

Ms. Gerhardt held the card up to her eyes. Squinting, she read the small print, *Sophia Angus* and then said the name out loud.

"Correct." Dr. Hanson nodded.

"What's going on here?" She asked, wondering if he had handed her the wrong card.

"After speaking with you, I believe Miss Sophia can be of help."

Another doctor, Ms. Gerhardt thought, dropping the card deep into her open purse.

Without inquiring, she zipped her purse shut. In a sarcastic tone, she said, "We're trying to have a life other than doctor visits."

"Oh," Dr. Hanson said, smiling. "Miss Sophia is not a doctor." He looked back and said, "Please just give her a call."

"Alright, shall we go," Ms. Gerhardt said, grabbing Willem by the hand.

Forcing a smile, Dr. Hanson held the door open. Ms. Gerhardt and Willem stepped out from the office, holding hands.

"Thank you," Willem said, returning the earplugs.

"You're very welcome," Dr. Hanson said, firmly.

ELEVEN

"WILLEM, COME BACK and sit down," said Ms. Gerhardt. "They did not call your name, yet." She squinted as she looked down at her wristwatch, wondering why the wait time had grown so long after having arrived promptly for their scheduled nine-o'clock appointment.

Impatient, Willem plopped himself back down on the chair beside Ms. Gerhardt and let out a prolonged sigh.

Finally, a nurse peeked out from a side door, revealing only her long narrow face. "Willem," she said, looking at her clipboard. Then more loudly said, "Gerhardt?"

Ms. Gerhardt stood and walked hand-in-hand with Willem through the doorway. Awaiting their entrance, Dr. Hanson stood just beyond the door with a chart tucked by his side.

"Follow me," he said in a serious tone. As they all stepped into his office, he said, "Have a seat." Ms. Gerhardt and Willem sat in wooden chairs set in front of a large mahogany desk. Dr. Hanson reached into the top sliding drawer and pulled out dark framed reading glasses. After placing his glasses onto the bridge of his nose, he opened the chart and spread X-ray images across the desk as if he were displaying a dark roadmap. Particularly interested in one particular X-ray, he lifted the image above his head toward the light.

Hesitant, Ms. Gerhardt asked, "Is everything okay?"

"So far, so good," Dr. Hanson said before placing the image back down. He leaned back and raised another X-ray above him.

Ms. Gerhardt looked up, as well.

"What is that?" She frantically asked, pointing toward the middle.

"That's the temporal lobe region." He used his index finger to make an imaginary circle around the mid portion of the slide.

"I meant, here," she said, pointing slightly below.

"Thalamus," Dr. Hanson said. "And speaking about the thalamus," he said, "let me take a closer look." He held the X-ray up to the light and alternated several times between opening and closing each eye.

"Oh," Ms. Gerhardt gasped, putting her open hand up to her mouth. "Is everything really okay?"

"Well, what I am doing now is examining the scans for nonsymmetrical areas that may be different in color, shape and size."

Unfamiliar with medical lingo, she wanted to know that all was fine.

"You and I had some time to talk last week during the testing. I also had the opportunity to speak with Dr. Weinman." Dr. Hanson paused for a moment and inserted the scanned images back into the chart.

"Is everything ok?" She asked, trembling.

"Well, I don't see anything remarkable in these test results."

"That's a good thing," Ms. Gerhardt said, looking around. She nervously asked, "Is it not?"

"Did you have a chance to reach out to Miss Sophia," Dr. Hanson inquired.

"No," Ms. Gerhardt said. "It was another busy week, just a lot going on." Her manner was nonchalant, suggesting she did not believe her own excuse.

Dr. Hanson nodded in an exaggerated slow-motion manner, realizing he faced resistance. He walked over to the filing cabinet and placed the chart back into a sliding file that was organized in alphabetical order. As he returned, he shook his head and sighed before he sat back down.

"I'm really not sure what to say at this point. Miss Sophia may be your answer."

"Well, I just feel like we are getting the run around," Ms. Gerhardt said.

"Well, I'm not quite sure what—"

"Excuse me," Ms. Gerhardt interrupted him. "The principal wants Willem to see the school nurse. The school nurse thinks he should see a psychiatrist. The psychiatrist recommends an adoption specialist and a neurologist." She dipped her head, seething, "And, you", she said, stuttering, "…you stuffed him into a tunnel machine with obnoxious noises."

"Oh-h-h Ms. Gerhardt," he said, defensively. He took a deep breath and exhaled.

"Let me finish," Ms. Gerhardt said, raising her voice. "Take him here and take him there and now it's time for him to see…" she said, pausing for a moment while reaching into her purse for the business card, then said "Sophia Angus?"

"Please, Ms. Gerhardt. I'm not suggesting that—"

Ms. Gerhardt interrupted the doctor, again, and read the name slowly out loud, "So-ph-ia An-gg-us."

"Please," he said, raising his hand, "just give it a chance." He looked toward the side. "Willem," he said, cupping his hands together to the sound of a soft clap.

"What?" Willem snapped, sounding annoyed.

In silence, Ms. Gerhardt sat with her arms tightly folded.

Dr. Hanson paused. "Well, Willem," he said, again, repeating his name. "Do you know things you should not know?"

"Sometimes," said Willem, without hesitating, looking away. His body stiffened as he stared at the wall.

"Do you feel people sometimes talk to you, even though no one is with you?"

"Yes," Willem snapped, looking up to the corner of the ceiling where the wallpaper had unraveled.

Dr. Hanson nodded his head in an emphatic way in-sync with each response. He got up and pushed his chair aside. Smiling, he stood with one leg crossed over the other, planting his elbow on the table to balance himself.

Ms. Gerhardt stood and walked toward the door at which time Willem followed closely behind her.

"Oh, Ms. Gerhardt," Dr. Hanson said, following behind her as well. He jogged ahead and grabbed hold of the doorknob. "You can spend Willem's childhood hopping from one doctor to the next, or you can take him to see Miss Sophia. It's really up to you."

Ms. Gerhardt nodded. She did not know anything about Miss Sophia, but realized that Dr. Hanson was persistent with the one and only recommendation he offered. As she looked down at the card again, she mouthed, *So-ph-ia An-gg-us.*

"I will call Miss Sophia," Ms. Gerhardt said softly, staring at Dr. Hanson. Nodding several times, she appeared to finally concede from exhaustion.

"Willem," Dr. Hanson said with his hand still affixed to the door knob. "I'm married. Do you know my wife's name?"

"I don't know," Willem said, clenching his fist and pausing for a moment. Then he looked up and said, "But, I think her name begins with an *E.*"

"E-m-i-l-y," Dr. Hanson stated, nodding in the direction of Ms. Gerhardt.

"Emily," he repeated, confirming with a full nod. He asked, "Do I have any pets?"

Willem looked up and said, "No." After a brief pause, he said, "But you used to."

Dr. Hanson thought *no* would have been sufficient. Willem's additional comment caused him to exhale and think about the recent passing of his dog. As he held the door open, Ms. Gerhardt and Willem exited.

"Oh Ms. Gerhardt," Dr. Hanson said in an elongated way as if he were singing out her name.

"Yes," she said, abruptly turning around. But, before he spoke, Ms. Gerhardt said, "I know… I know… I will make the call."

TWELVE

IN HIS PAJAMAS, Willem adjusted the bent rabbit-ear antenna that looped high along the wall. He dropped to his knees at a nose length from the black and white television encased in the large wooden shelf.

"Can you please turn the volume just a tad lower," Ms. Gerhardt said, her voice projecting from the kitchen where she stood emptying groceries from brown paper bags. She hurried to put a carton of milk, containers of yogurt and two-dozen eggs into the refrigerator.

"Thank you," she said, acknowledging the decrease in volume.

"You're welcome, mom," Willem said, twisting the fist-sized television knob clockwise, scrolling from one station to the next: *The Flintstones, The Partridge Family, The Brady Bunch, The Munsters, American Bandstand...*

"After I put away these groceries, I'd like to talk to you," Ms. Gerhardt said, stacking vegetable cans in the pantry.

Willem looked back, turning the knob even faster. Excited, he stopped channel surfing and stared at the game show.

"Wait, mom," he said, his voice reaching a higher pitch. "It's Joker's Wild!"

Smiling, Ms. Gerhardt stepped into the family room and stood above him. Well aware of his favorite show, she smiled and tapped her nails gently against the back of his neck.

"One of your very favorites," she said, kneeling down beside him. "I know it is."

"Uh-huh," Willem acknowledged, letting out a soft giggle.

"That's fine," she said, nodding, "but let me know when Joker's Wild comes to an end." Before returning to the kitchen, she said, "I want to talk."

Willem lay on his side, using an elbow to prop his head up from the carpet. A game contestant responded correctly and spun a mechanism that resembled a slot machine. Willem pumped his fist up high and cheered as the host, Jack Barry, enthusiastically shouted, *Joker*, three times in succession.

Ms. Gerhardt hurried back and stood by the doorway where she held onto the door panel as she poked her head in.

Willem rolled over and stared back at her from his side.

"He got it! ALL Jokers, mom," he said in excitement. "He just won five hundred dollars!" Willem held up five fingers as he spoke.

Ms. Gerhardt clapped and asked him to join her in the kitchen to which he agreed. In the background, Jack Barry invited the audience to tune in again, describing Joker's Wild as, *the game where knowledge is king and lady luck is queen*. Willem pulled the plug out from the wall socket just as Jack Barry waved goodbye.

"Okay," she said, smiling. "It's time to talk." Her manner was playful, though she was extremely eager to engage in conversation.

"Do you mind if we talk outside?" Willem asked.

"That's dandy," Ms. Gerhardt said, latching her hand around his thin wrist. "Watch your step."

Willem stepped into the garden and sprinted toward the jungle gym, composed of swings, ladders, monkey bars and an attached seesaw. He bent his knees and jumped onto the monkey bar. Ms.

Gerhardt watched him from a distance as he alternated hands from one bar to the next as his legs swung beneath him. After he arrived at the last horizontal bar, he dropped down to the ground with his hands straight up like a gymnast sticking the landing. He sprinted over to the tetherball pole and held the rope above his head.

"Willem, come sit with me," Ms. Gerhardt said. "You can play later."

Ms. Gerhardt sat on the red-painted seesaw where her weight had carried her down to the ground. As she pushed up, Willem sat upon the seat across from her on the opposite side. As a breeze whisked though the backyard, Willem used the back of his hand to brush his hair to the side.

"Do you need a haircut?"

"No, just less wind," he said, eliciting smiles from both.

Willem reached his arms above his head as his side of the seesaw hit its peak. At first, he glanced over the fence at the yard next door. He then panned up to the sky, focusing on a group of birds in flight.

"Is that a flock?" He asked, gazing toward the clouds.

"I believe so," Ms. Gerhardt said, using her hand to block out the glare from the sun. "So, you like birds?"

"I do, very much. It's just really amazing."

"What's amazing?" she asked.

"Birds stick together, like a family!"

"A family?" she said.

"Yea. I mean sometimes I wish I was a bird."

Willem kept his eyes glued on the dozens of birds flying together above in a V-formation. The flock circled the sky, chirping and fluttering their wings, each following the one in front, stride for stride amidst their journey.

Ms. Gerhardt kept her eyes glued on Willem, wondering the meaning behind his fascination. "For years," she said, "scientists have been trying to figure out why birds fly in the V-formation." She took a deep breath. "I sure don't think it is coincidental."

"Well," Willem said, "it is because it most likely saves them energy."

"Energy?" Ms. Gerhardt repeated. "In what way?"

"It will be discovered in the future," Willem said. "In time," he said, pausing, "in time, we will hear about V-formations and energy."

In her mind, she thought, *Energy?* Ms. Gerhardt just nodded in agreement amidst her inner confusion. "You do love them birds," Ms. Gerhardt said, "so much so that you wish you could be one?" She cleared her throat, awaiting his response while looking up toward the flock.

"Yeah, they are kind of cool. But I'm not sure I really want to be one."

"What do you like about birds?" Ms. Gerhardt asked.

"Let's see," he said, putting his finger to his forehead. "Birds are peaceful and they stay together. Oh, yeah—and, they can fly."

"Would you like to get a bird?" She asked, "Perhaps, a bird of your own."

"Well no," he said, shaking his head. "That wouldn't be a very good idea."

"No," Ms. Gerhardt said, wincing. She could not help but to ask, "Why not?"

"A life in a cage is never a good thing," he said, tucking his chin. He appeared to drift away in his thoughts. After a few moments, he lifted his head and muttered, "Never a good thing."

Ms. Gerhardt nodded as if she understood. She forced her end of the seesaw to touch the ground as Willem wiggled on his seat with his legs kicking out beneath him. Both were mesmerized by the chatty birds above, circling the neighborhood. Some drifted away, landing on tree tops while others landed on roofs. The original flock remained intact, though the formation had become a much smaller "v".

A seesaw may not be the best time or place for such sensitive conversations, she thought. *If not now, then when?* she wondered.

Thoughts raced in her mind with questions she long wanted to ask about: *his upbringing...the adoption... the scar on his eye...school incidents...the racetrack...his knowledge about her parents...the bird reference...and, energy?*

Willem noticed she was absorbed in thought. "It's okay," he said, shrugging. "You can ask me questions." He chuckled in a nervous way, "Ask away."

Ms. Gerhardt looked back at him with a closed mouthed smile. She felt relieved he was giving her the *green light* for inquiries like a teacher at the end of a lecture, who opens the floor for questions. Caught off guard, she was not sure where to begin, though felt delighted that he had offered.

"Do you ever wish you could fly away?" Ms. Gerhardt asked.

"Well," Willem said, blowing out air. "Can I be honest with you?"

Ms. Gerhardt's heart skipped a beat for a moment. She focused on a small dirt puddle below where bubbles had formed. *Honesty is the best policy*, she thought. But at the same time, unsure if she was prepared to hear truths. She cleared her throat and looked up. "Of course, honey," she said, "please be honest." Her speech slowed as she spoke softly.

"I don't feel like flying away. I am very happy here with you." Tears welled up in his eyes. "I just hope I'm with you forever." His eyes widened without blinking as he nodded. He then looked down and asked Ms. Gerhardt to lift up her side of the board so that they were, again, at an even level.

She stretched her bent knees and balanced the seesaw in the center. Willem looked away for a moment but continued to speak. "There was a time I wished I could fly away." He spoke through the cracks in his voice. "My life has not always been easy."

"Why's that"? She asked, maintaining the seesaw in a horizontal position.

"I used to stare out of my window at the birds above and wonder why I can't be a bird." Willem looked back at Ms. Gerhardt and exhaled. "To me, a bird means freedom." He used the top of his shirt to wipe away tears and the back part of his hand to wipe moisture beneath his nose. After a brief sigh, Willem continued, "I moved from one sad home to the next. My last name changed so many times."

Ms. Gerhardt sat still on the seesaw. Her knees buckled to point in which she could no longer press upward even if she wanted to. She was happy he felt comfortable enough to share, though also saddened by his disclosures.

"Why so many changes?" She asked.

Willem blew out a steady stream of air. "Well, I guess for the same reason you may want to get rid of me, too." He looked down with sorrow, pressing his head against his open palms.

"Willem, you have to realize—"

"I know, but—"

"Willem, give me chance—"

"I want to, if you—"

"Willem!" She said, raising her voice several notches higher.

He stopped talking for a moment, looking downward, again.

"Willem," Ms. Gerhardt repeated, pausing for a moment, waiting for him to look up. "You are forever a Gerhardt." Trying to reassure him, she nodded slowly with widened eyes.

Willem broke into a partial smile.

"Forever?" He asked.

"Forever!" She confirmed, pressing her lips together.

Willem used the bottom of his shirt to dry his damp chin. "I really don't mind all your questions," he said, smiling. "I feel like you care."

"Oh good, honey," she said with another firm nod. "I do care."

"Actually," he said, emphatically, "your questions remind me of the doctor I used to see in El Paso."

A doctor, Ms. Gerhardt thought. *Doctor,* echoed again in her mind. So many more questions flooded her head. She remained calm, realizing it was in his best interest.

"El Paso," She repeated.

Willem was surprised that she showed more of an interest in the city than the fact he had seen a doctor.

"Just outside of El Paso," he said, nodding, "I think."

"Oh," she said. In deep thought, she placed two fingers upon her chin, thinking, *so, he has been to a doctor…perhaps a psychologist?*

"Yea, good old El Paso," he said. After a brief pause, he said, "Not!"

"What do you mean?" She asked, wondering what he may be hiding.

Willem shrugged. It was as if he hit a roadblock in his thinking. He had seemed comfortable sharing, even in tidbits, though all of a sudden took a turn in reverse and shut down. Blankly staring, he looked up.

Sensing his discomfort, Ms. Gerhardt decided to just go along with the flow and look up along with him toward the empty sky.

"Willem?" She said, looking back down.

"Yea, mom," he said, whiplashing his head back toward her.

"Was your family from El Paso?"

"I did not live in El Paso for long. Well, I really did not live anywhere for long," he said with a nervous chuckle, bobbing his head.

"So, you were not born in El Paso?"

"Not sure where I was born," Willem said with a sigh. "But, I think I heard someone say something about a jail." He looked down and drifted into deep thought. "I don't think the jail was in El Paso, though."

Jail, she thought to herself. It was as if an alarm was set off in her body. Like an old record player with a broken needle, repeating lyrics, all she heard replaying in her mind was *jail...jail...jail...*

"Oh, jail," Ms. Gerhardt said out loud, trying to sound as casual as possible in her inquiry.

"Somebody said that," Willem said, shrugging. "But, I really don't know."

In her mind, she kept thinking about things teachers had said and the questions doctors had asked. She tried to envision what his parents look like, and what sort of legal problems had placed his mother behind bars. Her mind raced about every scenario imaginable.

"Oh, that's fine," Ms. Gerhardt snapped. "But how about the incidents in school? What happened at the track? How did you know what happened to my parents?" She knew her questions were like rapid fire, but at this point, she could not help herself. There were so many things she wanted to further understand. She wanted to know everything. And, she wanted to know, *now!*

Feeling vulnerable, Willem did not respond. One of his biggest fears was that he'd be judged. He trusted Ms. Gerhardt, but at the same time felt overwhelmed by her questions, especially one after another.

"Mom?"

"Yes," she responded softly, looking back toward him. She nodded as if to say, *it's okay.*

"Have you ever seen the clouds that planes leave behind?" His inquiry was more of a rhetorical question.

Ms. Gerhardt nodded and said, "Vapor trails."

Willem looked up and pointed to the sky. "Sometimes you see a plane. Then the vapor trails...Visible a few seconds and then they just disappear." He put his open hand in the air and made circular motions as if he were erasing a chalkboard. "All gone," he said, snapping his fingers, "but where do they go?" He shrugged in an exaggerated way with both palms up high.

Ms. Gerhardt stared back, nodding eagerly to hear what more he would say.

"Vapors disappear," Willem said, "just like my memories." He made a rumbling noise. "Here for one second, then gone the next." He looked up in deep thought. "Where do they go?" He closed his eyes for a moment and muttered, "Where, oh where do they go?"

Ms. Gerhardt listened without commenting, nodding as if she understood.

Willem opened his eyes wide with a sudden jolt. "Mom," he said, pausing for a moment, "let's get off."

Ms. Gerhardt pushed her weight down and slowly stepped off her side of the seesaw. As she stood up, she used her hands to slowly lift her side up as the other side gently touched the ground.

Willem hopped off and ran to the other side of the seesaw where Ms. Gerhardt greeted him with open arms. He stepped to the side for a moment and looked back toward Ms. Gerhardt in an awkward type way.

"Is everything, alright?" Ms. Gerhardt asked. She leaned forward and kissed his forehead.

In silence, Willem stared back. His eyebrows dipped as he stretched out his arm.

"You're it," he said, lunging toward her with his index finger. He sprinted to the side of the yard, looking back over his shoulder, hoping she was following in pursuit as he tried to engage her in a game of *tag*.

"Go ahead and play, honey" she said, waving her hand. "I am going to fix us some lunch." She blew him a kiss and walked back toward the house.

"I love you, mom," he shouted out.

Turning around, Ms. Gerhardt bunched her fingers to her lips and opened her palm in one motion. A sound of, *muah,* came out of her mouth as she extended her arm in a loving way toward him.

In the distance, Willem patted his fingers several times against his puckered lips, giggling.

THIRTEEN

"OH, HONEY," MS. Gerhardt called out, speaking over the loud humming sound resonating from the vacuum. "Can you please bring the potato chips and sour cream dip?" She pushed the vacuum over the family room carpet for a third time.

Willem stood up from the sofa and headed to the kitchen where he reached for the bag of chips and container of dip.

"Anything else, mom?" He asked, turning around and awaiting for her response.

As Ms. Gerhardt pushed the *off* button, the sound of the vacuum transitioned from a loud hum to a gradual whistle hum, then after a moment, reached complete silence.

"No, honey," she said. "I will get the drinks later."

"Okay, no problem, mom."

"We're having company," Ms. Gerhardt said, lifting a colorful feather duster along the corner crease of the wall.

Willem returned to the family room where he placed the container of dip onto the circular table before dumping the full bag of chips into a large glass bowl. Stoic, he looked down and then timidly asked, "Who is coming?"

"A friend," Ms. Gerhardt said, yanking at the vacuum plug several times until it finally dribbled out of the electric socket. She leaned the duster against the wall.

"What type of friend?" Willem asked, flashing two fingers up high gesturing an air quote as he said, *friend*. Before she could answer, he shook his head and sarcastically said, "A friend."

"Yes," Ms. Gerhardt said, "…a very nice man." She wound the vacuum cord around the upper handle.

After taking a deep breath, Willem exhaled.

"Oh, c'mon," Ms. Gerhardt said in an enthusiastic way, "you'll like him." *Lord, I hope so,* she thought to herself, strutting toward the kitchen.

Willem plopped back down on the sofa, watching the television news.

Ms. Gerhardt returned from the kitchen carrying vetiver-scented candles that she set down, one at a time, upon the glass table. She stepped toward the side wall where she reached for the switch to dim the recessed lighting over the fireplace.

The doorbell rang at a frenetic tempo to the tune of, "Happy Birthday." Ms. Gerhardt hurried to strike a match to light each candle. A few more consecutive raps on the door followed as the birthday melody played for a second time.

Willem stood and looked over toward the door.

"Don't worry. I'll get it, honey," said Ms. Gerhardt, waving her arm and mouthing to Willem, *sit back down*. Smiling, she opened the mesh curtains draped on the door and peeked out through the side glass panel.

"Robert is here," she said, unlocking the double bolt.

Robert? Willem mumbled, pushing his lower torso deeper into the sofa.

"Why, hello there," Ms. Gerhardt said, opening the door with a twinkle in her eyes.

"Hi, darling," Robert said, handing her a dozen roses. The petals were mostly bright red, though some had more of a pink-colored tint.

"Thank you," she said in a prolonged way, welcoming Robert with a quick hug followed by a soft kiss on his cheek. "You smell terrific," she whispered, tugging gently on the knot of his tie.

Ms. Gerhardt escorted him across the hallway toward the family room. At the entrance way, she rolled out her palm.

"A-n-d," she said, proudly, "this is Willem." She pointed with her chin toward the sofa.

Willem stood and extended his arm. Robert's gold nugget bracelet dangled below his wrist as they shook hands.

"It's nice to finally meet you," Robert said, nodding with a huge smile. "Your mom sure has told me so much about you."

Willem forced a smile of his own before he sat back down.

"Robert," Ms. Gerhardt said, pointing toward the other side of the sofa, "please, have a seat." She walked to the corner table and placed the flowers into a crystal vase.

"What are you watching?" Robert asked, "Anything good?" He leaned forward and grabbed a chip before sitting down upon the sofa.

Willem shook his head. "Just the weather."

"Weather is a good thing," Robert said.

"Depends on the weather," Willem snapped back.

"Or the weatherman," Robert said, smiling, "or, I should say, weatherwoman."

"Depends on the weather," Willem reiterated.

"This is true," Robert said, chewing, "I agree."

Smiling, Willem nodded hard back.

"I take it you are a Cowboys fan," Robert said, acknowledging the Tony Dorsett jersey Willem had on.

"You can say that," Willem said, flexing his chest to show off the thick embroidered familiar number 33.

"So, how's school going for you?" Robert asked.

"Fine," Willem said, shrugging. "I guess."

"You guess?" Robert pulled the dip toward him. "What's that supposed to mean?"

"It is what it is. It ain't what it ain't," Willem said, sighing.

"Have a favorite class?" Robert asked, crunching down on the dip-coated chip, "or, a favorite teacher?"

Changing the topic, Willem commented about the weather forecast. "It's strange how it could be raining and sunny in different parts of the same town," Willem said before grabbing a chip.

"Excuse me," Robert said, nodding. He stood up from the sofa with a chip in hand. "Beth, I'll be right back," he called out before taking a bite.

"Ok," Ms. Gerhardt said, smiling with her thumb up.

"I left something in the car," Robert said, winking toward her. He made his way to the front, leaving the door open behind him as he stepped out.

"Nice guy, right?" Ms. Gerhardt said, entering the room.

"I don't know," Willem said, looking back toward her.

Ms. Gerhardt kissed the top of his head. "Come on," she said, tapping her knuckles against the upper part of his back as if she were playing the drums.

"I'm b-a-c-k," Robert sang out, reentering.

"Oh, my," Ms. Gerhardt said, staring at a Labrador Retriever puppy, whose leash was triple looped around Robert's leg. Panting with a protruding tongue, the puppy stood on his hind legs, climbing up the wall.

Robert stooped to a knee. "Come over here. You can touch him."

Hesitant and acting shy, Willem rose from the sofa. From a distance he watched the puppy chase his own tail.

"Come," Robert said, louder. "He wants to see you."

"He's really cute," Willem said, stepping over. He stooped down and bent forward on both knees, allowing the puppy to lick his whole face.

"Watch this," Robert said. He pulled a small rope out from his back pocket and wiggled it along the floor. The puppy clutched onto the rope, tugging back and forth in a game of tug-of-war. "You do it," Robert said, handing him the rope.

Willem waved the rope from side to side as the puppy rolled over in circles on the tiled floor. After releasing the rope from his clenched jaw, the puppy lay on his back, paws straight up, begging for a tummy rub.

"Go ahead," Robert said, firmly. "Give 'em what he's asking for."

Willem gently massaged his belly. As he leaned down, he put his cheek flat against the puppy's stomach.

Chuckling, Ms. Gerhardt stood with her hands at her hips.

"Aww that is just so cute," she said, cooing, "I wish I had a camera." She put her hands together in the shape of a box and flicked her index finger, pretending to snap a shot.

Willem lifted himself up from the floor. His enthusiasm suddenly dimmed. His eyes peered over toward Robert and darted back toward Ms. Gerhardt in a rapid motion. Suddenly, he clenched his fists and walked briskly until he reached the foot of the stairway where he stopped and looked back for a moment before marching up the stairs with exaggerated stomps, one step at a time.

The high pitched, excited bark of the puppy transitioned into a soft whimper. Robert stooped down on a knee, comforting the sad puppy while shrugging in the direction of Ms. Gerhardt, who also wondered what had just happened.

With soft steps, Ms. Gerhardt made her way to the foyer. She looked up the stairway to where Willem was sitting at the midway point with his arms folded, head tucked between his bent knees.

"Is everything okay?" she asked.

"No," he said, sniffling. "Not okay." Through the space between the hardwood railings, Willem peered out in disgust.

Ms. Gerhardt stood on the very bottom step for a moment and then proceeded to make her way up the stairs.

"Just stop," Willem said, holding his hand up.

Confused, Ms. Gerhardt froze for a moment. "You were having fun with the pup." She threw her arms up. "Just what is going on here?"

Tears filled his eyes. "It was a test," Willem said, whimpering. "Wasn't it?"

"What do you mean, honey?"

Willem put his head back between his legs, using his knees as earmuffs to block out the world. He peered out for a moment, then asked, "Did I pass?" Frustrated and saddened, he straightened his body, stood up and stormed up the remaining stairs to his bedroom where he closed the door behind him.

Ms. Gerhardt blew out air as she looked across the room toward Robert. Saddened, she scratched the top of her head as she walked back toward the family room.

From the top banister, Willem reappeared.

"Mom," he called out. "Are you sure he is not married?" Without giving her a chance to respond to the rhetorical question, he stormed back to his bedroom.

FOURTEEN

IT WAS 3:37 in the afternoon. The sun had already started its descent. Intermittent bubbles rose to the top of the lake where recently stocked sunfish and bass swam beneath the slow moving ripples.

On the bench, Ms. Gerhardt sat shoulder-to-shoulder beside Willem, watching the water glistening beneath the late afternoon sun.

Willem lifted his legs and planted his mud-stained sneakers up on the bench. "Life is good," he said, hugging the top of his kneecaps.

Ms. Gerhardt curled her arm around him and rested her cheek on the top of his head. They sat, together as one, watching a family of eight quacking ducks move steadily across the lake, diving and dipping their heads beneath the surface.

Ms. Gerhardt hummed as she leaned back. It did not take long before Willem broke into a smile. She stood and quickly flattened the wrinkles on her bright green high-waist shorts as she hummed even louder. A gentle echo resonated across the peaceful lake as she sang out that she loved him. After the final echo completely faded, she leaned down and kissed him on the middle of his forehead.

Willem looked up through squinted eyes, using his forearm to block out the brightness generated by the descending sun. "I know you love me," he whispered.

Ms. Gerhardt took Willem by the hand and spun him around. She pulled him close to slow dance with him on the path, twirling several times together, then alternating dips beneath one another's arms.

"You're a good dancer," she said, tugging him back and forth like a rag doll. She rested her cheek on the top of his head while slowly rocking him tightly within the grasp of her arms.

Willem took a deep breath and stepped back for a moment.

"Mom," he said, "I have something I need to tell you."

Ms. Gerhardt felt uneasy. She realized there was so much she did not know. Inside, she thought, *some things are best unsaid. What she did not know wouldn't hurt her.*

"Tell me," she said, then whispered, "anything, honey."

"Well," he said, "I don't like animals."

"What?" She gasped. "What exactly do you mean by that?" She recoiled, trying to catch her breath.

"I don't like animals. I LOVE them," he shouted out, smiling.

"What am I going to do with you," Ms. Gerhardt said. Breaking into a smile of her own, she jabbed her fist gently into his ribs, playfully.

After a brief pause, her smile faded.

"Oh, Willem," she said, taking in a deep breath.

"Don't tell me," he sarcastically said, chuckling, "You don't like animals, either?"

As Ms. Gerhardt stroked her fingers through his fine hair, she said, "What made you say Robert is married?"

"Well, that's not e-x-a-c-t-l-y what I said, mom."

Ms. Gerhardt perked up. "Oh, really, that's not what you said?"

"No. Not exactly."

"Well, I thought I heard you—"

"I did not really say—"

"Well, you were RIGHT," Ms. Gerhardt said, interrupting. "Right, again."

She caressed his face and sang, "You and Me Against the World," by Helen Reddy. As she swung his limp arms in motion, she looked deeply into his eyes and sang the most meaningful lyrics.

They walked arm-in-arm along the dirt path that encircled the lake as their shadows followed in the lake beside them. Both inhaled the fresh aroma in the air from an assortment of colorful flowers that bordered the path.

"Nature is beautiful," Ms. Gerhardt said. She pointed to and named the flower types as they walked by: *Portulaca, Mexican Sunflower, Yellow Rose, Bluebonnet*. She stopped for a moment and explained how he will impress all of the girls if he remembers the flowers by name.

Willem giggled before reciting back each of the flowers by name.

"So, you are listening."

"I always listen," Willem said. He lifted their clenched hands and kissed her wrist.

"The Yellow Rose will make most people mention the song," Ms. Gerhardt said, pointing at the beautiful, bright colored flower. "But the song does not refer to the flower, but rather to a woman, instead."

Without saying a word, Willem absorbed the details.

Ms. Gerhardt turned and pointed to a different flower. Excited, she squatted and proudly said, "The bluebonnet!"

Intrigued, Willem leaned down and touched the surface of one of its leaves.

"I see you're noticing the five leaves," Ms. Gerhardt said. "You know they represent the five points of the Texas Lone Star."

Willem continued to examine and massage the flower. He said, *blue*, as he stooped all the way down to get a closer look at its stems.

"Bluebonnets are given special status as our state flower," Ms. Gerhardt explained. "While not always blue, as you see, they sometimes bloom in other colors as well."

On both his knees, Willem stuck his nose into the base of the bluebonnet flower, inhaling the attar through his widened nostrils.

"There is only one thing lovelier than a flower in bloom," she said, inhaling deeply, "The breathtaking scent of wildflowers!"

"Wow," Willem said, taking in a deep breath.

"Beautiful, aren't they?" Ms. Gerhardt said.

Around the bend of the lake, a small wooden dock was connected to a snack shed. Several canoes and rowboats swayed alongside the dock at their posts. Ms. Gerhardt and Willem jogged down the path toward the boats. An attendant, in his late teens, was wearing blue flip flops and a matching blue-striped bathing suit.

"Can I help y'all?" He asked, greeting them with a warm reception.

Ms. Gerhardt reached for her purse and inquired about the rates. The attendant flapped his wrist once and said, "Just go right on ahead, Ms. Gerhardt."

Well known throughout the Greater Houston area, people were often enamored with the Gerhardt family. The attendant was honored to have Ms. Gerhardt as a lake guest. All lake personnel either knew Ms. Gerhardt or, at least, knew of the Gerhardt lineage. Wealthy, yet extremely generous, *The Gerhardt's* had donated money over the past two decades for the purchase of picnic tables, benches, rowboats and canoes. Donations had also helped improve the overall landscape of the park.

Ms. Gerhardt escorted Willem toward the boat of his choice, a white rowboat, 12 feet long, three rows deep of sliding seats. Together, they rowed toward the center of the lake where a fountain sprayed water twenty feet high. Large oval-shaped floaters surrounded the sprayers. A large electronic warning sign flashed, *Wet Risk*.

On the boat, they watched the ducks from a closer distance, many of which swam beneath the water spray. Families and couples picnicked on blankets spread across the entire lake property.

As Ms. Gerhardt sat back, she rested the paddles to the side and closed her eyes, remembering times when her parents took her boating on the lake. She reminisced on the good memories spent on boats and afternoon picnics that included watermelon, celery sticks, sandwiches of all types and ice cream they had to always eat quickly. The landscape was less manicured back then, though the serenity and freshness of air remained.

"Oh, mom?"

Ms. Gerhardt opened her eyes. "Oh, W-i-l-l-e-m," she responded, smiling back toward him.

"What do you think about people who do bad things but with good intentions?"

Here we go again, she thought, leaning back with her arms folded tight. "Okay, fess up," she said, firmly. "What now?"

Willem smirked while reaching behind his back. Sustaining perfect eye contact, he watched her every move.

"Oh, my," she said, breathing deeply. "You look like the cat that ate the canary."

Willem rocked from side to side and extended his arm out from behind his back.

Exhaling, Ms. Gerhardt looked back in disappointment as Willem handed her a bluebonnet.

"Willem!" she said, gasping.

"For you," he said, smiling. "For you, mom."

"Where did you get this?"

"From before when—"

"You are not supposed to ever pick the flowers."

"Yeah, but I love—"

"There is no, yeah, but—"

"But, I just wanted to give—"

"You're not supposed to pick a bluebonnet," she said, firmly.

"Only because I really—"

"What made you even do something like that?"

"I really thought you would—"

"Would what? That really was not a good thing to do, honey."

"I know, I really wanted to—"

"The beauty of the flower goes beyond just the flower."

"It was just that I—"

"Willem," she said, putting her hand up. "Please, no more excuses."

Okay, he whimpered before going silent.

"I know why you picked it. But the flowers are here for everyone. Look at them, sniff them and absorb their beauty into the depths of your mind…But, don't ever pick them."

Willem nodded, but in silent disagreement. He put his head down and walked to the far side of the boat where he placed the flower on the boat bottom, beneath the sliding row of seats, next to an emergency kit.

Ms. Gerhardt dropped the paddles and walked to the last row of seats where she sat down while removing each sandal, one at a time. As she reclined, she reached down, picked up the bluebonnet and placed the stem behind her ear. She took a deep breath and smiled, then crossed her bare feet in front of her.

"These are memories we will look back on," she said smiling, "precious memories and many more to come." She took a deep breath and said, "I love you, son."

Sighing in relief, Willem scooted closer beside her and stared at the bluebonnet, dangling by her ear.

Nestled side-by-side, cheek-to-cheek, Ms. Gerhardt kissed his forehead and then wrapped her long arms around him. Both closed their eyes and snuggled, together as one, while the boat swayed to the rhythm of the gentle ripples. The sky glared a pale tint of orange before the sun dipped further beneath the horizon, vanishing.

FIFTEEN

RAIN DROPS TRICKLED down the windshield as Ms. Gerhardt drove along a winding road that led deeper into the woods. The song, "Rhinestone Cowboy," by Glen Campbell, played in the background to which she rocked her head and sang along. In the backseat, Willem pressed his face against the window, leaving an imprint of his nose upon the condensation on the glass.

"Where are we?" Willem asked, wiping away the mist with the ball of his palm. He tucked his hand inside of his coat and used the cuff of his sleeve to remove the smudge marks left behind.

Earlier, Ms. Gerhardt had stumbled upon the business card of Sophia Angus. Having had no plans for the day and knowing the weather forecast called for a high chance for precipitation, she felt this would be an ideal time to finally adhere to *medical advice*.

"Where are we?" Willem asked, again.

"Good question," Ms. Gerhardt said, smiling back at him in the rearview mirror. As she applied the brakes by a mail box, she said, "I think we are here!"

Willem looked through droplets on the windshield as Ms. Gerhardt drove up the looping driveway where she parked near the detached three-car garage.

"Is there an umbrella by your feet?" She asked, turning around and looking down at the backseat floor.

"I don't see one," Willem said, raising his legs. "I'm fine, though," he said, unbuckling his seatbelt. "It's only drizzling, mom."

Ms. Gerhardt looked out from her window at the tall brick home attached to a much smaller, single story building of wood construction in the rear. All curtains were shut in the front. A sign reading, *Use Rear Door*, was mounted beside a metal arrow that pointed toward the back.

They stepped out of the car and walked along a dark pavement looping around in a half circle toward the rear of the home. A Frisbee-shaped fluorescent orange sign with the words, *We Are Open*, hung on the middle of the door.

"What's going on?" Willem asked, repeatedly. Confused, he squinted, looking up through the corner of his eyes.

Smiling, Ms. Gerhardt shrugged her shoulders.

"Is it tunnel-time, again?" Willem asked, perking his head up.

"No," said Ms. Gerhardt, biting her upper lip to refrain from laughing.

"What now?" Willem whined.

"Relax," she said. "Everything is going to be fine." The tone of her voice was hesitant as if she were trying to reassure herself. She sucked in a deep breath and opened the door a crack.

"Hello?" she said as they stepped inside. "Is anybody here?"

"Yes, I am," a woman's voice called out.

With Willem by her side, Ms. Gerhardt pushed the door all the way open and then stepped inside.

A short, plump woman in her mid-fifties was seated at a long rectangular table with her arms folded. Her black sweater matched her black pants. A colorful beaded necklace was wound twice around her neck from which a large gold medallion dangled to the middle of her wide cleavage. Her thick framed glasses made her big brown eyes appear even larger beneath her unusually thin, curled eyebrows.

"I'm Miss Sophia," she said, stroking her fingers through the knots of her curly black hair that hung down to her waist.

"Oh, hi," said Ms. Gerhardt, introducing herself in a nervous way. She pushed Willem's damp hair to the side of his forehead before nudging him toward the table.

Miss Sophia stood and waved, revealing her long finger nails, curled at the tips. "Please have a seat," she said, rolling out her arms.

Ms. Gerhardt helped Willem free his arm from his tight coat sleeve. She easily removed her own raincoat before placing both coats over an extra chair.

"Oh, cool beans," Willem said, pointing toward the wall shelf.

"That is a lava lamp," Miss Sophia said, "Do you like it?"

Globs of blue oils swirled at the top of the cone-shaped glass. Beside it, another lava lamp with a pink-tinted liquid bubbled with foam. Willem directed his attention toward the middle of the table where several sticks of incense leaned against a long, canoe-shaped, wooden ash catcher that had a small Buddha attached at one end. A combined aroma of vanilla and coconut filled the room.

"Again, I'm Miss Sophia," she said, reaching out her hand to gently *shake fingers* with Ms. Gerhardt.

Still mesmerized by the lava lamp, Willem sat in silence, smiling with an open mouth.

"So what brings you here on such a rainy day?" Miss Sophia asked, leaning forward with her hands clasped together.

"Well, Dr. Hanson has been recommending we see you," Ms. Gerhardt said, shrugging. "So, we are hoping that you can provide some answers—or at least offer some guidance."

"A doctor referred you?" Miss Sophia questioned. Then more softly, she said, *Hanson*, sounding surprised.

"Yes," Ms. Gerhardt said, nodding hard.

Miss Sophia reached for a pile of cards and loudly tapped the stack against the table. After straightening the deck with both hands, she spread the cards out like a fan.

"What's going on here?" Ms. Gerhardt asked. With her head cocked, her eyes blinked fast.

"Cool," Willem said, pointing at the colorful patterns. Rather captivated by the art designs on the cards, he said, "Let's play War."

"No, honey," Ms. Gerhardt said, "We're not playing War."

"How about, Go Fish," Willem said, letting out an exuberant cackle.

"Please," Ms. Gerhardt said, staring up at Miss Sophia, "Just tell us what's going on here." Her speech was rapid, southern accent no longer identifiable.

"Cards, mom," Willem said, planting his elbows on the table, "We're playing cards."

"Please, Willem," Ms. Gerhardt said, exhaling in frustration. "We are not here to play cards." She leaned back and folded her arms, then asked, "Or, are we?" Impatiently, she awaited any form of response.

Miss Sophia reorganized the set of cards, placing some in the form of a lower case "t" and others in the shape of a cross. She added more cards so that the pattern was that of a Celtic Cross.

"Please, say something," Ms. Gerhardt pleaded.

After sticking a cigarette into her mouth, Miss Sophia used her thumb to roll the metal spark wheel of a BIC to light it up. She then pushed the Marlboro box to the side.

"Pick a card," she said, blowing out a steady stream of smoke.

"I love magic," Willem said, excitedly.

Ms. Gerhardt leaned back in her chair.

"You want me to pick a card?" Ms. Gerhardt said, rolling her eyes. Sounding annoyed, she asked, "Are you serious?"

In the background, Willem chanted, *Pick-a-card, Pick-a-card, Pick-a-card...*

Ms. Gerhardt finally touched a card.

Miss Sophia scooped up the chosen card and examined the front. "Really," she said with widened eyes, "Very interesting."

Annoyed, Ms. Gerhardt tilted her head to the side. "Just, what is going on here?" Her arms looped, forming the shape of a *W* as she shrugged high.

"Well," said Miss Sophia, "you chose a card that symbolizes wealth."

"We are here for Willem," Ms. Gerhardt said, leaning down and meticulously looking at the *tarot* card.

Squinting, Miss Sophia looked toward Willem. Appearing confused, she asked, "How old is he?"

"Eleven," said Ms. Gerhardt.

"Eleven?" Miss Sophia mumbled, placing a finger up to her chin. "And you brought him to see me?"

"Yes, I did—"

"So, you want him to know about his future and what his future may hold. Things like that?" Miss Sophia winced, crinkling her nose.

Ms. Gerhardt leaned back. "Well to be perfectly honest, I'd prefer to know about his past."

"Excuse me," Miss Sophia said.

After nodding in a dramatic way, Ms. Gerhardt said, "He was adopted."

Miss Sophia tapped her curled finger tips along the tabletop in an animated way.

"Well, ethically speaking, I cannot sit here and divulge to you, or anyone for that matter, anything about his past, or future. Certainly, I can speak to him about such things in private. But to sit here and tell you about his past would be like eavesdropping or snooping."

Miss Sophia had seen thousands of people over the course of her career, mainly adults of high economic or celebrity status. She had helped numerous clients gain a deeper understanding of the present while also *tapping* into the future by facilitating communication with loved ones who had passed on. Divulging information about a young boy's past to an adoptive mother was not something she had any desire to do.

"But, I am his mother," Ms. Gerhardt said, exhaling.

"I understand THAT. But, let me ask you a question." Miss Sophia paused for a moment while reclining back in her chair. "What is your concern?"

"He seems out of touch," Ms. Gerhardt said, rushing her response, "but at the same time very much in touch with the things he knows or senses."

Miss Sophia nodded her head several times while gripping the edge of the table. "Please tell me more."

"Well, he randomly says things and does things."

"Maybe he just likes the attention," Miss Sophia said, interrupting, "and, by all means, who doesn't." She fluttered her long eyelashes and sucked another drag from her cigarette.

Frustrated, Ms. Gerhardt shook her head in disagreement. "There are times when he will say things or just know things, whether it be at home, at school or even at the racetrack. I am not sure how to describe it and I'm not sure he does either. But there is certainly something uncanny—"

"Uncanny?" Miss Sophia interrupted.

"Yes, uncanny!" Ms. Gerhardt snapped. "And I'm not sure what happened to his eye."

"It is possible he has been silenced," Miss Sophia said, "especially if there is a significant past filled with trauma and secrets."

"Silenced?" Ms. Gerhardt repeated.

"Yes," Miss Sophia said loudly. "And if so, I am not the one to break anyone's silence." She looked up and politely said, "I'd like to meet with him alone."

"Alone?" Ms. Gerhardt said, sounding worried as she arched her back.

"Yes," Miss Sophia said softly, pressing her lips together.

Ms. Gerhardt snatched up her purse and walked with long rapid strides out of the room.

Willem wondered what this was all about. In his mind, he kept thinking about the lava lamps, envisioning them on his own dresser at home.

Miss Sophia spread the deck out, then said, "Pick a card."

Willem cupped his hand beneath his chin. "Do the cards really have meaning? Or is it like when a magician says to blow on his hand?"

"You are a very interesting, young man," Miss Sophia said, flicking the cigarette tip against the rim of the ashtray. "You are beyond your years, for sure." She stuck the cigarette back into her mouth and loudly sucked in another long drag.

"Thank you," he said, nodding with confidence as if he already knew.

Miss Sophia lifted her torso and repositioned her chair to face Willem.

"You know, you have a gift," Miss Sophia said, blowing out a steady stream of smoke towards the ceiling.

"A gift?" Willem said, chuckling. "That's what the man told me."

"What man?" Miss Sophia asked, "Dr. Hanson?" She jabbed her cigarette into the ashtray, snuffing it out, then exhaled one last stream of smoke out from her nose.

"Not him," Willem said, sighing. "The old man at the racetrack."

"Old man," she said, recoiling in confusion.

"I don't know," Willem said, "some old man with a cane with slime on his collar."

"Oh, impressive," Miss Sophia blurted out with a sourpuss expression. Leaning back, she repeated, "Slime?"

Willem nodded, giggling. "I really don't know. It may have been mustard or just very old ketchup. Maybe a combination?"

"Well, I don't know any old men at the track with condiment-painted collars." She smirked before breaking into a full smile. "But one thing I do know for sure," she said, pausing for a moment, "you do have a gift."

"Did you talk to the old man from the track?" Willem inquired.

"I did not," Miss Sophia said. She organized the cards into a neat square pile before setting them aside. "Uncanny, huh?"

Willem's eyes jittered, looking around sheepishly.

"What I'd like for you to do is just look at me," Miss Sophia said, "but, don't say a word." She held her index finger up to her lips as she pushed her chair closer toward him, staring him in the eye.

After thirty seconds, she interrupted the silence.

"Let me ask you," Miss Sophia said. "Do you know what I was thinking?"

"I think so," he said, grinning.

Miss Sophia nodded, wondering if he really knew.

"Okay, go ahead and show me," she snapped back.

Willem stood and walked to the back corner of the room. He reached in his mouth and removed a large wad of Bubblicious Bubble Gum. Letting out a groan, he dropped it into the trashcan beneath him.

"Telepathy," she shouted out, waving him back to the table. "That's telepathy."

Ms. Gerhardt knocked on the door. "Hello," she called out, knocking again.

"Please come in," Miss Sophia said, welcoming her back.

Ms. Gerhardt stepped in and rejoined them at the table. "Is

everything okay?" She asked, looking around, confused. A sound of worry resonated in her voice.

"Depends on the way you look at it," Miss Sophia said, expanding her chest.

"How so? Please tell me," Ms. Gerhardt said, shifty eyed.

Miss Sophia exhaled. "Well tell me more about some of these occurrences that have made your doctor concerned?"

Ms. Gerhardt did not know where to begin. Collecting her thoughts, she said, "He knows about my deceased parents—"

"Mediumship," Miss Sophia interrupted. "He is able to communicate with those who have passed on. What else?"

"He predicted all winners at the racetrack and then got a sense of urgency before a tragedy."

"Clairvoyance," Miss Sophia blurted out.

"Clairvoyance?" Ms. Gerhardt repeated.

"Yes," Miss Sophia said. "He has visions or precognitions and able to see things prior to their occurrence. What else?"

Ms. Gerhardt buried her head into her hands. "I don't remember everything. There is so much." She rocked her head back and forth for a moment. "He senses and just knows things," she said. "Letters, symbols, feelings—"

"Clairsentience," Miss Sophia interjected, "which is an overwhelming sense of connection, empathetic feelings and emotions from the spirit."

Unfamiliar with these terms, Ms. Gerhardt looked back in confusion. Exhausted, she rested her cheek on the top of her folded arms.

"Now what?" she asked, looking up. "What can we do?"

Miss Sophia lit up another cigarette. "It's plain and simple," she said, blowing a stream of smoke. "He has a gift, maybe several. I also have many of these same gifts."

"Is there a treatment for this?" Ms. Gerhardt asked, sounding worried. "It's causing a lot of problems for us."

"This is not something you can cure, nor should it be something you want to cure. It is something to be cherished." Miss Sophia smiled. She looked at Willem with a look of concern written on her face. "He does need to be very careful how he uses the information that comes to him. It'll be best if he just keeps his thoughts and feelings to himself. If not, many will think that he is sneaky, highly intrusive, or, like you mentioned before, uncanny."

Ms. Gerhardt looked over at Willem. "Did you hear what Miss Sophia just said?"

Willem nodded, agreeing to keep such thoughts and feelings to himself.

Miss Sophia stared back at him and said, "If you say all that comes to mind, you will scare people away with the things that you say and know. It is very intrusive." She broke into a smile and put her index finger up, "but I think you will be able to truly make good use of your gift in the future."

"Are you listening?" Ms. Gerhardt said, leaning toward Willem.

Miss Sophia cleared her throat. "Use it only when you need it. And, there will come a time when you will definitely need it."

Concerned, Ms. Gerhardt nodded in deep thought, wondering what the future may hold.

"Fine," said Willem. "But, one more thing, okay?"

"Maybe," Miss Sophia responded with a cautious smile.

"What am I thinking?" Willem asked, staring at her without blinking.

Chuckling, Miss Sophia stared back with widened eyes. "You are too funny," she said, extinguishing her half-smoked cigarette. "You want those lava lamps!"

"Tarapanthy!" Willem said, bouncing up off his chair.

"T-e-l-e-p-a-t-h-y," she said softly, correcting him.

SIXTEEN

"GERHARDT, WAKE-UP!"

Rousted from a deep sleep, Dr. Gerhardt opened his eyes and stared back at the brash prison guard who was standing above him, repeatedly screaming out his last name. Through blurry eyes, he saw Mr. O'Reilly in a shadow beside the burly officer.

"Willem," said Mr. O'Reilly, nodding, "I was able to get permission for you to visit your mother this morning, instead of tonight."

"Oh, good," Dr. Gerhardt said, rubbing his eyes. "How's mom doing?" He asked through a wide-mouthed yawn.

"Not well," Mr. O'Reilly explained. His voice dropped to a whisper. "She's dying."

"Dying?" Dr. Gerhardt gasped.

"Yes. This is your final chance to see her. It's basically now or never."

Several stocky guards unlocked the bolt and stepped inside of the cell where they formed a semicircle around Dr. Gerhardt.

"We have to do this," a guard said before applying shackles to his hands in the front.

"Are you kidding?" Dr. Gerhardt said. *This is how she has to see me during her final days*, he thought, shaking his head.

"Just go with the flow," Mr. O'Reilly advised from behind. "I was able to get you this special privilege." His comment suggested, *better than nothing.*

Guards escorted Dr. Gerhardt out from the prison facility to a large transport van in the back of the lot. Stepping into the van, Dr. Gerhardt ducked his head before sitting in the center row between two guards. At a close distance behind, Mr. O'Reilly drove in his dark blue Bentley convertible to Texas Medical Center.

Dr. Gerhardt sat with his head tucked down, eyes squeezed shut. He never fathomed he would be handcuffed and accompanied by maximum security guards during his final *goodbye* visit with his mother. In general, he never imagined he would ever be in cuffs, much less, consider prison his home.

The Texas Medical Center was a place he knew well, a facility where he had lectured and also treated patients on many floors over the past twenty years. Though, he had only been to the long term, palliative care unit, once before— during his clinical training decades prior. This visit was far different for him, much more personal and emotional, as he realized he was about to see his mother for the very last time. The van ride felt like an eternity, years of memories flooding his mind.

Twenty minutes later, guards escorted Dr. Gerhardt across the hospital parking lot and through a rotating, glass entrance door. As he stepped onto the elevator, a guard stood on each side, guns pinned to their belts. From behind, Mr. O'Reilly rested his hand on Dr. Gerhardt's shoulder as the *up* button and identifying number 9 was pressed for the ninth floor.

The elevator rattled upward as guards whispered instructions.

Taking mental notes, Mr. O'Reilly nodded in acknowledgment to each directive. "We are going to make this visit short and sweet," a guard said. Another guard explained that the entire visitation would be closely supervised.

As they stepped out of the elevator, guards escorted Dr. Gerhardt down the narrow dark corridor. In silence, all nodded in unison while passing the central nursing station. A brunette nurse, in her late-sixties, was seated behind the long desk, clutching a phone in one hand and a pen in the other. Scribbling notes in a chart, she looked up for moment and nodded once in acknowledgment.

The door of Room 902 was wide open. Surrounded by guards, Dr. Gerhardt peeked in. The walls were worn out, stained on the bottom and peeling at the top. The room had a scent of rubbing alcohol. A hint of body odor could also be detected over the stale, lemon air freshener. The bed was set in the middle of the room with a small wooden table by the bedside that had piles of adhesive bandages, gauze and loose swabs of cotton. The square shaped nurse call button device with television control capabilities was set on the side. A very large package, unstamped and unsealed, was neatly aligned along the edge of the small table.

"Mom," Dr. Gerhardt called out before entering the room.

Ms. Gerhardt's eyes were closed. Her head was perched up on two large pillows. A larger cushion was used to elevate her legs. One bruised bare foot stuck out from beyond the white sheet.

Dr. Gerhardt glanced down at a Dunkin Donuts cup with lipstick markings set beside **The Houston Chronicle** just under the seat where the staff nurse had been sitting prior to their entrance. The front page caption read, *Gerhardt Trial Set to Begin*. A full length article followed beneath it in a smaller font, *Scientists Discover V-Bird Formation Relates to Energy Conservation.*

Energy, Dr. Gerhardt mumbled, looking back toward his mother.

Mr. O'Reilly made a request that the guards step back a few feet to allow Dr. Gerhardt some personal space. With tears in his eyes, Dr. Gerhardt stared down at Ms. Gerhardt, whose lips were tinged blue, twitching as she breathed. Her nostrils expanded upon each breath she took through the nasal cannula that was attached to a wall connection by the front of her bed. At the bend by her elbow, purplish scabs swelled where she had previously received intravenous fluid therapy.

"Can you hear me, mom?" Dr. Gerhardt asked. As he looked her up and down, he realized she had lost quite a bit of weight since the last time he had seen her. A pendant, two hands clasped together, dangled from her narrow neck.

A staff nurse, wearing blue scrubs, stepped into the room.

"I'm Tara," she whispered. Her smile lit up the somber room. "And, you must be Willem," she said, reaching down to pick up her Dunkin Donuts cup before taking a sip.

"Hi," Dr. Gerhardt replied, nodding." Hands cuffed in the front, he waved from his waist.

In a vibrant way, Tara said, "It is so nice to finally meet you. I've heard tons about you." Her high spirit turned dim and her voice cracked as she said, "Your mom loves you so much."

Dr. Gerhardt nodded and dug his teeth into his lips to stop them from quivering.

"I'll let you spend some alone time with your mom," Tara said. She swallowed hard, trying to catch her breath. "Even though she does not have the strength to perk up, she can still hear you. I promise." She patted a tissue under Ms. Gerhardt's lower lip where she had drooled. "I'll give you some privacy." Tara used her hand to fan her own eyes before she stepped toward the door.

As Tara left the room, Dr. Gerhardt quickly panned back toward Ms. Gerhardt, who showed slight, intermittent movements by her chin.

"Mr. O'Reilly," Dr. Gerhardt called out. "Can you please come in?" Mr. O'Reilly entered the room, using a handkerchief to dry his own moist eyes. He had long been connected to the Gerhardt family, not only representing them legally, but also a close friend over the decades. He could not help but to think about the numerous family functions shared together including dinners, vacations, holiday celebrations and award events. He was also supportive to Ms. Gerhardt when tragedy had struck her parents. Bombarded by memories of his own— this was a difficult moment for him as well.

"Yes, Willem?" said Mr. O'Reilly, taking another step forward. As he stood beside Dr. Gerhardt, he offered him a comforting pat on the back.

"I need you to reach into my pocket," Dr. Gerhardt said.

"Right away," Mr. O'Reilly said, folding his handkerchief before stuffing it into his jacket pocket. He reached into Dr. Gerhardt's front pocket and pulled out a folded, frilly piece of paper, appearing to have been freshly torn out from a spiral notebook.

"Open it for me, please," Dr. Gerhardt said, then asked, "Can you please hold it up?"

Mr. O'Reilly unfolded the crinkled paper and flapped it several times in the air to flatten its creases. Without access to his reading glasses, Dr. Gerhardt squinted.

"Bring it closer, please," Dr. Gerhardt said, taking a deep breath. "I wrote you a poem, mom." He peered underneath the paper and looked down for a moment at her on the bed. Beyond her wrinkled skin, swollen eyelids, discoloration and medical attachments, he could still see that beautiful woman, standing with open arms, awaiting his first hug 38-years ago to the month.

Dr. Gerhardt took an exaggerated deep breath and proceeded to read:

As if it were just yesterday, I think about adoption day

I melted in your arms right away, neither one of us knew what to say

You sang to me, we danced and we sometimes even twirled,

You are my mom, my friend, my teammate, you and me against the world

Always by my side you were when life did not seem fair,

When doctors, teachers and a psychic did not seem to care.

Always as one together, not a day gone by apart,

I'm grateful mom, I'm appreciative

— Thank you with all my heart.

Struggling to catch his breath, tears dripped down his flushed face. Dr. Gerhardt had written much more, but felt too emotional to read on. He nodded and gave Mr. O'Reilly a nonverbal cue to put the paper down, then stepped closer to Ms. Gerhardt's bed where he planted his damp face beside hers on the pillow.

"I love you, mom," he whispered and then kissed her forehead, gently.

Tara reentered the room with a bounce in her step. Enthusiastic, she hustled to the bedside where she lifted a large package from the wooden bedside table.

"I spent a good amount of time with your mom over the past two weeks before she lost all her strength." Nervous, yet at the same time wearing a look of excitement, Tara hugged the package and raised her index finger. "I'll be right b-a-c-k," she said.

In silence, Dr. Gerhardt's eyes widened.

Tara hurried out of the room with the package tucked against her side. After several moments, she tiptoed back into the room, smiling giddily with her hands placed behind her back.

"What is it Tara?" Dr. Gerhardt asked, cocking his head from one side to the other. He took a deep breath, awaiting her response.

"Your mom wanted me to give this to you." Tara extended her arm out from behind her back. "Here you go," she said, holding up a bluebonnet.

Unbeknownst to him, Ms. Gerhardt had chemically preserved the flower for the past thirty-five years. He stood in awe, staring at the flower he had picked on a day spent at the lake. A preservation procedure had enabled the flower to maintain its original color and soft texture.

"The bluebonnet", he whispered, unable to speak through the lump in his throat. *These are memories we will look back on*, echoed in his mind, envisioning the moments after he had handed the flower to her.

"Thank you," he whispered.

Tara nodded in unison and then turned to the side to discretely wipe away her own tears.

"Tara," Dr. Gerhardt said, bowing his head.

"Yes," she said, turning back.

"Can you please," he said, stuttering, "…please, put it behind my ear?"

"I can," Tara said, bouncing up on the toes of her shoes. She stepped forward on her tippy toes and slid the long stem behind his ear.

Willem glanced over for one final time in the direction of Ms. Gerhardt. *I love you, mom,* he mouthed, puckering his lips.

The guards escorted him down the ninth floor corridor as Mr. O'Reilly trailed at a close distance behind. Willem had a smile on his face as he walked down the narrow hallway with the bluebonnet fastened behind his ear.

SEVENTEEN

IN THE CORNER of his cell, Dr. Gerhardt sat with his head tucked between his knees, facing the heartbreaking reality that he had seen his mother for the very last time. With mixed emotions, he was happy to have visited her on the previous day—her final day of life. It had only been the second time he had been on the ninth floor, palliative care unit. He had thought that his first visit, twenty years prior, would have been his last. He closed his eyes, reflecting back upon his clinical training.

The first time that he had been on the palliative care unit was during his very final year of the doctoral program as a required clinical internship. At the time, he had been assigned to see several patients on the long-term care unit. Willem never understood why palliative care was considered *long-term*, where in fact most patients did not live for a long period of time following admission. Back then, he had resolved in his mind that the unit descriptor, *long-term*, at least, sounded better than *Journey's End*.

Madeline, more affectionately known as Maddie, had been his

first assigned patient. When he had first arrived at the foot of her room, he heard an obnoxious banging noise originating from inside. When he stepped in, he saw Maddie pointing a remote toward a television mounted on a wall across from her bed.

"These batteries are dead," she cried out, banging the remote several times in succession against the metal bed frame.

Willem looked around the room, nodding gently with a smile.

As Maddie propped herself up on the bed, her mouth hung open. All Willem could see staring back at him were swollen lips and toothless gums.

"Sit down," she said with a lisp, motioning with her chin toward a chair.

Even though she was 86-years-old, Maddie was energetic and quite assertive. While her history was not fully known, it was clear that she was once a very *take-charge* type person.

Willem took a seat upon the vacant chair adjacent to the bed. "It's a pleasure to meet you," he said, smiling as he nodded.

Reaching for her bedside table, Maddie plunged her hand into a shallow dish filled with water. In one motion, she swung her hand up toward her mouth.

"And, you are?" She asked, chewing for a moment before revealing a full mouth of loose fitting, flapping choppers.

"I'm Willem. I'm a doctoral student assigned to this floor."

"So," she said, shrugging. "Are you here to study me?" She looked to the side for a moment before snapping her head back, anxiously awaiting a response.

Willem stuttered for a moment. He had never been asked that question before, but realized that she was more or less, right. Clinical internships had been geared towards enabling doctoral students to utilize clinical skills in the field, but to also provide field exposure to help in choosing populations with whom they would most like to work with in the future. Willem knew that his college professors would not be *thrilled* if he were to acknowledge that he was there more so for himself than for the patients.

Before Willem could respond, Maddie said, "Well, at least you sure are a cutie." After putting her finger up in the air, she quickly said, "A very handsome young man," correcting herself, trying to sound more *politically correct*.

Willem turned to the side, ignoring the compliment.

"Let's get started," she proposed. "Shall we?"

"Let's," Willem repeated in agreement.

"So, how old are you, doctor?" She interrupted, propping her head back and trying to take on the role of an interviewer.

From *Ethics* class, Willem knew that questions of a personal nature should be either *ignored* or *redirected*. Professor Ballantino had taught Ethics classes back in the day. He had always stressed the importance of maintaining professional boundaries when working with patients, especially patients of the opposite sex. Willem was confident, though not one hundred percent certain, that his old professor was not likely referring to 86-year-old women residing in palliative care units.

Willem leaned back and crossed his legs, using the top of the adjacent chair to rest his arm.

"Why don't you tell me a little bit about yourself?" He asked, trying to regain control of the conversation and redirect questions back to her.

"What can I tell you, doctor?" Maddie shrugged. Her high spirited energy suddenly turned dim. She turned over on her side and, for the first time, lost eye contact.

"Please share what you feel comfortable sharing." Willem's tone was firm, yet at the same time, encouraging.

"I've lived a full life…I've done many things…I've known many people." She sucked in a deep breath and sighed. "Now, people help feed me. I can't feel my toes."

"I understand—" Willem said, nodding.

"And this dark room here," she said, turning her body around, "is my home."

Willem was not sure how to respond. With a folder affixed to his restless lap and an anxious pen gripped between his fingers, he just nodded back in silence.

Maddie perked up and thrusted her neck forward. Her eyes blinked fast as she stared into his mouth. "Do you floss those teeth?"

Self-conscious, Willem leaned back and rolled the tip of his tongue along his upper gums. He used his pinky nail to scrape in-between his two front teeth.

"Your teeth are fine, doctor," she said. "It's good to floss though. After all, you really don't want to end up looking like me." She opened her mouth wide and smiled, showing her full set of dentures, loosely fitting and clicking as she forced a chuckle.

"You won't tell me your age," she said, extending her limp wrist out toward him. "But, I will show you a picture, anyway." She reached for the side table and snatched up a photo. "Are you single?" She asked, handing the picture to him.

Willem held the small picture up close to his eyes. The photograph was of a woman in her early twenties. She had long wavy brown hair and light brown eyes that sparkled above her cute dimples. Her teeth were bright white, smiling back at the photographer with ease. Her skin was clear and of an olive complexion.

Fascinated, Willem could not help but to smile as he stared at the photo. For a moment, he thought the woman was his "dream girl." *Could it be fate to have been assigned to this unit?* He wondered.

Willem had a fondness for brunettes. His mind raced, wondering if he should remain professional, or just blurt out his age and see where it takes him. After all, school had consumed most of his time and he was starting to find himself in somewhat of a lonely state of mind. A voice in his head said, *go for it*. In a mixed state of deep thoughts and emotions, he handed the picture back to her. He took another deep breath before swallowing hard.

"I saw you smiling," she said, raising her eyebrows and waving her index finger in the air. "Oh, yes…oh, yes, I did." Giggling, she set the picture down upon the bedside table next to her denture holder. "A pretty, pretty girl. Right?"

Willem did not respond. Lips pressed together, he nodded in friendly acknowledgment, figuring it was the least he could do.

"So Doc," she said, chuckling. "How old are yo-u-u-u?"

Willem tried to speak, but could not find his words. Conflicted in thought, he bit his tongue. *Silence is golden*, he recalled.

"You don't have to tell me your age," Maddie said, using a cloth to dry her moist eyes. She stuck her chin out in the direction of the picture. "She is 22-years-old, though," Maddie said. After pausing for a moment, she solemnly said, "A pretty, pretty girl I was."

"Excuse me," Willem said. His eyes widened, glancing back down at the photo.

"You heard me doctor," Maddie said. "That was me at twenty-two. How the years go by fast."

Gazing out the window, Maddie stared down at the bird-infested dumpsters below. She shook her head in silence, sighing as she looked around the room. *How the years go by so fast*, she said again, mumbling.

In his mind, Willem could not fathom that it was a picture of Maddie. "You were very pretty," he said, feeling more comfortable and loosening up a bit.

She laughed and clapped her thick, swollen hands. "I thank you," she said, looking back at him. "They say age is just a number. So, how old are you?"

Willem checked his watch and stood from his chair, realizing he needed to attend to other patients on the unit.

"Maddie," he said, "I must leave, now."

"Oh, doctor," she said, clearing her throat. "Please, do me a favor."

His eyebrows arched, awaiting her request. At this point, he was not sure whether or not he should stick around to hear what she was about to request.

"Y-e-s," he said in an elongated, nervous way. He then more bluntly said, "What is it?"

"When you work with older people," she said, sighing, "please ask to see pictures of them when they were younger." She paused for a moment, collecting her thoughts. "Sometimes, we are just seen for our immobility, dependence, grouchiness and less than appealing looks." As she nodded, she looked back at him. "We were once active and good looking…just like you, doctor."

She reached for the picture, held it up high and dropped it back down before patting her hand down once upon it. "How the years go by fast," she said, louder.

"Okay," Willem said softly, "it was nice to meet you." He breathed heavily as he walked toward the door.

"Oh, doctor," she called out.

Willem stopped in his tracks and spun his body around to face her.

"When you see someone's picture from their younger years," she said, nodding, "you see them in a new light." After she took a deep breath, she said, "Always remember that."

"Okay," said Willem, nodding in agreement. "Thank you, Maddie."

She waved her finger toward Willem. "Don't ever, ever get old." She shook her head and mouthed, *goodbye*, before removing her dentures and dropping them back into the dish.

Willem nodded his head while walking backwards out of the room. After exiting, he made his way down the corridor towards his next assignment, *Joe Doe*. Puzzled, Willem skimmed through his notes, wondering if the name was used as a placeholder for a patient whose true identity was withheld.

"Yea, who is it?" A male voice resonated after Willem had knocked on the door of room 907. "Just come in," the man shouted, sounding agitated.

Willem stepped in and extended his arm. "I'm Willem," he said, introducing himself in a business-like manner.

"Oh, hi there," the man replied, sitting up from his bed. "Have we met before? They say my memory is shot."

"Not sure," Willem said, chuckling for a moment. "What is your name?"

"It's Joe Dormienterechiano."

"Joe Doe?" Willem said.

"Yes, it's me," Joe said, sounding surprised. "You know me?"

"Not sure. Let me ask a few questions."

"What do you need Willie?"

"It's Willem," he said firmly, correcting him. He advised Joe to remain seated on the bed, explaining there was no need to stand up. "I just have a few, or perhaps more than a few, questions for you," Willem said, sliding a chair closer to the bed before he sat down.

"I've got plenty of time," Joe said, panning the bare room where many tiny holes remained after thumbtack removals. "You know," he said, nodding, "I used to do what you do?"

Uncertain what Joe meant, Willem just nodded in agreement, then asked, "Just what did you do?"

"I used to volunteer and visit people in hospitals," Joe said, sighing as he reflected back in time. "It's a weird thing to visit people during their final years." He paused for a second, then said, "Final days."

"I am going to be spending some time with you on the unit," Willem said, looking around the bare room. "Maybe we can get you a painting or two?"

"You're an interior designer?"

"Well, no," Willem snapped. "I am actually a doctoral student."

"You can get a doctorate degree in interior design?"

"Well, no—"

"I am kidding," Joe said, coughing up phlegm, laughing at his own humor. "You are more than welcome to spend time, here, Willie."

"So, tell me more about you," Willem said.

"Do you have time?" Joe asked, looking up toward the clock.

"I do," Willem said, striking his pen against the pad on his clipboard.

"I've been here two weeks. They say I'll be lucky to be here another month." Joe inhaled slowly. "Life's been good, though."

"Oh. Tell me about your life," Willem said, trying to keep the tone positive.

"Let's see." Joe shrugged, his voice dropped to a whisper. "I've lived life the right way."

"That's a good thing," Willem said, sounding perky. "I think."

"I've never smoked. I don't drink. I eat healthy. I've always exercised." Joe paused in deep thought, slumping down. "But, I guess you can't beat the aging process no matter how fast you pedal on the stationary bike."

At a loss for words, Willem pretended to jot down notes. He could not help but wonder what it would be like living out life's final days in isolation where even the most colorful paintings would not brighten the gloomy aura.

"How old are you?" Willem asked.

"I just turned fifty-eight."

Willem and Joe stared at one another, nodding in unison.

"Hello," a doctor called out, tapping a knuckle against the open door. "May I?"

"Of course," Willem said, gathering his belongings while rising up from the chair. He tucked the pen into his upper shirt pocket and walked toward the door.

The doctor stood by Joe, speaking at a slow pace with exaggerated head nods. Joe looked somber. After all, most news was bad news on the unit. The doctor offered Joe a comforting pat on the back before stepping out of the room.

"It's no surprise," Joe said, looking up. "The good news is that you can come back next week. Or if you have time, even sooner."

Willem nodded. "I'll be back soon."

"Hey, Willie," Joe said, coughing, "We all dread the hospital. It symbolizes the end. Are you sure you want to spend every day of your working life in a hospital? You'll be here someday. Take your time…Enjoy your life."

Nodding again, Willem stepped out and walked down the narrow ninth floor hallway, looking for Room 927.

"You look lost," a staff nurse said before guiding him in the right direction, just a few rooms down.

"Thank you so much," Willem said, feeling dazed. He knocked on the half-open door of Room 927 before entering.

The sound of a slight groan reverberated in the quiet room, surrounded by bare walls. The television was turned off. A man lay curled up on his bed.

"Hi, Max," Willem said, standing at the entranceway. "Are you up?"

"Jesus Christ," Max said. "What in the hell took you so damn long?"

Confused, Willem said, "Oh, you were expecting me?"

"I think so," Max said. "Are you Doctor Kevorkian?"

"I'm afraid not," Willem said, chuckling.

"Okay-y-y-y," he mumbled, gritting his teeth. "Who the hell are you?"

"I'm Willem."

"Well, Doc, I was hoping to see you. I got cramps in my legs, pains in my side and I can't move my bowels. My balls hurt, my ankles are swollen and the food tastes like shit." His speech was pressured as if he could not get the words out fast enough. "Don't just stand there," he said, sounding annoyed, "come on in, you're late."

Max was 78-years-old. He lay in a torn undershirt and dark brown boxer underwear. His black socks were stretched up just below his bruised boney knees. Max was frail, his movements slow. He had been on the unit for close to three-weeks.

Hesitant, Willem walked toward the bed.

"A pleasure to meet you, Max."

"Well," Max said in a prolonged way. "Are you going to order some tests?" The tone of his voice was harsh.

Willem set his briefcase down and sat in the vacant chair alongside the wall. "I'm a doctoral student," Willem said, retrieving a folder. "I have been assigned to work with you. I'm enrolled in the psychology program."

"That's wonderful," Max said, exhaling loudly, "real wonderful."

"I have some questions for you," Willem said.

"Of course you have questions," Max snapped back. "Let me guess. You want to know how it makes me feel to be in the hospital."

Willem glanced back. "Well, I really wanted—"

"Well, I feel like crap," Max said, interrupting. "Where is the real doctor," Max asked, looking up at the plain, square-shaped, wall clock. "I need something to happen. Not to just talk about it."

"I'm going to spend the next several months with you," Willem explained.

"In here?" Max gasped, looking around the small room. "Hell no, you're not moving in."

Willem sucked in a deep breath. "Well, no," Willem explained, "on a once a week basis." He reached in his pocket and pulled out a pen. "I would like to get to know you better, Max."

"Several months," Max mumbled, sounding surprised.

"Yes, just about," said Willem, nodding. "How about this—We will get to know each other."

"Oh," Max said. "Well, there is not much to get to know, really." He sounded curt in his response.

"I'm sure there is a lot to know." Smiling, Willem sounded optimistic. "For starters, what do you enjoy?"

"I used to enjoy movies, playing golf, traveling—" Max paused for a moment, appearing sad. "Now," he said, scratching the top of his head near a scab, "this is my life." He used his index finger to draw a full imaginary circle around the room. Again, he mumbled, *this is my life*.

"Tell me more about your life," Willem said, trying to remain optimistic.

"Like what?" Max said, choking up phlegm from the back of his throat.

Willem shrugged. "Ever been married? Have any kids?"

Jesus Christmas, Max said, chuckling. "You sound like you're hitting on me." After his laughter subsided, Max sternly asked, "Are you?"

"Never mind," Willem said. He thought to himself, *It's not worth it*. Willem took a deep breath and looked down for a moment. "Well, share all you feel comfortable in sharing."

"That's really about it, I'd say." Max clasped his hands together. "See, we did not need even need several months." He looked over to the wall clock, squinting. "Around, let's say, three minutes and a half."

Willem nodded, pretending to validate what Max had said.

"How about you doctor? Tell me your story." Max leaned back and cupped his hand by his better ear.

Willem did not respond, but instead, strategized in his racing mind how he could redirect the conversation back to Max. After an awkward moment of silence, Willem perked his head up and asked, "Do you have any pictures of yourself when you were younger?"

"What the Hell?" Max snapped. "Pictures of me?"

"Well, yes—"

"HELP," Max screamed out. He reached over to the side table and pressed several times on the nurse call button. "Can someone remove this queer?"

Dr. Gerhardt snapped back to the present. As he reopened his eyes, he stood up from the cold concrete floor and walked toward the front of his jail cell where he looked out toward the dark prison hallways. Feelings of emptiness took hold of him as he looked into the silence of darkness where in the shadows he saw moonlight shift guards sleeping, or at least, *resting*.

In his mind, he contemplated whether he should have just continued working with the elderly. Some had said it would be *easier* or *less stressful* with more downtime. His limited exposure in the hospital was not terrific, but somehow wondered if he would have had far less problems in the long run working with patients during their final months. Dr. Gerhardt made his way back toward the cot where he lay down and closed his eyes, awaiting the start of the trial.

EIGHTEEN

"ALL RISE," A bailiff called out as Judge Orton stepped into the court. All stood in adherence, then quickly sat back down as the judge settled into his seat on the bench.

In his late-forties, Judge Orton was wearing a white collared shirt that was only visible above the very top of his black robe. He looked out to the courtroom as the recessed lights reflected off his clean-shaven bald head. Nodding, he read the basic courtroom instructions and spoke more specifically about this particular trial.

"As we prepare," Judge Orton said, "for opening statements, I want to point out, as many of you already know, that there is extensive media coverage surrounding this trial." He continued, "All I ask is that you listen to the facts presented, and at the end, carefully weigh all of the testimony and evidence brought forth before you."

He straightened his robe and adjusted his chair.

"Counsel," he said, looking toward the prosecution table. "Counsel," he repeated, nodding in the direction of the defense table. "Let's proceed…"

The prosecutor stood and approached the podium where he removed his glasses before he spoke. "I'm Arthur Freeman," he said, turning around to face the jury as he introduced himself. "I am the lead prosecutor for the State of Texas." In his late fifties, Mr. Freeman was short in stature with a plump appearance. He wore a loose fitting checkered blazer and baggy beige pants that were held up by a belt beneath his protruding stomach. His Dockers were a slip-on type, neither matching his blazer nor his pants.

Mr. Freeman nodded in the direction of the prosecution table, at which time, Linda Jacobs, his co-prosecutor, stepped forward to introduce herself and describe her role. A slim brunette in her early thirties, Ms. Jacobs was wearing a purple blouse and a black skirt hiked up just below her thighs. As Mr. Freeman nodded, she returned to the table where she sat, reviewing papers.

Mr. Freeman took a sip from his glass and then continued.

We will be closely examining occurrences on the twelfth of October of last year, an important day in the lives of many related to this case. That is when Dr. Gerhardt had engaged in session with his patient, who was emotionally devastated after Jimmy Townsend, the man accused of raping her, had been acquitted. So what did Dr. Gerhardt do when his long time patient sought his support? He suddenly terminated sessions with her. And later on that evening, he urgently met with Tino Ballantino, an old time professor, who he had not seen in decades. The very next day, or, I should say, hours later, on Friday the 13th, the lifeless body of Jimmy Townsend was found face down.

We realize, and I want to further emphasize, that we have a challenge from the start. To convince a jury to convict a distinguished psychologist from a well-known family lineage is no easy task. We ask that you somehow set aside your previously held notions and carefully listen to the testimony and evidence presented before you. We will display a chart containing more specific sequences, in the form of a visual demonstration, which proves beyond a reasonable doubt Willem Gerhardt murdered Jimmy Townsend on the fatal day, October 13th.

As we proceed, you will be presented with significant details about

Willem Gerhardt's past, which is extremely significant to this case. The terms, emotional triggers and countertransference, will be introduced as we discuss a motive for murder. You will also have the opportunity to listen to key witnesses on the stand, including Dr. Gerhardt's young patient, as well as Tino Ballantino, who will both provide important testimony regarding occurrences on October 12th and October 13th.

"Thank you, counsel," Judge Orton said, folding his arms as he leaned back in his chair. Looking across the courtroom toward the defense table, he then asked, "Are you ready for your opening statement?"

Theodore O'Reilly stood and walked to the middle of the courtroom.

"My name is T.J. O'Reilly," he said introducing himself. "I am an attorney here in Houston." Nodding, he smiled. "I represent Dr. Willem Gerhardt."

Mr. O'Reilly was in his late sixties. Tall and slender, he looked distinguished in a three-piece suit. His white collared shirt was perfectly ironed, customized with his initials on the cuffs. As he spoke, he put his fingers through his full head of thick silver hair, which was feathered straight back, glistening beneath the recessed lighting. He stood in the center of the court where he nodded.

"I know this case is in the media spotlight," Mr. O'Reilly said, "being that anything having to do with a *Gerhardt* is in itself newsworthy." Mr. O'Reilly paused for a moment, then continued, "I ask that you all, as members of the jury, remain open minded as you hear the testimony and arguments. You will find during the course of the trial that Dr. Gerhardt has done no wrong doing in this concocted looks, smells and seems like it case."

Mr. O'Reilly used a lot of hand gestures as he spoke. "I want you all to be aware that Dr. Gerhardt is a well-known psychologist and moving forward, you will hear testimony that he is well respected amongst his peers and colleagues. He is also a multi-time award recipient for distinguished accomplishments in his field." Mr. O'Reilly nodded, proudly, then said, "From a standpoint of accolades and professional accomplishments, we will demonstrate that few others can be likened to the doctor we all have come to love." Mr. O'Reilly approached the podium where he continued to speak.

So that there are no surprises or disappointments in the end, please be advised that Dr. Gerhardt is not going to testify on the stand. Of course, a change of plan can occur later on down the line, if and when I determine such is needed. Bear in mind that the burden of proof is placed on the prosecution to prove beyond a reasonable doubt that Dr. Gerhardt is a murderer. Our case demonstrates this is not possible.

There are no triggers. There is no motive. Diving into personal records of Dr. Gerhardt's early childhood does not suggest that he is a murderer, but rather shows how he has overcome hardships in life, remained resilient and transitioned from darkness into the light.

There will likely be many twists and turns during this trial, which is typical when murder charges are launched against someone who did not commit a crime. I appreciate your dedication to this case, and again, I ask that you listen to all arguments and pay particular attention to the evidence of murder in the trial. There is none!

Mr. O'Reilly nodded toward the jury. "Thank you," he said, turning around and nodding hard in the direction of the judge before returning to the defense table.

NINETEEN

"GOOD AFTERNOON LADIES AND GENTLEMEN."

Arthur Freeman's voice was powerful, commanding full attention from the courtroom especially members of the jury seated within close proximity. He stood and approached the podium, while his co-prosecutor, Linda Jacobs, remained seated at the prosecution table reviewing materials and scribbling on a small spiral notepad.

On the day prior, a wide range of people had taken the stand, many of whom expressed the highest of accolades for Dr. Gerhardt. The defense team felt confident that witnesses helped establish a positive tone for jurors to sleep on at the end of the trial day. For nearly the final two hours of testimony, prominent members of the community and professional colleagues had spoken of Dr. Gerhardt's integrity, work ethic and *selfless* involvement in the entire community.

Dr. Gerhardt had kept his head dipped down for nearly the entire time, feeling invisible, yet at the same alive, as if he were sitting in attendance at his own funeral during praise-filled eulogy speeches.

A prestigious member of the River Oaks Baptist Church had

described Dr. Gerhardt as the *most loving people-person* he has ever known, shedding some light on the *exquisite relationship* Willem had with Ms. Gerhardt from the day of his adoption up until her recent passing.

A community director of volunteer services from the YMCA had told stories about how Dr. Gerhardt readily donated time and money to youths less fortunate. He went on to describe Dr. Gerhardt as *selfless* and *passionate* to the cause, specifically sharing how monetary donations to the mentor program helped provide services to thousands of inner city children across the Greater Houston area. He also shared how he had more personally gotten to know Dr. Gerhardt during weekend camping trips when he had volunteered his time to organize and monitor camp activities including fishing, hiking and basketball.

The President of the Texas Psychological Association had also taken the stand, testifying that Dr. Gerhardt *stands for absolutely everything this field embodies.* He went on to share how he had the distinct pleasure of presenting Dr. Gerhardt numerous recognition awards over the past twenty-years including the most prestigious award a psychologist can receive, *Distinguished Psychologist for Contributions to Psychology and Psychotherapy*, from the American Psychological Association.

On the day prior, Mr. Freeman had lodged many objections, feeling as though some witnesses had strayed beyond the original instructions provided by the judge. Judge Orton was unfazed by the objections, often overruling them and simply motioning with his hand each time to proceed on. On cross examination, one member of the church was stumped into silence when asked if he would have a changed opinion if he knew Dr. Gerhardt had abruptly terminated sessions with a young patient after she had disclosed to him that she had been sexually abused. Another witness created a buzz in the courtroom after she had recalled that Willem, during his younger years, had an intuitive ability, considered to be *enigmatic, mysterious and uncanny.*

Mr. Freeman and Ms. Jacobs did not cross examine all witnesses, fearing that increased attention could provide even more of an opportunity to praise Dr. Gerhardt who was universally adored. Mr. Freeman had stared at the jury box, examining the reactions of each of the jury members who listened to enthusiastic and charming commentary spoken on behalf of Dr. Gerhardt. He realized such testimony during trials often draw empathy from jurors, in general, but could perhaps even more so for Dr. Gerhardt, an esteemed psychologist with a well-known and long respected family lineage.

Recognizing that the momentum had shifted in favor of Dr. Gerhardt on the previous trial day, Mr. Freeman was eager to proceed.

"GOOD AFTERNOON," he said, again. "The prosecution would like to call upon Dr. Haggerty." Mr. Freeman nodded in a confident way, believing that introducing Dr. Haggerty, an expert witness, could not have come at a better time.

Dr. Haggerty approached the stand, wearing a dark purple blazer and a gold colored turtleneck beneath. He was in his early seventies, balding on the top, with thinning white hair, brushed all to one side. A full, white Santa Claus style beard covered his entire face including well beneath the bottom of his wide chin.

A bailiff stood before him and administered the oath.

As Dr. Haggerty raised his arm, the bailiff asked, "Do you solemnly swear to tell the truth, the whole truth, and nothing but the truth?"

"I do," said Dr. Haggerty, speaking in a gentle, yet deep voice.

Mr. Freeman shuffled papers at the podium. He then retrieved his glasses from his shirt pocket and placed the tip of the frame into his mouth. As he removed the tip, he said, "Can you please provide the court with your name, as well as your credentials?"

"I am Dr. Haggerty. I have my Ph.D. in clinical psychology and I also have a medical degree."

"Thank you. Do you go by any other name?"

"My name is Charles, but my close friends call me Charlie. My grandchildren call me Santa."

"Ok. You have both a doctorate and medical degree?"

"That is correct."

"Did you obtain these advanced degrees in the same program at one university setting?"

"No, I did not. I received my Ph.D. from University of Houston. And, I attended medical school and received my Doctor of Medicine at Johns Hopkins."

"What type setting do you work in Dr. Haggerty?"

Dr. Haggerty extended his wrists from beyond his blazer sleeve, revealing a shiny gold bracelet, dangling below his right wrist. "Are you referring to my work history or what I am doing now?"

"Please tell the court both," Mr. Freeman said, rolling out his arms in a circular manner.

"I have been in the field for 40-years," Dr. Haggerty explained. "I've been employed in various psychiatric hospitals here in Texas, as well as outpatient psychiatric clinics. I have a private practice and presently teach at the university here in Houston."

"So, would it be fair to assume that you are an expert and one of the elite in your field?" Mr. Freeman asked in a suggestive way.

Dr. Haggerty swayed his body around in his seat and tilted his head from side to side in a slow-motion, modest-type manner. "Well, I would say so."

"Is your main specialty related to boundaries within the scope of psychotherapy?"

Dr. Haggerty again shuffled his body around in his seat. "I am well versed in the overall therapeutic dynamic, both individual and family. But, yes-- I am very familiar with the significance of boundaries, as well as issues that may arise due to transference and countertransference."

"Have you specifically taught this material in your courses?"

Mr. O'Reilly stood up. "Objection Your Honor. That is a less than vague inquiry."

Judge Orton glanced over his reading glasses. "Objection, sustained. Rephrase your question."

"Can you please tell the court the extent to which you have taught about boundary issues, transference and countertransference."

"The courses I teach do include these important issues within the context of the much broader therapeutic dynamics of various treatment modalities and diagnosis."

"Thank you," Mr. Freeman acknowledged. He swayed back for a moment and then twirled his pen toward Dr. Haggerty. "I would like to ask you more specific questions about both countertransference and triggers as it relates to this case."

"Objection!" Mr. O'Reilly called out. "Your Honor, this is a presumptuous statement, rather leading. There is no justifiable reason at this point to solely speak about the phenomena of countertransference in this case without also discussing transference."

"Sustained," Judge Orton said.

"That's perfectly fine," Mr. Freeman said, acknowledging the good point with a nod. "Can you please explain the significance of transference and countertransference to the court?"

"Absolutely," Dr. Haggerty said, emphatically nodding his head. "Transference and countertransference can be described as being the alpha and omega of therapy."

"Can you please break that down into simple terms?" Mr. Freeman asked.

Dr. Haggerty glanced over to the jury.

"To further clarify," he explained, "transference is a term used in psychotherapy to describe the feelings or triggers that a patient develops toward a therapist." He then continued, "...and countertransference describes the emotional responses, or triggers, that a therapist has in reaction to a patient."

Mr. Freeman put a clenched fist up to his mouth as he looked down at his notes.

"So, in other words, both forms of transference refer to feelings and emotions that may arise between a clinician and client during the course of therapy?"

"Yes. That is correct," Dr. Haggerty said.

"Now, Dr. Haggerty," said Mr. Freeman, retreating back with a stutter step, "it sounds as though the emotions of both the therapist and the patient can be triggered in therapy."

"Absolutely, correct," Dr. Haggerty touted, as if to say, *now you get it.*

"Ok," Mr. Freeman responded, strutting his way back towards the main courtroom table. "Would it be fair to assume that once these triggers occur in therapy, it is unhealthy and therapy should be brought to an immediate halt?"

"Objection," Mr. O'Reilly said.

"Overruled!"

"Thank you, Your Honor," Mr. Freeman said. "Please go ahead and answer my question Dr. Haggerty."

Dr. Haggerty opened his arms and clasped his hands together in the form of a steeple. "Well, both are common within the scope of therapy. Triggers are bound to be elicited by both the therapist and a patient. This can actually be quite healthy for the therapeutic connection."

As Mr. Freeman approached Dr. Haggerty, he placed his clipboard on the side table and then crossed one leg over the other before resting his elbow on the table for support.

"Ok, let me make sure I'm getting this right," Mr. Freeman said, looking out above his reading glasses. "What you are saying is that transference refers to triggers generated within a patient during therapy. And countertransference refers to triggers experienced by a therapist."

"Yes," Dr. Haggerty responded.

Mr. Freeman paused for a moment and cocked his head. "In what way can triggers be healthy?"

"For establishing rapport," Dr. Haggerty said, bringing his hand made steeple gesture up toward his heavily bearded chin.

"By *rapport*, I assume you are referring to closeness?" Mr. Freeman inquired.

"Closeness…connection…rapport…," Dr. Haggerty replied. "These descriptors can all be used synonymously."

"Now, let's closely examine countertransference," Mr. Freeman said, twirling both index fingers in a backward circular motion. "Countertransference refers to the triggers or feelings that are generated within a therapist."

Dr. Haggerty nodded.

"I know you are nodding your head. Please say your response out loud for the court record," Mr. Freeman encouraged.

"Yes."

"And, countertransference is the most important phenomena we are discussing today, because it directly relates to the case being heard today with regard to the triggers of a therapist. Is that correct?"

"Objection!" Mr. O'Reilly shouted out, jumping to his feet with an arm fully stretched. "That is highly suggestive, presumptuous and misleading. Can I approach the bench, Your Honor?"

"Your Honor," Mr. Freeman touted. "We have key evidence and we are trying to prove our case by demonstrating to the jury a motive."

"Objection sustained and let's continue," the judge said as all stepped back from the bench. "Please, rephrase your question Mr. Freeman."

Mr. Freeman removed his reading glasses and slowly thumbed through pages bound in a yellow folder containing numerous documents. As he turned pages fast, he licked his index finger to create a fleeting glue-type effect that helped him proceed more easily.

"What do you think is important about countertransference within the scope of therapy?" Mr. Freeman asked

"Well, I think it is extremely important," Dr. Haggerty quickly suggested.

"And, how so?"

Dr. Haggerty looked around the courtroom and again, glanced over toward the jury. He extended his arms, palms faced upward.

"Countertransference in therapy gives rise to the emotions triggered within a therapist. And, this may include past experiences, unresolved issues, fantasies and a wide range of emotions." After pausing to take another sip of water, he then said, "Therapists must understand and be able to properly manage their own various personal triggers."

Mr. Freeman nodded. "So what you are saying is that countertransference is healthy for a therapist in developing a close connection and better rapport with patients."

"True," Dr. Haggerty responded. "For the therapeutic connection," he explained, again, "if indeed properly managed."

"So, when would you say that countertransference can be a negative?"

Dr. Haggerty dropped his hands to his lap. "There are times in which therapists have great difficulty managing emotions that arise within the scope of therapy." He motioned with both hands as he spoke. "Poorly managed countertransference can cause a therapist to be angry, depressed, jealous, opportunistic, controlling, manipulative, spiteful or reactive and the list of emotions goes on and on…"

"Thank you," Mr. Freeman said, nodding. "Once any of these emotions kick in for the therapist—is it fair to assume that a therapeutic relationship should come to an end?"

Dr. Haggerty shrugged, curling both arms in front of him. "Well this brings us to the topic of ethical dilemmas."

"Can you tell us more about that?" Mr. Freeman asked.

"Well," Dr. Haggerty said, pausing for a moment to gather his thoughts, "when a therapeutic relationship is no longer in the best interest of a patient, a conversation should occur between a therapist and patient. Termination should be considered, or at least discussed."

"Thank you," Mr. Freeman said, looking down at his handwritten notes. He snapped his head up, then said, "The therapeutic relationship between Dr. Gerhardt and Amanda Jensen seemed to come to an abrupt halt. Are you aware of this?"

"Objection, Your Honor. Dr. Haggerty is just serving as a consultant in an area of expertise."

"Overruled, continue…"

"Yes. I have been made aware of the sudden, unexpected termination of their therapeutic relationship."

"So, if in fact Dr. Gerhardt was triggered during his interaction with Amanda—it makes sense that sessions had stopped. Correct, Dr. Haggerty?"

"Objection, Your Honor. These are hypotheticals, nothing more than assumptions."

"Overruled," Judge Orton said, "please continue…"

Dr. Haggerty nodded. "Yes, that is correct. It would make sense that Dr. Gerhardt bring sessions to a halt if he felt emotionally triggered to the point in which his patient could be negatively impacted, or if he felt for whatever reason that he could no longer sit in a professional role."

Mr. Freeman clapped his hands together once. "The prosecution has no further questions at this time for Dr. Haggerty," he declared, tapping his folder against the podium.

At the defense table, Mr. O'Reilly sat, comparing notes with Dr. Gerhardt. Both nodded to one other before Mr. O'Reilly bounced up from the table and stood before the court. He wiped the bottom of his moist chin with the back of his shirt sleeve while approaching the podium.

"Dr. Haggerty," he said, clearing his throat. "How many years did you say that you have been in the field?"

Dr. Haggerty touched the front of his neck as he cleared his throat. "As I mentioned earlier, 40-years." He calculated with his fingers and then stared up toward the ceiling, counting. "It may actually be just shy of 40-years," he admitted, tilting his head from side to side.

"That is a long time to be in the field," Mr. O'Reilly said, gesturing a prolonged nod.

"It is," Dr. Haggerty said, acknowledging with several quick nods of his own.

"Is it fair to assume that you have actually been linked to the field even longer than your 40 professional years?"

"Well, I'm not quite sure what you mean by that?"

Mr. O'Reilly stuck his reading glasses back into his upper shirt pocket. He shrugged his shoulders and then said, "Well, what I mean is that you have been in the professional field for 40-years now. But if we include your undergraduate studies, graduate achievements in ascertaining both your Ph.D. and your medical degree—and I'm sure you had numerous clinical internships as well." Mr. O'Reilly turned and faced the jury, continuing to smile. "So, all in all-- you have actually been linked to your field of expertise for well more than 40-years."

"If you would like to put it like that—then, yes, I have."

"Dr. Haggerty," said Mr. O'Reilly, loudly. "Have you read your share of books on psychopathology?" Mr. O'Reilly held out a very thick text book, *Clinical Psychopathology: Diagnosis, Treatment and Sequel,* for all of the court to see.

"Yes, of course."

"A requirement in your field is to read many books that relate to diagnosing, psychopathology and human behaviors. Correct?"

"Yes, it is."

"Okay. So you have read numerous materials in the literature on psychopathology. You attended two excellent universities towards your doctorate and medical degree. You have been in the professional field for 40-years or we could say even more years than that as we discussed. Correct?"

Dr. Haggerty nodded, glancing over to the jury. "Correct," he responded.

"Is it fair to assume that in all your years in the field, you have seen a lot."

"Objection," Mr. Freeman interrupted. "Your Honor, the question is broad. It offers nothing in its vagueness".

"Sustained," Judge Orton said, nodding, "Mr. O'Reilly, please move forward with specificity."

"In all of your 40-years of professional experience, including all of the books and other publications you have examined…Can you tell the court today if you have ever heard of a psychologist being charged with first degree murder?"

"Objection, Your Honor. Asking a witness if he has ever heard—"

"Overruled," Judge Orton said, sounding more annoyed with each subsequent interruption.

"Please answer the question, Dr. Haggerty," Mr. O'Reilly urged. "Have you ever heard of a psychologist being charged with first degree murder?"

"No, I have not—"

"Thank you Dr. Haggerty," Mr. O'Reilly said, waving his pen in the air. "You suggested that it may be common for clinicians or patients to be triggered. Is this correct?"

"Well, I think it is more common than we realize."

"Okay. It may be more common than perhaps the literature even suggests. But as infrequent, or as frequent as triggers may occur, have you ever heard of the end result being a murder?"

Dr. Haggerty shrugged before panning the courtroom. "I have never heard of a murder due to therapeutic countertransference," he said, clasping his hands. "So, that is correct."

"Thank you very much, Dr. Haggerty. No further questions," Mr. O'Reilly said, retreating back to the defense table.

Mr. Freeman stood, pulling up his baggy pants as he approached the stand. "You mentioned earlier, Dr. Haggerty, that both transference and countertransference are common in therapy."

"Yes, I did."

"And, you also testified that it is common, sometimes very common, for triggers to occur within the scope of therapeutic treatment. Correct?"

"Correct," Dr. Haggerty said, nodding with confidence.

"Is it also common for therapeutic sessions between a psychologist and a long time patient to come to a sudden, unexpected end, initiated by a treating professional?"

Dr. Haggerty looked around the courtroom, appearing to breathe in an exaggerated way. "I would say, no," he said, shaking his head, "it is not common."

Mr. Freeman dipped his chin. "No further questions, Your Honor."

TWENTY

IN HIS JAIL cell, Dr. Gerhardt sat on the edge of his cot, thinking about *transference* and *countertransference*. He could not fathom how anyone could possibly call into question his work ethic, or challenge his boundaries.

Where did things go wrong? he wondered.

As he leaned back on the cot, he closed his eyes. The name, *Irene Skullman*, entered his mind. Again, he drifted back in time.

TWENTY-THREE YEARS PRIOR

In the waiting room area, Willem had been browsing through pages of one magazine after the next; *Psychology Today, New England Journal of Medicine, Lancet* and *Intrigue*. Feeling anxious about the whole idea of seeing another psychologist, he reached into his pocket, counting loose change. Just as he stood to approach the payphone mounted on the side wall, an office door opened and out stepped Dr. Irene Skullman.

"Hello," she said, embracing Willem's hand with both of hers. "Please, excuse me," she said, apologizing for running late as she glanced at the Sigmund Freud wall clock.

Willem stepped forward and looked all around at the artwork displayed across the office walls. With his mouth open in awe, he nodded in silence before sitting down upon the large brown couch set several feet in front of a reclining chair.

"Well, I am Dr. Skullman," she said, sitting down on her leather recliner, "but please call me, Irene."

"I'm Willem," he said, shrugging, "and, you can call me, Willem." Both smiled.

"Nice to meet you," he said before spinning his head back around to look at other displays of artwork. "Did you paint those pictures?"

"Well, no," Irene said, shaking her head, "I did not." She took a deep breath. "Many of my patients are very artistic." Looking back at the wall display, she asked, "Do you paint?"

"No", Willem said, "My artwork won't be appearing any time soon on your walls."

"I am not an artist, either," Irene giggled, cupping her hands together. She crossed her legs and leaned forward.

"So, what brings you here today, Willem?"

"I'm enrolled in the graduate program in psychology. And, we were all advised to participate in our own counseling."

"Well," she said, shrugging, "it's a matter of opinion." She paused for a moment, exhaling. "Personally, I think we should all engage in some form of counseling regardless of the field we pursue."

"True," Willem said, agreeing. Then mumbled, "I guess."

"Have you been in counseling before?"

"Well," he said, "I have—"

"You sound hesitant." Irene shrugged. "Tell me a little bit about your experiences."

"Well, I was much younger. I don't remember a whole lot about it."

Irene smiled. "How young were you, if I may ask?

Willem bobbed his head, trying to figure out his age at that time by using his adoption day at eight as a baseline for him to calculate.

"Well, it was before I was adopted," he explained. "So, I was younger than eight."

"Oh, you were adopted—"

"I was," he said, nodding.

Irene folded her arms and leaned back. "Was that one of the reasons you chose to enter the field of psychology to begin with?"

"What do you mean—?"

"Well," Irene said, pausing. "Do you hope to work with children who were adopted?"

"I'm not sure, yet," he said, shrugging.

Irene flapped her wrist. "You have plenty of time to decide." She thought for a moment and then asked, "What would you like to gain from our sessions?"

"Well, everyone keeps saying that it is important to resolve issues of your own before addressing issues of others." Willem motioned with his thumb toward himself as he spoke.

"Certainly makes sense," Irene said. "Do you have any pressing things going on right now or anything that may be affecting you from the past?"

"I don't think much of the past. Only really focus on after I was adopted."

Squinting, Irene stared just below his eyelid.

"May I ask what happened to your eye?"

Nervously, Willem laughed. "It's a long story."

"Just how long of a story," Irene said, suggesting she had all the time in the world.

"Fine," Willem said. "It happened after I mistakenly gave the Heimlich maneuver to someone who was not choking."

"You did what—?" Irene snapped with widened eyes.

"I'm only kidding," Willem said, chuckling.

"I was about to say," Irene said, sighing. "Well, at least we know you have a sense of humor. And that is a must in this field."

"That I do have," Willem acknowledged. He clasped his hands together as he stretched back.

"Ok, so what really happened?" Irene asked, leaned forward in the most attentive way.

Willem squeezed his palm into a fist. "A long time ago," he said, hesitantly, "it was an accident."

"An accident?" Irene said, tilting her head to the side.

"Yea—an accident," Willem said loudly, nodding. He muttered, "Just an accident."

"By whose account was it an accident?"

Willem looked down in silence. Nodding, his leg began to shake.

Irene sensed he was not ready to *go there*. She pumped her own brakes and immediately shifted gears.

"How was your relationship with your mother?" She asked in a casual way.

"Which one?" he asked.

"Well," Irene said, stuttering. Confused, she repeated, "Which one??"

"That's okay," Willem said, putting his hand up. "I've had many, but the only one I truly consider to be my mother is Ms. Gerhardt."

Oh, *Gerhardt,* Irene parroted back. "Umm... Beth Gerhardt?" She said, curiously.

"Oh, you know my mom," Willem said, then asked, "Do you?"

Irene grinned with both arms shrugged up high. "We all know your mother," she nodded, then said, "well...your family!"

Willem nodded back in silence.

"Wonderful family," Irene touted.

"Well, yeah—"

"Great," Irene said warmly, touching her heart. "So, you want to enter the field of psychology," she said in an enthusiastic, encouraging way.

"I do, I do." His voice was higher pitched, matching her enthusiasm.

"But, before you enter—You want to do a little more introspection," she said, putting words in his mouth before sipping from her coffee mug. "And, that's understandable," she said nodding.

"You can say introspection," he said, "and, perhaps even some direction."

Irene nodded with her head dipped down before she said, "Guidance." Curious, she looked up and asked, "Do you have any idea with which population you would like to work with?" Not wanting Willem to feel pressured, she paused for a moment, then quickly said, "Well, you certainly have a lot of time to decide."

"Maybe with children," Willem said, shrugging. "Children and adolescents," he said, continuing the thought.

"A wonderful population," Irene said, smiling. "Would you consider working with the elderly? There is a growing need now that people are living much longer than ever before."

"Sure is a growing need," he said in firm agreement, "but, not really sure it's for me."

"That's fine," Irene said, her voice reaching an even higher pitch. "Working with young ones is truly special. There is also a growing need for working with children and the challenges kids face, today." After taking another sip of coffee, she enthusiastically said, "We psychologists are certainly in demand."

"Oh good," Willem said, taking another glance over at the displays of art.

"For you to work with children—it is important to overcome or address issues that you may have had during your childhood." Irene leaned back and folded her arms. "Well, let me ask— would you consider working with adopted children."

"Not sure," Willem said, hesitantly. "Probably just with children in general."

"How was your childhood?" She asked, "What was it like?"

"It was okay." Willem looked down, losing eye contact for a moment.

"How was your relationship with Ms. Gerhardt?"

"Oh, it was great," he touted, perking up. After a moment, he slumped back down.

"But—?" Irene said, using her hands and prodding him to continue.

"No, but," he said, smiling. "It has been incredible." He spoke in a soft voice.

Irene nodded in slow motion. "B-u-t-t-t—" she said, again, in a prolonged way.

"It's just that—" Willem paused midsentence.

"That?" she winced, then snapped, "That what...?"

"I have never felt so loved...so secure...so wanted...so supported... and, to be a Gerhardt means the world to me."

"And?" Irene said softly, leaning forward.

"And, I've always worried that all can change. I just want to know that I will forever be a Gerhardt."

Irene nodded in deep thought. "Have you gone through a lot of transitions in your life?"

"I have," Willem acknowledged. "Well, that was before I came to Ms. Gerhardt."

"You may be having what we call a fear of abandonment," Irene explained, leaning backwards and placing her hands behind her neck. "It is actually common in children who have been adopted."

Willem sat in silence, taking mental notes. "Even at my age?" he asked.

"Yes, even at your age," she said, reaching to tap his knee, then pulling away to respect his personal space. "If not fully resolved," she added, "issues may come up."

"Growing up as a *Gerhardt* was an honor, but there is always a part of me that worries—"

"What is it that worries you?"

Willem exhaled, gathering his thoughts. "I was so used to change," he said, "so even when things were stable...a part of me always anticipated the next change to come."

"Did change come?"

"No. Not after I became a Gerhardt."

"Ok," Irene said, "that has to be at least somewhat reassuring." After pausing for a moment, she said, "Right?"

"It is," Willem said, hesitantly. "But, I still sometimes worry what if." He stopped midsentence, then said, "Anyway..."

"What if?" Irene challenged, recoiling.

"I'm not really sure," Willem said softly. He dropped his head and shut down for a moment as if he could not explain his own train of thought.

"Well, these are the type issues that will be important to address and unravel as you enter the field," Irene said, matter-of-factly. Nodding, she continued, "Especially if you are to work with children."

Willem listened, absorbing her wisdom.

"Regardless of the patient population with whom you choose to work," she said, softly, "you must be able to sit with people's emotions and not allow yourself to be triggered to the point in which something has an effect on the well-being of your patients or even upon you."

"I understand," Willem said softly, nodding.

"The past is important to dissect and address. Understanding it and being able to move forward," she explained, "is ever so important."

Willem nodded in silence. He realized the importance of the past, at least according to all the text books he had already read. In his mind, he thought about the famous words of Winston Churchill, "The farther backward you can look, the farther forward you can see." He stared blankly back at Irene. Conflicted, he also thought about the memorable Dionne Warwick lyric, "A fool will lose tomorrow, reaching back for yesterday."

"You can go your whole life and get pats on your back," Irene said, sighing, "but confronting truths is what life is really all about."

"Do you think the past or the present is more important?" Willem asked.

"Of equal importance," Irene touted.

Willem nodded in agreement.

TWENTY ONE

"YOUR HONOR," SAID Mr. Freeman, looking down at an open folder. "We would like to call to the stand, Amanda Jensen."

Judge Orton nodded and instructed a bailiff to escort her into the courtroom. As the side entrance door opened, Amanda stepped into the court walking with a perfect posture. Her pink tie dye shirt had a purple princess crown embroidered in the middle. The blue looped buckle straps on her shoes matched her tight blue jeans.

Another bailiff greeted her with his hand held up high.

"Please raise your right hand," he said, nodding. "Do you solemnly swear to tell the truth, the whole truth and nothing but the truth?"

Amanda held her right hand up high, emphatically nodding as her colorful beaded bracelet dangled beneath her wrist.

Upon prompting, she then verbally said, "Yes." Peering out toward the crowded courtroom, she took the stand while completely ignoring the presence of Dr. Gerhardt.

Mr. Freeman stepped toward the middle of the courtroom with the open folder resting upon his forearm.

"Hello," he said, smiling.

"Hello, everybody," she said, waving out to the courtroom while nodding in the direction of the jury. After this awkward moment, she finally placed her waving hand back down.

"What is your name?" Mr. Freeman asked, clearing his throat.

"My name is Amanda," she said, bowing her head several more times as if she were in a beauty pageant greeting a panel of judges for the first time. Her voice was high pitched, somewhat squeaky, as if she had inhaled a dose of helium. Several members of the jury could not help but to shuffle in their seats refraining from smiling back.

Mr. Freeman sensed her discomfort, though, in his mind, wondered if she was also basking in the attention.

"It's okay. You can just speak to me." He put his arm straight up to redirect her focus. "Can you please state your first and your last name?"

"Fine," she said, pushing her long, fine blonde hair to the side. "Well, my name is Amanda Jensen." She scooted all the way back in the seat as her blue eyes darted across the courtroom.

"Thank you, Amanda. Can you please state your age?"

"I just turned eleven."

"Can you explain in what capacity you know Dr. Gerhardt? Or, I should ask... How do you know Dr. Gerhardt?"

"He was my doctor."

"And you met with Dr. Gerhardt in his office?"

"Yes," she said, nodding with her lips pressed together.

"Did you meet anywhere besides his office?"

"What?"

"Have you ever seen Dr. Gerhardt in any other location? Or, just in his office?

"No."

"No what?"

"Yes. Only in his office—"

"Ok. And where is his office?"

"It's near the Dairy Queen."

Some members of the jury, once again, stirred in their seats. Judge

Orton waved his hand in an effort to *hush* the jury box and sustain order within the courtroom.

"For the record," Mr. Freeman said, "I would like to indicate that his office is in the River Oaks section of Houston, which for the record is in fact very close to a Dairy Queen."

Clueless, Amanda nodded hard in agreement.

"How many times have you seen Dr. Gerhardt?" Mr. Freeman asked.

Amanda sat on her hands, rocking back and forth. Squinting, she counted softly out loud and then pulled her hands out from beneath her to use her fingers to more carefully calculate.

"I really dunno…Maybe like, ten or eleven times," she said. "I'm really not sure. It could be twelve times." She shrugged, appearing embarrassed.

"Did you see Dr. Gerhardt during the week?"

"Yes, I used to see him during the week," she said, shaking her head up and down. "In the past," she added.

"So—let me make sure I am following. You used to see Dr. Gerhardt in the past?"

"Yes."

"And, how old were you?"

"When I was like 10-years-old."

"Ok. But, then you stopped for a while? Correct?"

"Yes. Then I saw him after that again just one time."

"So you had been seeing Dr. Gerhardt every week. Then you stopped for a while during the court proceedings and saw him only once more just after Jimmy Townsend was acquitted."

"Yes, only the one time."

"Only one last time," Mr. Freeman repeated, sounding surprised. "What made you see Dr. Gerhardt this one last time after the acquittal?"

"Objection," Mr. O'Reilly called out. "She was 10-years-old. I am sure she did not initiate the appointment."

"Your Honor," Mr. Freeman said, "I'm introducing evidence to show motive." He threw his arms up. "This final session occurred on October 12th. The murder of Jimmy Townsend occurred the very next day."

Judge Orton said, "Proceed…"

Nodding, Mr. Freeman asked, "Who would bring you to see Dr. Gerhardt?"

"Well, my mom."

"Objection, Your Honor." Once again, Mr. O'Reilly stood up.

"Overruled, please move forward toward your purpose in your line of questioning unless you believe her transportation has relevance."

"Thank you, Your Honor," Mr. Freeman, said acknowledging. Did you ever see Dr. Gerhardt in your house?"

"In my house," Amanda said. "No!" She spoke in a prolonged way, rolling her eyes.

"Have you ever been to his house?"

"No," Amanda snapped back, sounding annoyed.

"Objection," Mr. O'Reilly shouted out. "The witness has already answered the question."

"Your Honor," Mr. Freeman explained, "I'm demonstrating to the court a doctor-patient interaction that goes well beyond the professional relationship."

"Overruled. Continue—"

"Did Dr. Gerhardt ever call either you or your mother on the telephone?"

"Nope."

"Did you ever see your mother with Dr. Gerhardt."

"N-o-o-o," she said, again in an elongated way, sounding grossed out.

"Okay. So, your mom would bring you to see Dr. Gerhardt. What did you talk to him about?"

"Objection. This oversteps the bounds of doctor-patient privilege," Mr. O'Reilly said, approaching the judge.

"This does not infringe upon privilege, Your Honor," Mr. Freeman countered, flailing his arms out. "This has nothing to do with privilege. The patient herself is here testifying on the stand. We're not asking Dr. Gerhardt to reveal what she disclosed."

"Overruled," Judge Orton said. "Just be more specific in your questioning counsel."

Disgusted, Mr. O'Reilly turned around and retreated back toward the defense table.

Mr. Freeman exhaled. "Well, did you ever speak to Dr. Gerhardt about Jimmy Townsend?"

"Objection," Mr. O'Reilly called out.

"Overruled!" Judge Orton said, losing his patience. "Please, answer the question."

"Did you ever speak to your doctor about Jimmy Townsend?" Mr. Freeman repeated.

"Yes, I did."

"Did you tell Dr. Gerhardt all of the horrible things Jimmy Townsend had done to you?"

"Yes," Amanda said, nodding. "I did."

"Did you ever tell anybody else besides Dr. Gerhardt about the horrible things Jimmy had done to you?"

"No." She shook her head, then again, said, "No."

"When I asked if you had ever told anyone else, I mean did you tell any-y-y-y-one?"

"Well, I did tell some other people."

"Thank you," Mr. Freeman said. "And, who were these other people?"

"I told my mother and the children's team what had happened to me."

"The children's team?" Mr. Freeman said, sounding perplexed. "Did this team visit with you in your home?"

"Yes," Amanda said.

Mr. Freeman scratched the bottom of his chin. "I assume you are referring to DFPS, which is the Department of Family and Protective Services in The State of Texas," he said, realizing what she had meant.

Amanda shrugged, panning the courtroom.

"So you had told your mother and the children's team. Then after and in more detail, you had been discussing this all with Dr. Gerhardt during your sessions. Is that correct?"

"Yes," Amanda said, nodding her head as fast she could.

"Did you tell the same story and share the same details with the workers that you shared with Dr. Gerhardt?"

"Yes," she said as she looked across the courtroom. Without further prompting, she then even more emphatically said, "Yes, I did."

"And Jimmy Townsend was arrested a short time later. Is this correct?"

"Oh. I don't really know." She shrugged her shoulders in an overly dramatic way.

"Objection Your Honor," said Mr. O'Reilly. "How can she be expected to know the legal sequence of events at 10 years-old?"

"She said she does not know," Judge Orton pointed out, "Proceed, counsel..."

Mr. Freeman looked over toward the jury box.

"As a matter for the record," Mr. Freeman said loudly, addressing the courtroom, "Jimmy Townsend was arrested a short time later and formally charged with sexual assault, endangering a minor to various degrees and in varying forms." Mr. Freeman nodded in the direction of Amanda. "And that is when you went to court, as you recall, and testified in court all he had done to you."

"Yes," Amanda said, looking downward, losing all eye contact.

"Okay, we will not re-enact the trial today," Mr. Freeman said. "But, you do recall telling the court the horrible things Jimmy Townsend had done to you?"

Amanda nodded. In a soft voice, she said, "Yes."

"For the record," Mr. Freeman said, "I was the prosecutor in the case brought forward against Jimmy Townsend. And after all was said and done, a jury of his peers acquitted Jimmy Townsend and found him not guilty on all charges."

Amanda tucked her head down and dug her front teeth into the lower part of her lip.

"Some time after the day he was acquitted, you returned to see Dr. Gerhardt for what ended up being your very final session. Is that correct?"

"Yes," she said. After looking down for a moment, Amanda looked out toward her mother, seated on the far side of the courtroom. "Yes, I wanted to see him again," she said, pressing her lower torso toward the back of the chair.

"Jimmy Townsend was found not guilty by a jury of his peers. I assume there was an important reason that made you want to see Dr. Gerhardt, again. Am I right?"

"Yes."

"Ok. I will not make you reveal details. But, I would like to ask you about the last session you had with Dr. Gerhardt." He paused for a minute and whispered into the ear of his co-prosecutor, Linda Jacobs, who had just stepped up to the podium.

"Amanda?" Ms. Jacobs said.

Without responding, Amanda dipped her head down.

"Amanda," Ms. Jacobs repeated. "I have a few questions."

Amanda closed her eyes for a moment, drifting off in deep thought.

She recalled the last time that Jimmy intruded upon her. His breath had reeked of a combination of some form of alcohol. As he had done many times before, he opened the door leading into her bedroom. She remembered how terrified she had felt upon hearing the pitchy, creaking sound of the door as it opened. She recalled how Jimmy had opened the door slowly and then closed it just as carefully. Her memories brought her back to the moment he had crawled from beneath the sheets up toward her from the foot of the bed as she pretended to be asleep. She remembered feeling his hands and his body parts, touching her in all the wrong places. She recalled squeezing her eyes shut, trying to disguise a grimace with a stretch as she heard his heavy breathing inside of her ear. She could not recall all details, though remembered waking up the next day, as usual, to blood-stained bedsheets.

Infuriated, yet feeling helpless, Amanda lifted her head and stared back at the co-prosecutor who stood just a few feet away. No longer timid, Amanda appeared more animated and fidgety on the stand, riven in conflicting emotions.

"Amanda," Ms. Jacobs said, again. "I would like to ask you about the last visit you had with Dr. Gerhardt on October 12th. This is extremely important. Please answer the best you can."

Nodding, Amanda looked down for a moment. She had anticipated this question, but somehow still felt unprepared.

Ms. Jacobs made her way back to the prosecutor's table where she whispered to Mr. Freeman as they fumbled through transcript pages from the previous trial, *State of Texas versus Jimmy Townsend*.

The pending question about her last session with Dr. Gerhardt set Amanda back to that day. She closed her eyes, again, and drifted back into vivid memories.

FINAL SESSION ON OCTOBER 12TH

She recalled sitting in that final session with Dr. Gerhardt while her mother sat in the waiting room. She remembered the anger she felt toward Jimmy Townsend and that empty feeling after having been completely let down by the court. In tears, she had told Dr. Gerhardt that her life had been ruined. All choked-up, barely able to breathe, she remembered having difficulty getting the words out. Dr. Gerhardt had picked up the glass from which he had been drinking and slammed the glass to the floor. She remembered he had told her that he was also devastated beyond belief by the not-guilty court decision. She recalled the tears in his eyes and how he had embraced her with a warm hug, comforting her for all she had been through. She remembered his gentle kiss on her forehead and the warmth she felt as he gently rubbed her back. It was then when he promised in the best way he could that everything was going to be okay. She remembered that he had also informed her that their sessions must come to an end, at least for now...

"Amanda. Are you alright?" Ms. Jacobs asked. She repeated, "Amanda," a tad louder. At the podium, Ms. Jacobs impatiently awaited a response with her hands cupped to her hips.

Forcing her eyes open, Amanda clasped her hands together on her lap. She nodded her head in an uncertain, wobbly way.

"Yes, I remember the last session," she said. Looking around the court room, she took a deep breath and stretched out her trembling arms.

"Asking you to recall this session is emotionally not easy. Please share what happened on October 12th when you met Dr. Gerhardt for your last session."

Amanda tucked her head into her chest.

"Well, I told him I had a secret."

"A secret," Ms. Jacobs repeated, looking down, yet sustaining eye contact. "And what did he say to you when you told him you had this secret?"

"Well, he just listened."

"Okay, fair enough. And, then what happened?" Ms. Jacobs stared at Amanda with widened eyes. "Did you ever tell him the secret?"

"Yes, I did," Amanda said, head flipping her hair back.

"Can you please tell the court about the secret you told Dr. Gerhardt?"

"Yes, I can," Amanda said softly. "I told him that I had lied about the whole story."

"About what whole story," Ms. Jacobs said, her voice reaching a higher pitch.

"Well, I told him that I had lied about what had happened to me." Amanda nodded, taking in a deep breath. "I admitted Jimmy never did anything to me."

"Excuse me," Ms. Jacobs gasped. "Then what happened?"

"That's when he threw a glass on the floor—"

"Wait. What do you mean?" Ms. Jacobs sounded confused. "Was he angry at you?"

"You can say that," Amanda responded in a firm tone. She looked down and muttered, "Very angry with me."

"Ok, then what?"

"Well, he just told me how he felt."

"How he felt?" Ms. Jacobs said, crinkling her nose. Baffled, she cocked her head and looked back toward Mr. Freeman through squinted eyes.

"Yes. He just told me that he felt tricked and never wanted to see me again."

"He never wanted to see you, again?" Ms. Jacobs looked around the silent courtroom. "Are you trying to say he was not angry at Jimmy?"

Amanda shrugged, squeezing her shoulder up high.

"I really don't know. He never said anything about Jimmy. He seemed angry at me." Amanda took another deep breath and said, "I can understand why."

Ms. Jacobs knew from her days back at law school that a prosecutor should never ask a question without first knowing the answer. However, she was convinced she knew the answers that would follow in response to her line of questioning. She looked back, again, toward Mr. Freeman and shrugged, as if to say, *Now what?*

"Is there a reason you had made up these lies about Jimmy Townsend?"

"Objection Your Honor," Mr. O'Reilly cried out. "If there are any questions surrounding the accuracy of her prior testimony, or any possible perjury, she deserves the right for legal representation. She is not on trial. And, Jimmy was found not guilty."

"Sustained for now," Judge Orton said in agreement.

"How do we know she is not committing perjury right now?" Ms. Jacobs said, her eyebrows arching high.

"Please proceed," Judge Orton advised, holding the potential perjury problem *in abeyance* for now.

"Your Honor, we have no further questions," Ms. Jacobs said.

At the defense table, Dr. Gerhardt spoke softly with Mr. O'Reilly. After Mr. O'Reilly nodded hard, he then stood. The manner in which he hopped up off his chair suggested he was confident. His convex chest appeared fully barreled out.

"Amanda," Mr. O'Reilly said, before reaching the podium, "So, Jimmy never did anything to you?"

Amanda drifted into thoughts about how Jimmy Townsend had changed her life and lives of many of those around her. *If only* thoughts raced in her mind.

If only she had not attended the horse riding camp operated by Jimmy Townsend.

If only she had not decided to enroll in the sleep-over camp option.

If only she did not allow Jimmy to do bad things to her, perhaps this was her fault

If only she had not returned to meet with Dr. Gerhardt for that one last session...

Amanda shrugged. "No. He did not do anything to me. I just like attention on me." Nodding, she said, "I used objects that caused damage and bruises to my own genitals."

Mr. O'Reilly stretched out his arms with open palms and nodded. "Thank you, Amanda," he said before looking back over toward the judge. "Your Honor, we have no further questions at this time."

TWENTY TWO

"GOOD MORNING," JUDGE Orton called out from the bench before sipping water from a glass. Looking over toward the defendant's table, he said, "Let's proceed…"

Mr. O'Reilly stood, holding a thin binder in his hand as he approached the front of the courtroom. "We would like to call to the stand, Carol Smith."

A short woman in her mid-forties approached, walking slowly with small steps, waddling in a penguin-like manner. Her red hair was elevated high upon her head and at the very top, placed in the form of a bun. A bailiff greeted her and kindly asked that she raise her right hand before he proceeded to recite the courtroom oath. She agreed with a courteous smile, then after the oath, dropped her arm to her side before taking a seat on the stand.

Mr. O'Reilly took out his reading glasses, then said, "Please state your full name for the court."

"I'm Carol Anne Smith."

"Thank you, Ms. Smith. Can you tell me if you are currently employed?"

"Yes," she said, enthusiastically, "I am…"

"And for the record," he said, nodding, "Who is your employer?"

"Department of Family and Protective Services, or DFPS."

"Okay," Mr. O'Reilly said, rocking to the side as he spoke. "How long have you been working for DFPS?"

"Sixteen years come next month."

"Oh," Mr. O'Reilly said, opening a plastic binder. "Are you familiar with the case surrounding Amanda Jensen?"

"I am."

"In what capacity are you familiar with the case?"

"I was the assigned caseworker."

"Thank you. And, you were called to testify in the case, *The State of Texas versus Jimmy Townsend*. Correct?"

"Yes. Correct."

"And, for the record," Mr. O'Reilly said, looking around the court, "these court proceedings took place after Jimmy Townsend was charged for sexually assaulting Amanda Jensen." He closed the binder for a moment and looked up toward Ms. Smith. "Why did DFPS open the case?"

"Well, initially an anonymous caller contacted our department to make an allegation. Many incoming calls reporting abuse do come in anonymously. We responded, as we usually do, by going out and doing an initial investigation."

"Okay. So, when the initial report came to the department by means of an anonymous caller—what was the actual alleged complaint?"

"Accusation of sexual assault," Ms. Smith said.

"Did you personally go out on this initial investigation?"

"No, I did not."

"Do you recall who all went on the initial investigation?"

"I don't recall. It could have been one or a few of many investigators on our team. I can find out."

"Okay," Mr. O'Reilly said, looping his index finger around his chin. "What we know is that after the investigation—a case was opened, and it was then assigned to you. Correct?"

"Correct," Ms. Smith said, nodding, "And the police were immediately contacted, as well."

"During the time you spent following-up with Amanda—did she ever share anything with you regarding things that were done to her by Jimmy Townsend."

"She did."

"Can you share with the court some of the things that Amanda claimed?"

"Objection!" Mr. Freeman stood up, shouting. "Your Honor, we are not here to retry the case of Jimmy Townsend. I tried the case against Mr. Townsend, and the case is over. Asking open-ended questions is like retrying a case that has already been ruled upon. The defendant's counsel has the transcripts from the court proceedings. If needed, they should be used if there is something specific that we need to allude to."

"Sustained," Judge Orton said softly, peering out. "I am trying to maintain a succinct proceeding here. Revisiting a previous case with general questions is likely to confuse the jury. Please be specific in your line of questioning, and if in fact this witness did testify at a previous hearing—let's make use of transcripts if they are available. We are not here to test the memory of the witness or determine her credibility."

As he reopened the thin plastic binder, Mr. O'Reilly asked, "May I approach the witness?" After approval, he stepped forward and handed Ms. Smith a stack of fifteen pages, double-stapled together on the side. He then walked back to the podium.

"Your Honor," Mr. O'Reilly said, "I have handed the witness a copy of the transcript for the testimony that she specifically provided during *The State of Texas versus Jimmy Townsend*. I have a copy in front of me as well. And, I'll be referring to this document as we proceed."

"Fine," Judge Orton said, appearing content. "Please, proceed."

Mr. O'Reilly peered out above his reading glasses. "Can you please find page 14 and read it out loud for the court to hear?"

Ms. Smith reached for her purse and pulled out her reading glasses, then placed the large red frames over the very tip of her nose. After licking the tip of her index finger, she turned the pages fast until reaching the page 14.

"Of course," Ms. Smith said, looking down. *That's when I knew—*"

"Excuse me," Mr. O'Reilly interrupted. "Can you please read the statements you made that are legally documented on lines 11 and 12?"

"Sure," Ms. Smith said, shrugging. She proceeded to read.

We believe that Amanda was attention-seeking and that she used objects that caused self-inflicted damage to her genitals, which would explain significant bruising to her labia minora and labia majora.

"Thank you very much, Ms. Smith. And likely due to this specific testimony that you provided, Jimmy Townsend was then found not guilty."

"Objection." Mr. Freeman stood up. "We don't know which factors contributed most in the jury's decision for an acquittal."

"Overruled."

"Thank you, Your Honor." Mr. O'Reilly sounded appreciative and relieved. "This testimony by DFPS was crucial to the case. After all, DFPS is the entity in Texas that oversees all reported cases of child abuse. And if representatives of DFPS, whom I refer to as *child protectors*, are themselves taking the stand and reporting that they do not believe a particular sexual abuse allegation—we must take these experts seriously."

In silence, Ms. Smith sat on the stand. Shifty-eyed, she looked around the courtroom.

"In your 16-years, Ms. Smith, what percentage of those cases brought to DFPS were in the end not substantiated for abuse?"

Ms. Smith shrugged before she looked down, then said, "I really don't know the statistics or different percentages."

"I don't need to know exact percentages, Ms. Smith." Mr. O'Reilly wiggled his hand in the air. "Approximately, give or take—how many cases out of every five are, in the end, not substantiated for sexual abuse?"

Ms. Smith bobbed her head back and forth for a moment. "It's hard to say." She patted her hand down, sounding unsure. "Maybe around four."

"Thank you, Ms. Smith. So, in other words, only about one out of five cases of sexual abuse are in the end substantiated."

"Four out of five are not substantiated," she mumbled. "So, yes—one out of five are substantiated." She looked embarrassed, using her fingers to do the math.

"So, is it fair to assume that a large percentage of cases, including the cases you see, are in the end not substantiated for sexual abuse."

"Yes. That is correct," she said, confidently. "I don't have official documentation, but these numbers are very close to the percentages."

. "I found in my research as well," Mr. O'Reilly said, nodding back toward Ms. Smith, "sexual abuse reports are often unfounded." His head tilted, looking over toward Judge Orton. "I have no further questions."

Mr. Freeman pulled his pants up high as he stood up by the prosecution table. As Ms. Jacobs stood beside him, she whispered into his ear before nudging him toward the podium.

"Just a few more questions," Mr. Freeman said, approaching the podium.

"That's fine," Ms. Smith said with a put-on smile.

"You recently spoke about the approximate percentages of reported abuse. And, the large number of cases that are unsubstantiated, after all is said and done."

Mr. Freeman stepped out from beyond the podium and approached the stand. He closed his eyes for a moment before bouncing up on his heels with a hand in the air.

"Is it possible that in cases that go unsubstantiated…abuse did in fact occur?" He asked, twirling around once, looking down.

"Not sure what you mean," Ms. Smith said.

"Rephrase your question, counsel," Judge Orton encouraged.

Mr. Freeman stepped back, gathering his thoughts, then walked back to the podium where he glanced down at notes that Ms. Jacobs had handed him. Blinking fast, he scanned over documents and transcripts from previous court testimony.

"Do you believe that there are situations in which a child did in fact endure sexual abuse, but after an investigation— it was mistakenly determined that abuse did not occur?"

"Yes, I imagine this happens."

"Why would you say this happens? Or, for what reasons may this occur?"

Ms. Smith emphatically nodded, acknowledging she understood his line of questioning. "Well, children will at times recant their stories," she said, "and when this occurs, we can no longer proceed."

"What would be reasons as to why children would recant their stories?"

"I can't get into a child's mind," Ms. Smith said, shrugging, "but, I assume it is often because the story was a lie to begin with."

"Would you agree children may also recant because of fear, or to protect someone," he said, leaning back, "whomever that someone may be?"

"Yes," Ms. Smith said, "I suppose."

"Do children at times recant in the courtroom?"

Nodding, she said, "Yes, they do."

"Thank you, Ms. Smith," Mr. Freeman said, gathering his documents. Exhaling, he walked back to the prosecution table.

TWENTY THREE

MR. FREEMAN STEPPED forward. He stood before the witness who had already acknowledged the oath.

"Can you please state your full name, including the spelling of your last name for the record?" Mr. Freeman said, holding his reading glasses in the air as he spoke.

"Yes, my name is Lucinda Delvecchio," she said, then loudly, like a cheerleader, spelled out her last name, "D-E-L-V-E-C-C-H-I-O."

Lucinda had dark brown hair, draped past her shoulders. She wore thick brown framed glasses over her large dark brown eyes. She had full dimpled cheeks and a large mouth. She appeared happy, breaking out into a full smile every time she spoke.

"Thank you Ms. Delvecchio," Mr. Freeman said, nodding. "Can you please state your job title and position?"

"Yes. I work for Texas Department of State Health Services."

"And, you work specifically within the adoption division…Is this correct?"

"Yes, I do," she said with enthusiasm.

"And you have access to the adoption records of Willem Gerhardt. Is this true?"

"Yes, I do."

"So are these records readily accessible?"

She nodded and then explained, "The Texas Vital Statistics Central Adoption Registry is part of a voluntary mutual-consent registry system mandated during the State of Texas' 68th Legislative Session in 1983."

"For the record," Mr. Freeman said, "what does that all mean?"

"Well," she said, smiling, "it means we have been granted access to his records."

"Wonderful," Mr. Freeman said. "That's really all I need to know." He shuffled through papers that he had spread across the podium. Peering out over his glasses, he then asked, "Can you tell the court about Willem's biological parents?"

"Excuse me," Ms. Delvecchio said, cupping her mouth to muffle out the sound of her dry cough. She cleared her throat before she continued. "Willem was the biological son of William and Emily," she paused for a moment, gesturing with her hand, "which may explain the origin of his name."

Mr. Freeman shrugged. "Did he live with both parents upon his birth?"

"Well, no," Ms. Delvecchio said, her voice dropping to a whisper. "He was born in jail." Uncomfortable, she gazed out in the direction of Dr. Gerhardt, who was sitting at the defense table, breathing hard and staring right back at her.

"I see," Mr. Freeman said, lifting a hand to his cheek. "So, if his mother, Emily, was incarcerated at the time of his birth, was he raised by his father, William?"

Ms. Delvecchio sighed. "Well, no," she said. "He was not."

"Why not?" Mr. Freeman asked. He squinted, acting surprised.

"There were many problems related to substance abuse and legal problems. And besides Emily, William had also served time in prison."

"Okay, so where was Willem placed after his birth?"

"He was placed into foster care," Ms. Delvecchio explained.

"For how long?"

"I'm not quite sure. I do know that he was placed back into the care of his mother, Emily, upon her release from prison."

"So, was he then basically raised by his mother?"

"Well, no."

"Please explain why." Mr. Freeman said, stepping back for a moment.

"Willem and all of his siblings needed to be placed into the foster care system after allegations were substantiated surrounding lack of supervision and neglect when his mother was having babies, one after the other."

"Can you be more specific?"

"Sure," Ms. Delvecchio said. "Emily had ten babies in a nine-year time period."

Mr. Freeman nodded, trying to do the math in his head. "The numbers don't seem to add up." He calculated using his fingers while bobbing his head in confusion.

Ms. Delvecchio rolled up her sleeves before neatly folding her cuffs. "Emily birthed ten children, including sets of twins, one of which was Willem."

"Was he abused by his parents?"

"There were no reports of abuse. But, supervision was an ongoing concern. Again, both parents had substance abuse issues and legal problems."

Mr. Freeman put a fist under his chin. "Can you tell us about Willem's siblings? Was there anything in particular that stood out?"

Mr. O'Reilly sat at the defense table, engaging Dr. Gerhardt in a full length conversation, alternating between speaking into one another's ears. Mr. O'Reilly nodded his head in agreement while jotting notes at a frenetic pace.

"Your Honor," Mr. O'Reilly called out, raising his arm. "I'd like to object to the open-ended inquiry about Willem's siblings. First, that's one big family. And asking a state representative to give a blow-by-blow description of each sibling offers little if anything, anyhow, to this case." Mr. O'Reilly paused for a moment. "Even the most accurate Family Tree or genogram, in the end, adds little, if anything at all, to the charges brought against Dr. Gerhardt."

Judge Orton peered out from his reading glasses. His eyes darted back and forth between Mr. Freeman, who was standing at the podium, and Mr. O'Reilly, who was calling out from the defense table.

"I'm assuming, counsel, that you have a purpose in your line of questioning," Judge Orton said, looking toward Mr. Freeman. "Please be more specific in your questioning and proceed more narrowly along your strategic path."

Mr. Freeman looked over the top of his reading glasses, nodding back in acknowledgment as the judge spoke. He exhaled quietly while reading typewritten pages that had scribbled reminders penciled outside of the margins.

"Can you tell the court the name of Willem's twin?"

"Amy," said Ms. Delvecchio.

"Did Willem live with Amy?"

"He did. The Division transitioned Willem from one foster home to another over the years. But DFPS always made sure that Willem and his twin sister, Amy, transitioned together."

"So, Willem grew up with his sister?"

Ms. Delvecchio looked down for a moment, rubbing her eyes. "He did," she said, then paused for a moment, "until—"

Mr. Freeman snapped his head up, glaring around the courtroom.

"Until," he repeated in suspense. In silence, he stared back at Ms. Delvecchio, awaiting the continuation of her thought.

"Yes, until Amy was murdered," Ms. Delvecchio said with her

hand over her throat, appearing choked-up.

There was an awkward sudden stir in the courtroom. Many attendees shuffled in their seats. Exaggerated gasps resonated from jury members who looked at one another, including a female juror in her early thirties, who dropped her head into her open hands. At the defense table, Dr. Gerhardt had lost all eye contact.

Judge Orton waved a firm hand in an effort to maintain order in the courtroom.

"Do we know how she was murdered?" Mr. Freeman asked.

Mr. O'Reilly stood up, waving. "Objection, Your Honor! The means by which a sibling was murdered over thirty-seven years ago has no relevance to this case."

Mr. Freeman stood his ground, tapping his hand down on the podium. "We think it is has enormous relevance, Your Honor."

"Overruled," Judge Orton stated. "Proceed—"

Ms. Delvecchio nodded and continued to testify. "All we know was that she was sexually assaulted before she was murdered. The medical records indicate that she died by means of strangulation," she said, shaking her head in disgust.

The courtroom was silent. Not a person moved. The jury appeared stoic, frozen in place. Mr. O'Reilly and Dr. Gerhardt were at the defense table, whispering and comparing notes.

Mr. Freeman looked through his reading glasses, turning over pages at the podium, one by one. "Did Willem know the specifics surrounding his sister's murder?"

Ms. Delvecchio shrugged. "I am not sure exactly how much he really knew."

"How old was Willem at the time?"

"He was eight."

Mr. Freeman glared back. "She was his twin sister, and they always lived together. Correct?"

"Yes, that's correct."

"If he was eight and he was living together with his twin sister, then how could he not know she was murdered?"

"I thought you asked if he knew the specifics about the sexual assault she had endured and the means by which she died."

"Okay. So, we don't know whether or not he knew that she had been sexually assaulted?" Mr. Freeman said.

"Well, no. The records don't indicate the depths of his insight related to her sexual assault or strangulation."

"Are there any reports in the records of any allegations that Willem was sexually abused?" Mr. Freeman inquired.

"No, there is no such indication."

"Is there any hint in the records that Willem showed any signs of emotional distress after this tragedy?"

She fidgeted in her seat as she spoke. "Well, we do not know the full impact it had upon him. We know that he had been seeing a psychologist prior to this tragedy."

"Do you have any progress notes or psychological assessments from these visits?"

"No, we do not."

"Okay, but we know for sure he received psychological services before the death of his sister. Correct?"

"Prior," she said, "that is correct." Ms. Delvecchio went on to inform the court about the adoption process at large and their limited involvement post-adoption. She also reiterated that Willem had been adopted very soon after the tragedy.

"Do we know why Willem transitioned so many times from one foster home to the next?"

"The reports indicate that Willem was intrusive," Ms. Delvecchio said, pausing for a moment. "And, foster parents often described him as *uncanny*."

"Was his twin sister also disruptive in these foster homes or described in this same way?"

"No, she was not."

"Okay. Our notes indicate that just a short time after the tragedy, Willem was adopted by Elizabeth Gerhardt. Correct?"

"That is correct. After the tragedy, Willem was rapidly placed out of the foster home. Ms. Gerhardt was contacted very early the next morning, just several hours later, and Willem was permanently placed into her custody."

"Do you have any reports or documentation of any problems or, as you put it, intrusive or uncanny behaviors exhibited by Willem after he was adopted by Ms. Gerhardt?"

Ms. Delvecchio exhaled, thinking for a moment. "After a child is adopted, there is no in-depth tracking or substantial case follow-up." She paused for a moment. "Adoption is considered permanent placement. We do not have any documentation following his transition to Ms. Gerhardt, other than that the transition went well."

Mr. Freeman nodded and thanked Ms. Delvecchio. Gathering materials spread across the podium, he said, "No more questions, Your Honor."

From the defense table, Mr. O'Reilly offered an emphatic nod. He stood and walked with quick strides to the podium where he dropped a folder and set his reading glasses down upon it.

"You had mentioned earlier that Willem received psychological services before his sister was murdered. Is that Correct?"

"Yes, that is correct," said Ms. Delvecchio.

Mr. O'Reilly affixed his reading glasses to the bridge of his nose and skimmed over notes that Dr. Gerhardt had scribbled.

"Isn't it true that most children in foster care are often connected to counseling?"

"I am not sure what you mean by often," she said, shrugging, "but

I can say that it is not uncommon for children within foster care to receive counseling."

"What are some of the issues for which children in the foster care system receive psychological assistance?"

"Oh," Ms. Delvecchio said, "there are so many reasons."

"Can you tell us some reasons that come to mind?"

"Adjustment, anxiety, attachment issues, depression," Ms. Delvecchio motioned with her hand as she spoke, flashing each finger, separately, as she went down a checklist in her mind.

"These issues you just mentioned are common," Mr. O'Reilly said, nodding, "or, at least not uncommon as you indicated for children in foster care. Correct?"

"Correct," she acknowledged.

"Did Willem's sister, Amy, also receive counseling?"

"Yes, she did."

"Aside from being criticized for being intrusive and uncanny—were there any reports suggesting that Willem was aggressive or violent?"

Ms. Delvecchio squinted, reading her official documents. "He was never out of control. He just made families feel uncomfortable at times."

"Thank you, Ms. Delvecchio." Mr. O'Reilly looked up, nodding. "Thank you, Your Honor. We have no further questions."

Judge Orton leaned back and nodded. "We are going to conclude testimony for today," he said, pushing his reading glasses to the side and shuffling loose papers. "We will proceed first thing Monday morning."

TWENTY FOUR

SILENCE FOLLOWED THE loud shut-lock, reverberating sound upon the slamming of the last cell door at the end of the hallway. It was 10:31 on Friday evening. For Dr. Gerhardt, this night was no different from any other night; quiet and lonely with too much time to ruminate. As he lay on his cot, he stared blankly at the bare walls that confined him. Restlessly, he wondered how he would get through the long weekend, awaiting the resumption of the trial.

Earlier in the day, Mr. O'Reilly had explained that Dr. Tino Ballantino was scheduled to testify first thing Monday morning, likely as the final witness.

Dr. Ballantino was one of Dr. Gerhardt's professors during the final semester of the doctoral program. Dr. Gerhardt cherished him as one of the very best professors he had ever had.

Dr. Gerhardt rolled over on his side and sunk his head onto his forearm. He closed his eyes, thinking about Dr. Ballantino including the enthusiasm his ole' professor exuded up until the very final day of the doctoral program, close to twenty years prior.

It was the latter part of May in 1996 and Willem was sitting in his very last class on the final day of the doctoral program. For all intents and purposes, the doctoral program was over. Professor Ballantino was sitting on a tall metal stool in the middle of the room. In a semi-circle two rows deep, twenty-two students faced the professor at various degrees of angles, listening with great intensity, absorbing every last word the professor had to say. He was more or less putting his very final touches on a course well-taught, but even more, collectively spilling out final advice and wisdom to graduating students for the very last time. The professor presented more like a football coach, giving that one and very final pep-talk just before a team takes the field.

Professor Ballantino stood up from the stool. Standing 6 feet 5 inches tall, he had jet black hair that was, as usual, slicked straight back with gel in a fresh out of the shower type look. His thick mustache was curled at the ends underneath his hooked nose. His height coupled with his stocky build gave him an appearance more typical of a football coach or a nightclub bouncer rather than a university professor who had been selected Professor of the Year for a third consecutive time. All of his students had known he was Italian, not only from his accent and revealing last name, but also because he had kept promising all semester that Italy would win the World Cup during the month that followed.

Known for his high level of energy and passion, Professor Ballantino was also known for his bright shining ring, one he wore upon his middle finger. As he lectured, he often walked around the classroom tapping the shiny ring against the side of desks, involving students in discussion and mental exercises. He had a deep voice that projected across the classroom and he often used hand gestures to further reiterate points he made.

On that final day of class, he had alternated between both sitting and standing up from the stool as his ring glistened upon every hand gesture he had made. On that day in particular, he had spoken in a rapid and thorough manner as if he were trying to summarize the entire purpose of the doctoral program during the very final hour on the very final day.

"I'd like to congratulate you all," he had said nodding as he stood up from the stool. Usually dressed in a formal suit, he was wearing a black T-shirt and beige cargo shorts that draped just below his knees. His shirt hugged tight around his shoulders creating a masculine silhouette that further accentuated his V shape. A diamond cut gold chain sparkled around his neck adding further glimmer to his appearance beyond the shiny middle finger ring.

Professor Ballantino leaned back against the stool, exhaling. "Earning your doctorate degree is a huge accomplishment," he said, nodding in a confident way. "Though, entering the field is only the beginning and far from the end-all of your accomplishment."

Students sat in silence, without notebooks or pens, eager to just listen and absorb every last tidbit of his knowledge and guidance offered.

"Some of you may work in hospitals, schools, private practices or in university settings." He paused for a moment and raised his forefinger, then continued, "Wherever it is you find yourself, you must never forget about the basics of our field."

Professor Ballantino propped himself up on the stool with his hands neatly folded upon his lap. "You are all about to embark upon fragile territory," he said, looking out to the semi-circles of students. "You will spend time with those who are depressed, angry, anxiety-ridden and buried deep in conflicts at work or within the home. You will sit face-to-face with those who have done the unthinkable…or, those who have been victims," he said, pausing for a moment, "and, it won't be easy." He continued, "You must be able to set aside your past triggers, long held belief systems and everyday personal life stress."

Professor Ballantino was straightforward and direct, not wanting to be interrupted. He had so much to say, yet so little time left.

"Are you able to set aside the emotions that you have in your everyday lives for those moments," he asked, reiterating, "those ever so precious moments, you spend with patients who sit before you?" He rhetorically asked, nodding in a pensive frame of mind. "Your typical feelings, knee-jerk reactions, facial expressions, long held values and belief systems have to be kept in-check. Can you shuffle them all to the side?" He asked, shrugging. "But, most importantly, I ask, will you be able to manage your emotions in the professional world, maintain boundaries, and recognize and address the triggers that arise?" He looked around at all the students and sighed. "It won't be easy. As you know from this class and others, your boundaries and emotions will be tested."

He stretched his arms out, then for a moment, lifted his legs off the floor.

"There are so many reasons why people enter this field. But, what we all have in common are good intentions and a burning desire to help others." He smiled, nodding. "But, what happens when you work with a patient who either has done something or has had something done to them that touches your every last nerve?"

Dr. Gerhardt snapped his head up from the cot. Squinting, he tried to shield his eyes from the bright light seeping in from the double-barred window. He leaped up and walked over to the front of the cell, gazing out to bareness as his hands gripped the vertical steel bars.

His *good ole'* professor was still on his mind. He recalled just how much Dr. Ballantino had cared about his students up until the very final day of class when he had given out his personal telephone number to all students, sincerely encouraging all to *reach out* anytime with any questions, concerns or dilemmas. His *open-door* offer was comforting to those who were graduating.

It was a great *send-off*, Dr. Gerhardt remembered. His professor's very final words rung in his mind, "It's not all peaches out there folks—you will be tested."

After pacing around the tight quarters, Dr. Gerhardt retreated back to his cot where he lay with his hands clasped behind his head, analyzing in a retrospective manner how things may have gone wrong. Confused, he shook his head and thought to himself, *professor said there would be times like these.*

TWENTY FIVE

JUDGE ORTON MOTIONED to introduce the next witness. Quickly adhering, a bailiff hustled over to the corridor where he stood and offered assistance by a side entrance door.

A loud humming sound slowly decreased in volume as the motorized wheelchair slowed before coming to a full stop by the front of the court. Buckled in his seat, a man with quadriplegia acknowledged the oath and then proceeded toward the stand, using specific tongue movements to maneuver and control the speed of his power chair.

At the witness stand, the man dribbled a stick out from his mouth before turning to face the packed courtroom. In his late fifties, he had salt and pepper hair that was, with the aid of gel, neatly brushed straight back in a meticulous fresh out of the shower look. Clean shaven on the sides, he had a thick grey mustache, curled downward at the tips beneath his hooked nose. His Italian accent stood out, even at the onset, when he said, "Yes, I do," after a bailiff had administered the oath.

As Mr. Freeman approached the podium, he reached for his reading glasses that were fastened to the outer part of his shirt pocket.

"Can you state your full name for the court? And, please spell your last name."

"I'm Tino Ballantino…B-a-l-l-a-n-t-i-n-o."

"Thank you, Tino. And what is your job title?"

"I'm a professor. But, I have since retired. I had taught Ethics courses at local universities."

"Thank you, professor," said Mr. Freeman. "Can you state for the record the name of your handicapped condition?"

Dr. Ballantino loudly exhaled, appearing uncomfortable by the question. His neck was fully supported. His strapped wrists were limp, dangling over cushioned armrests of the electric wheelchair.

"Objection," Mr. O'Reilly called out. "His physical condition or any health problem he may have is personal and irrelevant to this case."

"Your Honor," Mr. Freeman said, chiming in. "We believe it is relevant and it is one of the main reasons we are calling upon Dr. Ballantino to testify."

"Overruled," Judge Orton called out. "Please proceed—"

"Thank you, Your Honor. "Can you please state for the court record the name of your handicapped condition?"

"Yes, I have quadriplegia."

"Thank you, professor." Mr. Freeman bowed down, appreciating the quick response to a sensitive question. "Do you know him?" Mr. Freeman asked, motioning with his chin in the direction of Dr. Gerhardt.

Mr. O'Reilly stood. "I object to the reference, Your Honor. This is no time for Dr. Gerhardt or anyone for that matter to be referred to as, *him.*"

"I agree," Judge Orton said, "proceed with respect…"

Nodding, Mr. Freeman then asked, "Do you know Willem Gerhardt?"

"Yes, I know Dr. Gerhardt," Professor Ballantino said, his voice projecting.

"Can you tell the court in what capacity?"

Professor Ballantino then spoke in a deep voice and at a slower pace. "Dr. Gerhardt was a student of mine. He was enrolled in my courses."

How many years ago?"

"I don't recall exactly," Professor Ballantino said, pausing for a moment. "But I do know it was just before Italy won the World Cup," he said, looking up mumbling, "which was in 1996, which I guess, makes it around 20 years ago."

"I see we have an Italian soccer fan in the court today," Mr. Freeman said, smiling.

Not finding humor in the moment, Professor Ballantino remained stoic.

After an awkward moment of silence, Mr. Freeman continued. "So, we are speaking about 20 years ago. That was a long time ago, professor."

In silence, Dr. Ballantino awaited the next question.

"And, after all these years, you actually remember having taught Willem Gerhardt in your classes?" Mr. Freeman phrased the question in a sarcastic, challenging tone.

"Yes, I do remember," Dr. Ballantino said matter-of-factly.

Mr. Freeman removed his reading glasses from his shirt pocket and held the frames up high. "Just what is it that you remember about him?"

Fidgeting, Professor Ballantino blew out some air. "Well, he was an excellent student and he always had an unquenchable thirst for knowledge."

Mr. Freeman nodded. "Would it be fair to assume that doctoral students are generally excellent students, possessing, what you refer to as, a thirst for knowledge?"

"Yes," Dr. Ballantino said, agreeing.

"Okay," Mr. Freeman said, sighing. "I am trying to further understand what stood out about Willem Gerhardt so much so that you would remember him 20 years later?"

"He certainly was a passionate student. And, we all know, or at least know of the Gerhardt family."

"Did he keep in contact with you after graduating?"

"Yes, he did."

"And for what reasons did he remain in contact?"

"Objection," Mr. O'Reilly said, jumping to his feet. "This line of questioning is intrusive. It would be like asking why someone has chosen you as a friend."

Mr. Freeman countered, "Your Honor, I am trying to demonstrate to the court that the defendant's desire to remain in contact with his former professor had little, if anything, to do with a friendship."

Judge Orton listened to each argument with attentive ears, nodding. As he peered over his reading glasses, he said, "Overruled, but, please be more specific in your line of questioning, counsel."

"Let's fast forward if we could," Mr. Freeman said, looking down at his notes. He shuffled through papers and then pulled out a page from the bottom of his thick pile. "During the month of October of last year, on the 12th to be exact, Dr. Gerhardt contacted you and requested that you meet with him. Is that Correct?"

"Correct. He did contact me."

"Can you please tell the court what time, or about what time, you received his phone call?"

"I'm not quite sure."

"Professor," Mr. Freeman said, sounding annoyed, "Just an approximate time, please."

"It was about 9:30."

"When you say 9:30— Are you referring to the morning, or evening?"

"Evening."

"So, that's 9:30 at night. And, you ended up meeting the defendant, Dr. Gerhardt, at Rice University that same evening. Is that correct?"

Professor Ballantino froze in silence. His eyes shuffled, ignoring the question as if he were about to *plead the Fifth*.

Mr. Freeman planted his elbows against the podium.

"For the record and as a courtesy to the witness, I want to make it known that we have obtained video footage from that evening you met with Dr. Gerhardt on the university campus."

Mr. O'Reilly stood. "It sounds like the prosecution team is trying to pull a fast one." From the table, he appeared angry, expressing his discontent to the judge with regard to video evidence. "What ever happened to adhering to the rules of admissibility?"

"Your Honor," Mr. Freeman said, interrupting, "I'm not looking to introduce video evidence, but wanted to inform the witness what we have obtained so that he is aware prior to making his statement." He folded his arms and nodded, then said, "I don't want to put the witness in a position where he may commit perjury. Then we'd have an additional problem on our hands."

Judge Orton tapped his palm down, "Let's proceed."

"After you spoke to Dr. Gerhardt on the phone at, or about, 9:30—did you meet with him on the Rice campus?"

"Not exactly," said Dr. Ballantino.

"Not exactly?" Mr. Freeman repeated, sounding perplexed. "Meaning what?"

"Well, we had planned to have a meeting," Dr. Ballantino said. "But it never happened."

"Professor Ballantino, I am having a hard time following. Can you just tell the court what happened after you received Dr. Gerhardt's phone call?" Mr. Freeman was blunt in his questioning.

A bailiff stepped forward with a glass of water. With assistance, Dr.

Ballantino sipped from an elongated straw as the bailiff dabbed a tissue on water beads that had formed just above the professor's mustache.

"Take your time," Mr. Freeman said, turning around and glancing back toward his co-prosecutor, Ms. Jacobs. He nodded toward her in a confident way as she thumbed through notes at the table.

"Thank you," Dr. Ballantino said, after swallowing one last gulp of water.

"You said that you met, but you really did not meet. Can you take us through what all happened after you received the phone call from Dr. Gerhardt."

Dr. Ballantino cleared his throat before he spoke. "He asked if I could meet with him. We agreed to meet at Rice University at 10:30."

Mr. Freeman stepped in front of the podium and stood within a foot from the professor. "Can you," he said, pleading, "share with the court the specifics of that night?"

"I got in touch with my personal assistant, and she came to my home. She helped me change back into the clothes that she had earlier helped me remove. I got ready and then we headed over to campus."

"I see," said Mr. Freeman. "Okay, so you drove to the campus—then, what?"

"Well, my assistant drove me in the van to the campus. Then we parked just outside of Sewall Hall."

"Does she usually drive you around?"

"Irrelevant, Your Honor," Mr. O'Really said.

"Sustained," Judge Orton agreed without giving it much thought.

"Do people with quadriplegia usually drive?" Mr. Freeman asked.

"Objection, Your Honor." Annoyed, Mr. O'Reilly stood with his hand help up high. "He is not here as a representative of the quadriplegia community. If the prosecutor is in need of information on quadriplegia, we can connect him to the university library."

"Sustained," Judge Orton said, leaning back on the bench before folding his arms. "Let's keep order in this courtroom, gentlemen."

"Was Dr. Gerhardt already at the campus when you arrived?"

"As we pulled into the lot, I saw Dr. Gerhardt standing just outside the entrance door."

"Did he come to your van?"

"I don't think he knew it was me," Dr. Ballantino said, rocking in his chair. "It was dark and there were many other cars in the lot. He looked over at our van, but he had no reaction."

"Okay, then what happened," Mr. Freeman asked.

"I went across the parking lot and saw him standing by the doors of Sewall Hall."

"Was he happy to see you?"

"It's hard to say," Dr. Ballantino said.

"Why do you say that?" Mr. Freeman squinted, appearing confused.

"To me, he looked sad."

"Sad? Or, would you say, distraught?"

"Sad," Dr. Ballantino reiterated, nodding slowly.

"Okay, moving along…Did you then enter the building?"

"No, we did not. The doors were locked."

Mr. Freeman stepped away from the podium and approached the professor. "Did you ever get to talk to Dr. Gerhardt?"

"We could not get into the building," Dr. Ballantino explained.

Well aware of the locked building, Mr. Freeman nodded, concurring with the testimony. After all, he had access to the video footage, which had showed Dr. Gerhardt walking around the outside of Sewall Hall, unable to enter as the drenched professor rolled behind.

"So, you never got to speak to each other," Mr. Freeman said.

"No, we did not. He told me that he would contact me the next day."

"Did he?" Mr. Freeman asked.

"No, he did not."

"Did you speak at all to Dr. Gerhardt on the phone on the evening of October 12th, after you all could not gain entry into the building?"

"Not really," Dr. Ballantino said.

"Not really?" Mr. Freeman questioned. "We have access to phone records."

Dr. Ballantino exhaled. "Yes, we did talk on the phone, briefly."

"Briefly?" Mr. Freeman repeated, letting out a sarcastic chuckle. "What was this conversation about?"

"Objection," Mr. O'Reilly called out. "This line of questioning is very intrusive."

"Overruled," Judge Orton said. "If you could, please, at least, speak in general terms about the nature of your dialogue."

"Thank you, Your Honor," Mr. Freeman said. "Professor, can you share in general terms about this late night phone conversation on October 12th?"

Dr. Ballantino shrugged. "It was an enjoyable chat. It was great catching-up."

"So," Mr. Freeman said, "What you are suggesting is that it was like telephone conversations that most people have?"

"I suppose, yes."

"I want to make it clear to the court that you seem to be suggesting that it was just an everyday phone chat," Mr. Freeman said, "like no big deal."

"Absolutely," Dr. Ballantino said.

"Our records indicate that your telephone conversation began after 11:15 in the evening and the duration was 2-hours and 17-minutes."

"Objection," Mr. O'Reilly called out.

"Overruled," Judge Orton responded.

Mr. Freeman then asked, "Are you aware that Jimmy Townsend

was murdered the very next day? Shortly after your phone call."

"I am aware. But, I never linked the two."

Mr. Freeman shrugged, rolling his eyes. "Well, I did not ask if you linked the two, just whether or not you were aware...which, you have now made perfectly clear."

Dr. Ballantino shuffled around, visibly restless in his motorized chair.

"Are you aware that Dr. Gerhardt suddenly terminated his sessions with a long time patient earlier in the day?"

"I did not know at the time. I was informed later."

"Do you usually meet with former students so late at night?" Mr. Freeman asked, rolling up his shirt sleeves. "Do you usually speak to former students for 2 hours and 17 minutes during the wee hours of the morning? Do you ever speak to anyone for such a long period of time?"

"Objection," Mr. O'Reilly called out. "He needs the opportunity to answer the question, Your Honor."

"Please ask one question at a time, counsel," Judge Orton, said. "And keep your questions pertinent."

"Do you usually speak to or meet with students at such late times in the evening?" Mr. Freeman asked.

"Well," Dr. Ballantino said, swaying, "I have always had an open-door policy."

"Meaning what, professor?"

"Well, I am available 24-hours a day— to not only my students, but anyone, really."

"That's very nice of you. But have you ever met with a student so late or, shall I say, so early in the morning?"

"Objection, Your Honor."

Without hesitating, Judge Orton said, "Overruled."

Mr. Freeman repeated, "Have you, professor?"

"Yes, I have," Professor Ballantino said before requesting more water.

"I am surprised that Dr. Gerhardt wanted to drag you out at that time of the night." Mr. Freeman placed his finger on his chin. "Just how was the weather like on that evening?"

"Oh, I don't remember," Dr. Ballantino said. "That was a long time ago." With assistance from the bailiff, he sipped more water from a straw.

"It was not that long ago, professor—and again, keep in mind, we do have footage."

"I think it may have been raining," Dr. Ballantino said, wiggling in his chair.

"RAINING?" Mr. Freeman said, gasping. "It was SEVERE thunderstorms. If it were not for your assistant who shielded you with an umbrella, you would have been even more drenched in your clothes."

Like a school boy scolded by a teacher, Dr. Ballantino dipped his head, then mumbled, *true.*

"Knowing that you have a physical disability, I am surprised that Dr. Gerhardt needed to drag you out so late at night, especially amidst torrential thunderstorms."

"Well, Dr. Gerhardt did not know about my physical condition."

"Excuse me? Can you be more specific?" Mr. Freeman appeared perplexed.

"Well, he did not know I have quadriplegia."

"Dr. Gerhardt did not know you are a quadriplegic?" Mr. Freeman bluntly questioned, then returned to the podium where he shuffled papers. "I am confused, professor."

"No. He did not know about my accident." Professor Ballantino sounded subdued in his response.

"How many years ago did your accident happen?"

"It has been seven years…"

"In other words, you have not spoken to the defendant in many years," he said, pausing for a moment, "or, I should say, in at least seven years."

Professor Ballantino swayed during the moment of silence. "After the accident, I decided to stay in Italy."

"Where do you live now?"

"Italy," Dr. Ballantino said matter-of-factly.

"In October of last year, on the 12th to be exact," Mr. Freeman said, "you were here in Texas. Correct?"

"That is correct."

"What brought you to Texas at that point in time?"

"I still have a place here. I come back to visit family and friends." Dr. Ballantino spoke in a slow manner.

Mr. Freeman stepped forward and glared directly at Dr. Ballantino. "Were your travels from Italy to Texas in October in some capacity related to the struggles of Dr. Gerhardt?"

"No, I did not know of any of his struggles."

"Did you and your assistant stay in the home of Dr. Gerhardt in October?"

"No, we did not."

"Just where did you stay Dr. Ballantino?"

"Objection, Your Honor," Mr. O'Reilly called out. "It is irrelevant where he vacationed or with whom he stayed. The question was answered. He did not stay with Dr. Gerhardt."

"Sustained," Judge Orton said, "If he did not stay with Dr. Gerhardt, it does not seem relevant to explore his vacation itinerary."

"When was the last time that you had spoken to Dr. Gerhardt?"

"I really don't recall."

"So what you are basically saying is that he did not keep in much touch with you after he graduated or after you moved to Italy?"

"Well, most students don't," Dr. Ballantino said. He sounded somber as if he wished more students had. "We did remain in some contact over the years."

"Why do people call on the phone," Mr. Freeman said, gathering papers, "especially when it's out of the blue?" He then nodded toward the jury box before answering his own question. "It's when they need something!"

He then continued, "And when people want to meet out of the blue, late at night amidst thunderstorms with former professors from Italy," he said, nodding, "they REALLY need something." He slapped the stack of papers down. "It sure sounds as though Dr. Gerhardt was not doing emotionally well on that evening. No further questions, Your Honor." Nodding, he stepped to the side.

"Shall we take a recess?" Judge Orton inquired.

Mr. O'Reilly stood up from the defense table. "I'd like to proceed without a break, Your Honor," he said, trying to promptly cease the prosecutor's momentum. As he stepped forward, he brushed against Mr. Freeman as he hurried toward the podium.

"Good morning, Dr. Ballantino."

"Morning," he responded, squirming.

Mr. O'Reilly looked down for a moment, organizing a tall stack of newsletters printed by the American Psychological Association dating back twenty years.

"Professor," Mr. O'Reilly said, looking up, "you have been awarded numerous honors in the field throughout the last two decades. Is this true?"

Dr. Ballantino appeared in deep thought.

He recalled his teaching days and the interactions he used to have with his students. He thought about the times he would walk around the classroom instructing students, yet, at the time, learning from them. The awards and recognitions he had received over the years flashed in his mind, though the intrinsic reward of simply teaching mattered most.

"Professor?" Mr. O'Reilly said.

"Yes," Dr. Ballantino said, modestly. "I have won many awards." His voice was soft. More than just humble, he sounded somber in his response.

"You were a very fine professor, Dr. Ballantino," Mr. O'Reilly said.

The professor sucked in a full breath, before slowly exhaling.

"Is it true that Dr. Gerhardt went on to win many of these very same honors and recognition awards?"

"He sure did," said Professor Ballantino, breaking into a smile.

"So, when you said earlier that Dr. Gerhardt was enthusiastic with a thirst for knowledge," Mr. O'Reilly said twirling his pen, "you really weren't kidding."

"He was remarkable," Dr. Ballantino touted.

Mr. O'Reilly held up old newsletters that contained photographs of Dr. Ballantino receiving prestigious recognition awards in the field. He followed up by showing the court more recent newsletters, containing photos of Dr. Gerhardt receiving these very same awards.

Acknowledging the newsletters, Dr. Ballantino reiterated, "Truly remarkable."

Mr. O'Reilly pushed the stack of newsletters to the side of the podium. "How did you feel, professor, when Dr. Gerhardt contacted you late in the evening?"

Dr. Ballantino shrugged. "How did I feel?" he said, collecting his thoughts. "Well, I was happy to hear from him."

"Were you concerned?"

"Not really."

"Well, what were you thinking?" Mr. O'Reilly asked.

"I just figured he had some questions that he wanted to run by me, which, by all accounts, was fine with me."

"Was the time of the evening alarming to you?"

Dr. Ballantino shrugged, looking around the courtroom. "Dr. Gerhardt always knew that my days were very busy. I taught classes in both the morning and the afternoon. And I would see patients in the early evening as part of my private practice. So, evenings were the very best time to reach me."

Mr. O'Reilly peered out above his reading glasses with an open folder in his hand. "You mentioned earlier that Dr. Gerhardt appeared sad when you met him on campus. Can you be more specific?"

"I don't know for sure. It was just a feeling I had at the time."

Mr. O'Reilly set the folder down. "Were you worried that something had happened or something was seriously wrong?"

"It's difficult to worry about Dr. Gerhardt. He handles himself so well in both his personal and professional life. He is a passionate leader, a go-getter and someone who can be described as cool, calm, and collected."

Mr. O'Reilly shrugged. "So, you just thought he was sad."

"I may have had a self-centered intuition, but I thought he may have looked sad to see me in a wheelchair for the first time." Dr. Ballantino looked over toward the defense table where Dr. Gerhardt sat with his head dipped down. "Many appear sad when they see me in the chair, especially for the first time," he said softly.

Dr. Gerhardt stirred in his seat with his hands cupped solidly to his kneecaps as his legs shook beneath him. He could not fathom that his former exuberant professor was confined within the confines of a wheelchair, no longer even able to sip water on his own. He stared for a moment at the shiny gold nugget ring on the professor's middle finger, which immediately brought back *shiny* memories. *My problems pale in comparison*, Dr. Gerhardt thought to himself.

"As you know, professor, the prosecution is trying to establish a case that Dr. Gerhardt was affected by a phenomena described as countertransference, suggesting that he was unable to manage his emotions." Mr. O'Reilly paused for a moment. "Are you familiar with the term countertransference?"

"Of course, I am familiar."

"What are your thoughts on countertransference related murder?"

Fidgeting in his chair, Dr. Ballantino said, "First off, I have never heard of countertransference resulting in a murder."

Mr. O'Reilly folded his arms, rocking from side to side. "Is it fair to assume the case makes no sense?"

"Objection, Your Honor," Mr. Freeman said, bouncing to his feet.

"Sustained."

"In your wildest imagination, is it possible for a psychologist to commit murder based upon countertransference?" Mr. Freeman then added, "Or, commit murder in general?"

Dr. Ballantino swayed in his chair. "Is it possible?" He said with widened eyes. "Well, Dr. Gerhardt was not only a practicing psychologist, but he also taught this very material. So, is it possible?" He spoke in a prolonged way, with a puzzled expression.

"By your expression, I assume you are implying it would be highly unlikely?" Mr. O'Reilly suggested.

Mr. Freeman hopped off his seat. "Leading question, Your Honor," he said, "I am sure the professor is fully capable of speaking for himself."

"Sustained!"

Mr. O'Reilly chuckled as he placed a pen behind his ear. "Go on professor, please speak for yourself."

Dr. Ballantino exhaled. "It's simple," he said, "And, I'll put it like this—"

"Is it *possible* for an alcoholic to extol the virtues of abstinence?"

"Is it *possible* for the commissioner of the anti-bullying movement to become a bully himself?"

"Is it *possible* for an outwardly loving and happy law abiding citizen to drive up to a building with a truck full with explosives?"

"Is it *possible* for an unblemished, well-known and universally-respected psychologist who teaches Ethics to commit murder?"

"Yes, it is possible." Dr. Ballantino said. "But, HIGHLY unlikely."

Mr. O'Reilly nodded once and thanked the professor before retreating toward the defense table.

Judge Orton requested that the courtroom be cleared and that both sides of counsel approach the bench. Members of the jury stood, looking back silently at one another before walking in single file out of the jury box.

As everyone else was leaving the courtroom, Mr. O'Reilly and Mr. Freeman gathered belongings from their respective tables and then stepped forward.

"Gentlemen," Judge Orton said, leaning back sighing. "As we move into final deliberations, I have a decision I must make." Both lawyers leaned against the bench, listening carefully. "I may need to omit all statements made by Amanda Jensen."

"But, you just can't—" Mr. O'Reilly tried to speak.

"Let me finish," Judge Orton said, putting his hand up.

Sighing in frustration, he continued. "Testimony must be disregarded when a witness is caught making contradictory statements. And, it is clear that she has at some point in time lied. At this point, she lacks all credibility."

"She was the most important person to take the stand," Mr. O'Reilly challenged.

"The most important person to take the stand would have been Dr. Gerhardt," Judge Orton responded in a way that suggested that he was curious as to what the doctor had to say for himself. "I am not sure how I could possibly allow her story, which completely changed from the last trial. She can't just change her testimony from one court case to the next."

"Let me understand this," Mr. Freeman said. "You're planning to only omit statements made by Amanda during this trial." He paused for a moment. "Correct?"

Mr. O'Reilly quickly chimed in. "Well, I'd assume you would also omit transcripts of her testimony from the previous trial, as well, being as it was also shared with the jury."

"I only have control of this hearing," Judge Orton said. "It's too late to challenge anything Amanda said during any previous trial."

"Understood," Mr. O'Reilly said, sounding frustrated, "but if you are moving forward toward omission, it would only make sense to omit all her testimony, which would include the court transcripts alluding to prior statements."

"I don't think I can possibly do that," Judge Orton said, shaking his head.

Growing more frustrated, Mr. O'Reilly said fiercely, "It would make it impossible to address one testimony without addressing the other. Most of the trial has been about the intermingling of both of her testimonies. You won't be able to omit her testimony unless you also remove all testimonies of those who addressed it."

Judge Orton matter-of-factly responded, "But her story changed."

"But we really don't know at which juncture the lie occurred," Mr. Freeman pointed out. "Did she lie during the previous trial? Or, is she lying during this trial?" He gave the judge a tight-lipped stare back.

Mr. O'Reilly took a deep breath, feeling frustrated that his point was not getting across. "If we remove the present testimony, citing perjury—this would suggest that her testimony during the previous testimony was the truth. However, Jimmy Townsend was found not guilty, because her testimony back then supposedly lacked credibility, at least according to the verdict. Our case rests on the premise that her testimony is actually truthful, now."

"Alright, enough," Judge Orton said, picking up a pen while leaning back in his seat. "Would barring present testimony be in the best interest of justice," he rhetorically said aloud, twirling the pen around. "That's the decision I am faced with." He put on reading glasses, then glanced down at the transcripts of both Amanda Jensen and Carol Smith, both of which he had inked asterisks by the upper corners of each page.

Mr. O'Reilly aired his thoughts, "I think it would be a big mistake to omit any testimonies at this point. We would be confusing the jury by basically saying to forget everything they have heard thus far."

"When testimony is stricken, it can on the contrary, make it all the more memorable for the jury," Mr. Freeman suggested.

Both attorneys continued to make their points known, neither of whom encouraged any form of omission. On the contrary, both found the testimony of Amanda Jensen to be advantageous, in different ways, to each of their cases approaching closing arguments.

"Listen," Mr. Freeman said, "it is an impossible task for the jury to compartmentalize all of this information up until this point and then simply disregard an immeasurable portion."

"I couldn't agree more," Mr. O'Reilly concurred.

Open to suggestions, Judge Orton listened to all feedback. Appearing conflicted in thought, he took in deep breaths while scratching the top of his bald head. Not quite sure how to proceed, Judge Orton was determined to do the *right* thing. He realized it would be an impossible task to ask that jurors remove a majority of the testimony from their minds.

Judge Orton cleared his throat. "I have until the jury returns a verdict to declare a mistrial. We'll proceed, as is, with the deliberations, tomorrow."

TWENTY SIX

SECURITY PERSONNEL TURNED away crowds who swarmed around the front entrance, trying to push their way into the courthouse. Concerned about the influence brought on by the media attention surrounding the trial, Judge Orton refused to allow any cameras into the court. Reporters lined up against the back wall, holding various electronic communication devices. Undercover guards, who had been called in for safety precautions, were stationed at different locations throughout the packed, standing room only courtroom.

Judge Orton announced that deliberations would begin promptly following closing arguments. In preparation, media crews representing a wide range of both local and national affiliates were camped out on streets. The Houston Police Department used yellow tape and portable gates to keep people away from the immediate courtyard premises.

Inside, Judge Orton shuffled around some items and made himself more comfortable on the bench. After looking at his watch, he banged the gavel and then enthusiastically said, "Let's proceed."

Mr. Freeman stepped toward the middle of the courtroom where he looked over toward the jury box.

"Ladies and gentleman," he said, cupping his hands together. "I know the defense team has tried to paint a pretty picture of Willem Gerhardt." He looked down for a moment and shrugged, then casually said, "That is their job."

He turned around and made his way toward the prosecution table where he retrieved his reading glasses and a thick legal size pad before returning to the podium.

"I hope that you are able to clearly see Dr. Gerhardt beyond his previous accomplishments or family surname, and for the person who he has become," Mr. Freeman said, holding out his glasses. After pausing for a moment, he said, "He's become an emotionally triggered doctor who drowned in the circumstances of one of his patients."

Mr. Freeman slipped on his glasses. His voice deepened.

"LOOK," he said, loudly, "We are not here to determine if Dr. Gerhardt had a successful career or if he has kindness in his heart. To work in his field, a good heart is a prerequisite."

"His empathetic heart," Mr. Freeman said, looking around the courtroom, "may have actually been his pitfall leading up to the murder." Rising up on the toes of his shoes, he said, "In other words, ladies and gentlemen, he committed this murder because he was actually TOO caring." Mr. Freeman made his way back to the table where he dropped off his pad and removed his glasses. He then stepped over toward the jury box and stood with his arms tightly folded, rocking back and forth on his heels.

"I have known this defendant for many years. I can wholeheartedly say that he truly cares about the patients he sees. He is the type of person who takes his work home with him. And as for the descriptors we heard spoken by witnesses, indeed, he is a loving people-person, compassionate, caring and selfless." Mr. Freeman turned around to face the defense table. "Up until he committed murder, he had a great sense of integrity."

After nodding for a moment in silence, he turned back to face the jury box and looked into the eyes of the full panel of jurors.

"Keeping this all in perspective," he said, "Dr. Gerhardt did not commit murder because he is some madman, evil-spirited or an individual far different from the person we all know. But, he is a person who was triggered. And, we all are triggered in different ways at different points in time. After all, we all heard about his horrific upbringing."

Mr. Freeman returned to the podium where he pulled a pen out from behind his ear while turning over several pages on his clipboard. He scribbled notes before refocusing on members of the jury.

"Bear in mind," he said briskly, "the murder happened on October 13th, the very day after he suddenly terminated sessions with a beloved patient, Amanda Jensen, for reasons that remain unknown." He panned his eyes on each member of the jury, individually, as he spoke. Restless, he walked over toward the jury box.

"We heard character witnesses speak on the defendant's behalf, one after another," he said, pausing for a moment. Shrugging, he said, "Nobody here is in any way doubting the defendant's remarkable work history, people skills or reputation. Willem Gerhardt had an unblemished professional life before he committed murder."

Mr. Freeman raised his index finger and then softly said, "But, murder is still murder, no matter how much the defense tries to divert it."

He crossed his arms. "Nobody here is saying that Willem Gerhardt was not a good doctor. Nobody here is saying that he does not care about people." Mr. Freeman sighed, appearing conflicted in thought. After regaining eye contact with the jury, Mr. Freeman said, "I do believe that Dr. Gerhardt is a caring person, perhaps too much of a caring person as he now stands here on trial for murdering a man who did some very bad things to a young girl that Dr. Gerhardt adored."

Mr. Freeman paused for a moment and cupped his hand to his

chin. "No one can doubt the defendant had dedication to his field of work. No one can ever deny that he treats his patients well," he said, emphatically nodding, "and his character witnesses all described him in basically the same way, as a very good person."

Mr. Freeman turned to the side, and walked back to the podium where he said loudly, "However." He slapped an open hand on the podium, then continued, "Sometimes good people make mistakes." Nodding hard, he shouted out, "BIG MISTAKES!"

After turning several pages over, he used a paper clip to fasten previous pages he had already reviewed.

Jimmy Townsend may have done terrible things to Amanda Jensen. The case was heard before the higher courts and Jimmy Townsend was acquitted on all charges. Does his exoneration mean he did not commit the crime? Absolutely not! I was the prosecutor on the case. My frustration level was at a high upon the verdict and I recall Dr. Gerhardt was very emotional as well. But at the end of the day, you can't just go ahead and murder a person even if he was wrongly acquitted. An eye for an eye is not acceptable in the beautiful country in which we live...

Mr. Freeman paused, then retreated back to the defense table where he consulted with Linda Jacobs who handed him court transcripts with Roman numerals and asterisks drawn by the margins. After gathering the documents, he slipped on reading glasses before returning to the podium.

"Ladies and gentleman," he said, loudly, "a sequence of events diagram will help demonstrate that Willem Gerhardt is guilty beyond any reasonable doubt."

Bailiffs helped carry a large easel into the court where it was set down in front of the jury box. Linda Jacobs stepped forward with a large flipchart before she returned to the prosecution table.

Mr. Freeman uncapped a thick, black marker and approached with confidence. Jury members watched his every move including when he oddly sniffed the tip of the marker after removing the cap.

"Please follow along," Mr. Freeman said, bending over to write. "I will capture some of the witnesses who took the stand." He then wrote, *Dr. Haggerty*, on the flipchart.

"We all recall when Dr. Haggerty took the stand," he said, nodding. "He shared his experience in the field which extends beyond 40-years." Mr. Freeman looked up to the ceiling while mouthing, *forty*. "Countertransference is what he discussed," he said, while writing the term. As he set the marker down, Mr. Freeman clapped his hands together once. "Countertransference," he repeated, "is where the problem began." Mr. Freeman stepped forward before the jury.

"Dr. Gerhardt had an emotional relationship with his patient, Amanda Jensen, whereby he was unable to separate his emotions from the traumatized patient who sat before him." Mr. Freeman walked back toward the easel, nodding.

"Then, we heard from the patient, herself, Amanda Jensen." Mr. Freeman vehemently nodded as he wrote out her name, all in capital letters. He drew a diagonal line attaching her name to the term, *countertransference*.

Nodding, he said, "We saw Amanda on the stand, changing her story a few times. It is understandable, as she is young and she is scared. She may also feel guilty, knowing that had she not told Dr. Gerhardt what happened to her, he would not be sitting here today, nor would any of us be present in this courtroom." Mr. Freeman cupped his hands together and made his way back to the jury box.

"She changed her story on the stand," he said, shrugging, "but who can blame her?" He spun around and looked down for a moment. "She is covering-up for Dr. Gerhardt, knowing that he committed murder just hours after their final session. Why else would her story suddenly change?"

Mr. Freeman held a hand in the air as his voice hit a higher octave.

"Don't catch me wrong," he said, turning toward the jury. "No one is blaming her for the murder, but she may be blaming herself."

After pausing for a moment, he said, "We are presently looking further into who may have advised Amanda prior to her most recent, manipulated testimony."

Mr. Freeman shuffled through papers including recent transcripts. Reading through his glasses, he said, "Then we heard Lucinda Delvecchio. You will all recall that she was from Texas Department of State Health Services." He wrote her name and then drew a line with an arrow pointing toward the name, Dr. Haggerty, printed near the top.

"Ms. Delvecchio had access to Willem's adoption records with important information about his upbringing," Mr. Freeman said, pressing the marker cap on to the sound of a pop. "And we were informed that he had a twin sister who was sexually assaulted and murdered." He puckered his lips while staring in the direction of the jury box.

"Willem's twin sister was raped as a child, then murdered," he said, looking at the floor, "and, now fast forwarding to the present— Willem sits in an office with a young girl who pleas for help, because her rapist was acquitted."

As Mr. Freeman raised his glasses, he asked, "Was this perhaps the motive?" He then said, "I would say there certainly seems to be a strong connection."

Mr. Freeman leaned toward the easel and once again, removed the marker cap before he wrote the name, *Tino Ballantino*. After he drew a straight line back up to Amanda's name in the middle, he set the marker down and walked to the side of the courtroom where he flashed a laser pointer back toward the flipchart.

"Ladies and gentlemen," he said, motioning with a shaky hand, "it is crystal clear." He nodded as his voice got deeper. "After Dr.

Gerhardt met with Amanda on October 12th, he needed to quickly terminate services."

Mr. Freeman cleared his throat. "Why would a psychologist need to end sessions with a long time patient who is desperately seeking his help after a sexual assault?" He posed the question in a rhetorical manner. Shrugging, he twirled and glanced around the courtroom. At this point, his serious expression could be mistaken for anger.

"Dr. Haggerty had previously stated on the stand that it would make sense for termination to occur if Dr. Gerhardt felt emotionally triggered and no longer able to sit in a professional role."

Mr. Freeman marched over to the prosecution table where he briefly consulted with Linda Jacobs. He looked over some notes, then returned to the podium and proceeded.

"On the very same day that Dr. Gerhardt abruptly terminated sessions, he contacted Dr. Tino Ballantino, an ethics professor who he had not spoken to in years...well, at least seven-years, perhaps even longer."

Mr. Freeman stepped forward and flashed the laser back to the chart, then smiled in a sarcastic way. "An abrupt therapeutic termination on October 12th followed by an impromptu meeting with an old time, now quadriplegic professor, at an unusual time of the evening during torrential weather conditions." Shaking his head, he looked down at the floor. "Do you notice a pattern of urgency?" His voice was soft, yet firm.

"Ladies and gentlemen," Mr. Freeman said, sounding melancholic. "The very next day, October 13th, Jimmy Townsend was found murdered."

Mr. Freeman stood before the jury box with an open folder. He pointed the laser toward the flipchart one last time before stuffing it back into his shirt pocket. After taking a deep breath, he turned over several pages from the stack he held and read a prewritten statement that Ms. Jacobs helped compose.

Everything we have heard throughout the trial points to Willem Gerhardt as the only suspect for the murder of Jimmy Townsend. There is a reason why Houston detectives are not out there searching for any persons of interest at this time. The defense will say that it was just a coincidence that Jimmy Townsend was murdered the day after a distraught patient of Dr. Gerhardt had entered his office. And, it was just a coincidence that Dr. Gerhardt suddenly terminated sessions. And, it was just a coincidence that Dr. Gerhardt wanted to meet with a professor who taught his ethics course twenty-years ago, a professor he had not spoken to in at least seven years. The defense will say that it was not significant that Dr. Gerhardt scheduled the meeting in the evening on a locked, desolate campus during some of the most significant thunder storms this area has seen since the mass floods in the early 1980s.

Everything is just coincidental. It's the good ole, coincidental defense. We know that something happened when Amanda met with Dr. Gerhardt during their last therapeutic treatment session. And, we know that something happened that made Dr. Gerhardt abruptly terminate sessions. Something made Dr. Gerhardt contact his old professor that very same day to meet late in the evening despite going years without contact. We believe a 2-hour and 17-minute phone conversation during the wee hours is significant.

We know that Jimmy Townsend was found dead the very next day. Our case proves that Willem Gerhardt is guilty of murder.

TWENTY SEVEN

"MAKE IT BRIEF," Judge Orton said, granting permission for Mr. O'Reilly to privately engage Dr. Gerhardt prior to delivering their closing argument. After expressing his appreciation, Mr. O'Reilly quickly led Dr. Gerhardt to a small conference room across the hall.

Dr. Gerhardt stared across at an exhausted, Mr. O'Reilly, who had his elbows planted on the table with his chin resting upon a clenched fist.

"Now what?" Dr. Gerhardt asked, looking around the small meeting room. "What's the plan?" His voice lacked enthusiasm.

"Well, it's our turn," Mr. O'Reilly explained nervously, stretching his arms back behind his head. "It's now or never. I am not sure we have a slam dunk closing argument."

Dr. Gerhardt flailed his arms up, gasping. "I'm not sure what—"

"Well," Mr. O'Reilly said, interrupting, "you did not testify, which does not in and of itself legally suggest guilt, though still leaves the jury with many questions." He let out a sigh before hitting his knuckles against the table.

"It's more a wait and see, you're saying?" Dr. Gerhardt asked, sounding worried.

"It may have been best to just put you on the stand." Mr. O'Reilly said, raking his fingers through his feathered hair. "But, burden of proof is still their obligation."

"I'd still like to speak," Dr. Gerhardt said, "If I may…"

"Well, it is just a tad too late at this point," Mr. O'Reilly explained, shaking his head. "The proceedings end following our closing argument."

Dr. Gerhardt stuck out his chin and nodded several times while leaning forward in the chair. "I know some things about the jury. I'd like to tap into their emotions."

"I'm not sure what you are saying," Mr. O'Reilly said, leaning back, squinting.

"Well, I have a gift."

"Excuse me?" Mr. O'Reilly said, lifting his head. Perplexed, yet sounding annoyed, he repeated, "A GIFT?"

"Well, yes," Dr. Gerhardt said confidently. "Have you ever heard of Sophia Angus?"

"The plant?" said Mr. O'Reilly.

"No," Dr. Gerhardt said, blowing out air. "Miss Sophia."

"I have no idea what you are talking about, Willem." Grimacing, Mr. O'Reilly breathed heavily, glancing down at his watch. "Listen, we don't have much time, here. It's really now or never."

"I have a gift," Dr. Gerhardt explained. I don't talk about it much and I only use it when needed. I know about the members of the jury. I'd like to present the closing argument." Dr. Gerhardt sounded confident, nodding convincingly.

"What?" Mr. O'Reilly gasped, appearing alarmed.

Dr. Gerhardt smiled, perking up. "Listen," he said, his eyes opening wide, "I know about the lives of the jury members and I can communicate with their loved ones who have passed on. I know all the right things to say."

Mr. O'Reilly leaned back, shaking his head. "Willem," he said, looking through the corner of his eyes, "if we turn this court hearing into a spiritual séance, you will scare the living shit out of everyone."

"Listen, we must give it a try," Dr. Gerhardt said in the form of a whisper, fearing their private discussion may not be so private.

"We can't start manipulating the process," Mr. O'Reilly said, his voice growing stern. "Frankly," he said, "you are starting to worry me."

Dr. Gerhardt sat in dismay, looking around the room as his restless legs shook beneath him.

"Please stop shaking the table," Mr. O'Reilly said, concentrating on the prepared closing statement, typewritten on legal size paper that had folds at the corners.

"The two ladies sitting on the left side of the jury, side by side," Dr. Gerhardt said, "were sexually molested as small girls." He sighed, then said, "They may actually be happy Jimmy was murdered."

"Amanda has taken us in a new direction," Mr. O'Reilly said, before pausing. "In her most updated testimony, she claims on October 12th that she told you that Jimmy did nothing to her and that your anger was due to her fabricated assault story."

Dr. Gerhardt nodded, then mouthed, *true.*

"So," Mr. O'Reilly explained, "There really is no countertransference trigger related basis for the prosecution to hang their hat on." The passion in his voice suggested that his lost confidence was beginning to revive.

"Yeah but—" Dr. Gerhardt said, before being interrupted.

"No yeah, but—," Mr. O'Reilly said, "I can try to present a case and defend you in a professional way, or we can do it your way with a spiritual séance by dimming all the lights and introducing motive candles peppered with incense."

"I never said—"

Mr. O'Reilly quickly lifted his hand to stop Dr. Gerhardt in his tracks. "Listen," he said, tucking his chin, "you will raise some serious red flags in this courtroom if, on the most important day of your life, you transform into an Edgar Cayce wannabe and engage the court in some funny hypnotic, psychic game."

"But, I never said that I—"

"Willem," said Mr. O'Reilly, raising an open palm, "it'll be a circus in here if I were to ask everybody to close their eyes, because my client who has been charged with murder would like to relive his childhood by introducing his Magic 8-Ball."

Dr. Gerhardt nodded in resigned agreement.

After several taps, a bailiff, standing on the other side of the closed door, explained that the judge was looking to recommence.

Mr. O'Reilly escorted Dr. Gerhardt back to the defense table, where he whispered one last comment before approaching the podium.

"Good Morning," Mr. O'Reilly said, checking his watch, "well, I should say, good afternoon." He stood at the podium, wearing a navy suit. As usual, his pocket handkerchief was neatly folded, slightly showing at the top of his breast pocket. His Rolex watch sparkled from the recessed courtroom lights, especially when he used expressive hand gestures to further emphasize points.

"Ladies and gentlemen," he said with a resonating voice, cupping his hands together, "it is up to the prosecution to prove beyond a reasonable doubt that Dr. Gerhardt is guilty." His voice was firm and matter-of-fact. "The state has not satisfied burden of proof."

Mr. O'Reilly made his way to the podium where, after reaching into his shirt pocket, he pulled out reading glasses. In slow motion, he looked out to the jury box before adjusting the frames on the very tip of his nose.

"It is impossible to satisfy burden of proof," he said, softly, "when someone did not commit murder." He shrugged in an exaggerated way before he said, "It is that simple."

He stepped out from the podium and made his way back toward

the jury box where jury members sat scribbling notes on their handheld notepads.

"This is actually a no-win trial for Dr. Gerhardt. If convicted, it will be a tragedy for him to be incarcerated for a crime he did not commit. If acquitted, he will be properly exonerated, though unable to return to his former life."

Mr. O'Reilly pressed his lips together.

"The prosecution claims Dr. Gerhardt committed murder. But all they really did to support their case is suggest it looks like it, smells like it and seems like it, as I forewarned you from the very start." He shrugged and then stated, "In the end, it is a case that has no merit. It is really questionable as to why there was ever an indictment to begin with."

After shoving his hand into the back pocket of his pants, he pulled out a handkerchief before patting it against his moist forehead. After stuffing the handkerchief back into his pocket, he stood before the jury, swaying back and forth.

"The prosecution cannot prove their case," Mr. O'Reilly said, shaking his head, "but can only at this point try to convince the jury to falsely believe that Dr. Gerhardt is guilty."

Mr. O'Reilly made his way back to the podium where he shuffled through some papers before pulling out dictation pages from earlier testimony.

"We saw Dr. Haggerty take the stand and speak at length about the term, *countertransference*, which he described in layman's terms as the rise of triggers that are experienced by a psychologist." Mr. O'Reilly tapped his hand down. "The prosecution is not only frivolously accusing Dr. Gerhardt of murder, but also randomly basing a motive by attaching fancy lingo from the Sigmund Freud era." After sighing, he said, "It is much simpler than all of that ladies and gentleman. The beloved doctor we all know did not commit murder."

Mr. O'Reilly cleared his throat. "Dr. Gerhardt has worked over the years with numerous children and adolescents who have been sexually abused." He paused for a moment and raised his index finger. "He has also worked on the other side with the perpetrators who have done the unthinkable. Dr. Gerhardt cares about ALL people."

Mr. O'Reilly continued, "We know that the prosecution requested the release of Dr. Gerhardt's adoption records in their attempt to dig-up skeletons in his closet." After shrugging several times, Mr. O'Reilly then said, "For what?"

After a brief pause, he said, "Is it fair to assume he is a murderer because his twin sister was murdered 35-years ago?" He sighed, muttering, "It makes no sense."

Mr. O'Reilly stepped out to the middle of the courtroom holding papers by his side.

"We have to bear in mind," he said, looking towards the jury box, "Dr. Gerhardt was not only a practicing psychologist, but also a Professor of Ethics. And, the mere suggestion made by the prosecution that Dr. Gerhardt was unable to manage the basics of the very fundamentals that he teaches, once again, has no merit."

Mr. O'Reilly turned around and walked back to the podium where he spread dictation notes across the wooden structure. "We heard testimony from Amanda Jensen, who explained that during her last session, she confessed to Dr. Gerhardt that she had lied about her entire story of having been assaulted." Mr. O'Reilly nodded, looking back at the jury. "And, the prosecution tried to convince the court that Amanda was just covering up for the doctor she loved and that something of a different occurrence happened on that day."

Mr. O'Reilly's voice got louder as he motioned with his hands in an emphatic manner. "There was no cover-up" he said, pausing, "you want to know why?" He looked around briefly, then loudly said, "Because there was nothing to cover-up." He stepped back for a moment and looked at the jury box. "Amanda has clearly admitted on the stand, what we all knew to begin with. Nothing ever happened." Mr. O'Reilly nodded. "And this is what Carol Smith had previously stated in her testimony during the rape trial and why Jimmy Townsend was acquitted."

Cupping his hands together, Mr. O'Reilly said, "You will recall Carol Smith, a DFPS worker and expert in the field, who read word for word from a transcript taken from Amanda Jensen's testimony during the rape trial against Jimmy Townsend." Mr. O'Reilly pulled out her testimony, slipped on his glasses, then read it verbatim out loud for the jury.

We believe that Amanda was attention-seeking and that she used objects that caused self-inflicted damage to her genitals, which would explain significant bruising to her labia minora and labia majora.

Mr. O'Reilly removed his reading glasses, then set the transcript down on the podium. He pointed in the direction of Mr. Freeman and Ms. Jacobs who were shuffling in their seats by the prosecution table.

"The prosecution ridiculed and tagged Dr. Gerhardt as a murderer because he planned to meet with his old professor, who beyond just a professor was also a peer. After all, they both taught ethics." After pausing for a moment, he then said, "How does a planned meeting with an old professor or colleague in any way link Dr. Gerhardt to a murder?"

He stepped out from beyond the podium and faced the judge before turning around to address the jury.

"They met at a time in the evening that the prosecution described as unusual. Although 10:30 p.m. may be considered late by some, it still does not link Dr. Gerhardt to a murder. Let's say they had met at 6:00 in the evening. Would he no longer be considered a suspect?"

Mr. O'Reilly sounded angry as he spoke while pacing around the center area of the court, shaking his head in disgust.

"Dr. Gerhardt had some questions for his old professor, and the time of their scheduled meeting was mutually convenient, neither of whom knew of the torrential weather conditions in store for them, much the same way neither knew that the doors of the building would be locked."

Mr. O'Reilly looked over toward the jury box and then said, "Dr. Gerhardt has not done any wrong doing and the prosecution has not presented anything substantial that in any way suggests he has committed murder." He looked at the judge and nodded, walking back to the defense table,

Tight lipped, Judge Orton folded his arms and nodded. "Ladies and gentlemen," Judge Orton said, standing up, "that will conclude—"

"Your Honor," Mr. O'Reilly interrupted from the defense table where he was bent over reading a message on his cell phone and also listening to Dr. Gerhardt who was whispering into his ear. "One more thing," said Mr. O'Reilly, snapping his fingers. "I'm not quite done."

Judge Orton nodded in acknowledgment, settling back into his seat on the bench.

"Ladies and gentlemen," Mr. O'Reilly said, tapping Dr. Gerhardt on the shoulder while adamantly shaking his head, "A few more things." He returned to the center of the court where he turned around and faced the prosecution table.

"The prosecution stated that the Houston Police Department is not seeking out any other suspects for the murder of Jimmy Townsend," Mr. O'Reilly said firmly. Then, more softly said, "This is true."

Nodding, Mr. O'Reilly looked back at the defense table where Dr. Gerhardt sat with his arms folded close to his chest.

"And the prosecutor previously stated that the murderer is not a madman or evil spirited. He even went so far as to say that the murderer is not far different from the person we all know." Nodding in the direction of Dr. Gerhardt, Mr. O'Reilly said, "I agree."

He sighed before approaching the jury box where he stood before the jurors with his fingers touching beneath his chin. "The prosecution suggested that the murderer was emotionally triggered and unable to sit in a professional role." Waving his arms up in dramatic fashion, he commanded full attention of the courtroom and then said, "And I absolutely agree!"

Curiously, Judge Orton peered over his reading glasses at Mr. O'Reilly who walked with quick strides over to the defense table. Restless in their seats, jurors panned across the courtroom, trying to understand why Mr. O'Reilly seemed to take on more of a passive approach, perhaps about to concede the case. Some wondered if Mr. O'Reilly was somehow preparing to make a plea deal, though it seemed much too late in the game for any such negotiation. Others speculated that the defense attorney had come to the realization of his weak case, thus trying to at least soften up the jury before a sentence determination.

Judge Orton said, "Does that conclude your closing statement?"

Mr. O'Reilly stepped back to the defense table where he bent down and listened to Dr. Gerhardt who spoke at a frenetic pace. With a hand raised, Mr. O'Reilly said, "Not quite yet, Your Honor."

Judge Orton sighed while looking down at his watch.

Mr. O'Reilly escorted Dr. Gerhardt to the front of the courtroom where they stood, side-by-side, before the jury box.

"Ladies and Gentlemen," Mr. O'Reilly said, "The murderer is not a madman. He is not evil spirited. He is not far different from the person we all know…" Mr. O'Reilly put his hand over Dr. Gerhardt's shoulder and walked him over toward the podium. In a moment never seen in a courtroom, both stood facing the prosecution table, back sides toward the judge.

"The murderer was indeed emotionally triggered," Mr. O'Reilly said, pausing for a moment, before saying, "Good people make mistakes. Big Mistakes!"

Mr. Freeman sat with Linda Jacobs at the prosecution table in a two person huddle, face-to-face, engaging in deep discussion.

"The murderer was very closely bonded to Amanda Jensen," Mr. O'Reilly continued, "and unable to set aside his emotions." Nodding, he put his arm around Dr. Gerhardt's upper back. "When you are emotionally triggered, it is sometimes very difficult to sit in the professional role."

Growing restless at the prosecution table, Mr. Freeman started to scratch the top of his head. Linda Jacobs' eyes were darting across the courtroom, unsure what was unfolding.

"The prosecution suggested that had Amanda Jensen not seen Dr. Gerhardt for that last session, we all would not be here today." Mr. O'Reilly patted Dr. Gerhardt on the back. "The truth of the matter is that had Carol Smith simply provided an honest testimony at the Jimmy Townsend trial, he would have been convicted and we would not need to be present here today." Shaking his head in disgust, he said, "Self-inflicted bruising?"

Seated beside Linda Jacobs, Mr. Freeman nervously picked at his clothes as if he were removing invisible lint.

"That's right ladies and gentlemen," Mr. O'Reilly said in a somber tone. "Amanda Jensen was sexually assaulted. We all know that. What more can I say."

Exhaling, Mr. O'Reilly motioned for Dr. Gerhardt to return to his seat and then waited for a moment as the beloved doctor settled back at the defense table.

"Mr. Freeman was the prosecutor in the case against Jimmy Townsend," Mr. O'Reilly said, "and he knows she was assaulted." His voice projected loudly.

At the defense table, Mr. Freeman leaned to the side of his chair with his hand partially covering his mouth as he whispered to Ms. Jacobs.

"Having a daughter, actually two—both of a similar age to Amanda Jensen, Mr. Freeman was absolutely devastated." Mr. O'Reilly pulled out a handkerchief and patted his forehead. "As the prosecutor, Mr. Freeman had spent nearly a full year with Amanda, trying the best he could to convict the rapist."

Mr. O'Reilly turned, and walked toward the jury box. Motioning with his hands, he said, "After much hard work and many tear-filled evenings, his efforts to convict Jimmy Townsend were unsuccessful."

His voice got louder when he said, "But, it was not his fault. He presented a very strong case." Appearing sad, Mr. O'Reilly said, "In the end, Jimmy Townsend was acquitted, then freed."

Mr. Freeman clasped his hands together around the back of his neck.

"So when Mr. Freeman alludes to or speaks about triggers and countertransference, or difficulty sitting in the professional role…it sure sounds as though he his speaking about himself." Without any notes in hand, Mr. O'Reilly folded his arms and delivered his final thoughts.

Mr. Freeman did not have to pass the blame on to Dr. Gerhardt, who has done nothing but the best in his work role and for our community. To falsely concoct such a murder case charging Dr. Gerhardt is unforgivable and tragic. Dr. Gerhardt's dear patient, Amanda, -- as if she needed any more trauma in her life, felt compelled to now lie on the stand to protect Dr. Gerhardt, who she was led to believe had committed the murder. Dr. Gerhardt's life has been taken from him in every way. Handcuffed, he was not even able to embrace the most important person in his life, his mother-- the late Ms. Gerhardt, during those final precious moments of her life. He was only able to recite a poem that someone else held up for him. And that someone else was me. As you heard in the testimony provided by Lucinda Delvecchio, Dr. Gerhardt had a difficult early childhood marked by the murder of his twin sister. But, he was resilient and, once again, found a way to move forward in his life.

The Texas Attorney General is investigating Carol Smith and her testimony. It is believed, yet not completely confirmed, that she was an acquaintance of Jimmy Townsend and the entire Townsend family.

"Thank you, Your Honor." He then looked in the direction of the jury box and bowed down. "To the members of the jury, I thank you as well."

The judge nodded back and removed his glasses while jury members squirmed restlessly in their seats while writing their final notes.

Mr. O'Reilly walked back to the defense table, glancing up at members of the media lined up in the rear. He pointed his finger toward Mr. Freeman and said, "There is your murderer."

In the front of the court, several bailiffs gathered before Judge Orton, whispering loudly. A look of astonishment crossed the judge's face as he looked out from the bench with widened eyes.

From the prosecution table, Mr. Freeman and Ms. Jacobs stared back at the judge before snapping their heads in the direction of where doors had flung open.

"What's going on here," Mr. Freeman said, watching as guards sprinted toward him. "I've been framed," he said. As he was escorted out of the court, he angrily shouted, "Is this a kangaroo court?"

"Ladies and gentlemen," Judge Orton said, "I can't say too much at this time." He nodded gently. "I want to extend my appreciation for your service on the jury." He continued to nod in appreciation as he stood from the bench. "This concludes our trial. Thank you. You may be excused." He quickly stepped back toward his chambers.

TWENTY EIGHT

TOGETHER, MR. O'REILLY and Dr. Gerhardt stepped out of the courthouse and walked along the sidewalk, leading toward Main Street. At a close distance behind, a court guard carried large duffel bags. Mr. O'Reilly opened the passenger side door of the Bentley that was parallel parked in-between several large orange cones near the front. As Dr. Gerhardt sat down and buckled up in the front passenger seat, a guard carefully placed personal item bags upon the vacant backseat.

Numerous reporters stood, leaning against the car with outstretched microphones. One reporter shouted, "How does it feel?" Another raised her thumb, cheering, "Can you speak, now?"

Mr. O'Reilly pressed several buttons on the GPS before shifting the car into gear. Police escorts assisted as they drove away from the immediate court premises.

After a twenty minute ride, Mr. O'Reilly pulled up to the entrance gate surrounding, *Heaven of All Heavens Cemetery*, then parked along the nearest curbside.

Dr. Gerhardt opened the door and hopped out of the car.

"I'll be right back," he said, then walked quickly in the direction of the fading sun as the dusk sky glared a tinge of pink. On the side of the path, wild flowers and an assortment of shrubs were fed by in-ground sprinkler systems. As usual, the property was quiet, even though many walked around the larger circular path that outlined the entire cemetery grounds.

Dr. Gerhardt rushed along the path as if he were *a man on a mission.* He strutted around a small pool of water, stopping for a moment to observe large goldfish swimming beneath free-floating lily pads. The landscape mimicked that of a European park, possessing numerous fountains, statues and a colorful assortment of floral displays. Native and exotic plants bordered the long, winding path.

His pace slowed briefly, then picked up again when he thought he recognized the Gerhardt plot set by the fence, in a most serene location at the furthermost point from the entrance. Maneuvering toward the plot, he could not help but to read some of the headstones, some of which dated back over one-hundred years. One of the tombstones was of a former military hero, who had the nickname, "sharp shooter," engraved just below his name. A large mausoleum was at the foot of the attached plot with the name, *GERHARDT,* engraved at the top, followed by etchings of babies with wings and birds in flight. Stepping forward, he noticed a commemoration for Ms. Gerhardt's father.

ALVIN GERHARDT
Oil Man Alvie - October 1976
Lived Life Rich in Every Way

Willem then looked slightly over to the side, whereupon he read a commemoration for Ms. Gerhardt's mother.

ELLEN GERHARDT
An Angel Amongst Us Always - October 1976

It had been many years since he had last visited his grandparents' cemetery plots. Breathing at a faster tempo, he stepped to the side where he became emotional, recalling wonderful memories of times spent with his mother. The nervous feeling in the pit of his stomach brought him back to his adoption day. He then fast forwarded to the day he visited her in the hospital.

After closing his eyes, he swallowed hard and then ever so softly said, "I love you, mom." After touching the granite, he stepped to the side before reopening his eyes. As he stared up, he read the engraved words out loud to himself.

ELIZABETH GERHARDT
WILLEM'S MOM

He kissed the shiny granite and rubbed his outstretched hand in a circular motion upon it before kissing it, again. His eyes overflowed with tears as he extended his open palm out toward the mausoleum.

After several minutes, he returned to the walking path where he took a moment to look at a cluster of well-manicured wild flowers that bordered the entire fence. He stepped toward the garden of flowers where he stooped down near the colorful assortment, smiling as he noticed a bluebonnet. He reached down and squeezed it by its root, then listened carefully to a message in his mind saying, *Absorb their beauty into the depths of your mind…but, don't pick them.* After easing his grip on the stem, he gently let go.

"Willem," a man's voice called out from behind him. "I was expecting you."

"Yes?" Dr. Gerhardt said, turning his head around.

"I'm Dan Myers," he said, "I thought you may be coming around here."

"Oh," Dr. Gerhardt said, quizzically. "May I ask who you are?"

"I am the Cemetery Director," he said, extending his right hand for a handshake. "You don't know me, but I know you and your family." He reached into the inner pocket of his blazer and pulled out a plain white envelope, sealed, but not stamped. "This is for you," he said, handing him the letter.

Nodding, Dr. Gerhardt took the letter and brought it toward him. Softly, he said, "Thank you," then glanced at the outside of the envelope before tucking it into his pocket.

"Tara had dropped it off," he said, smiling. "She works at some hospital and explained that it was very important to your mom this letter finds its way to you."

Dr. Gerhardt turned around to make his way back to the main path to retrace his route. He walked with a bounce in his step back toward the front entrance. Curious, he stopped in his tracks along the flowery path and retrieved the letter from his pocket. Using the back of his pinky, he unsealed the envelope and removed the enclosed triple-folded stationary. He paused for a moment and looked up to the sky. Then after taking a deep breath, he began to read the short, yet ever so meaningful note, written in calligraphy of enormous beauty.

You are Forever a Gerhardt!
P.S. Yes, Forever!

Teary eyed, yet at the same time feeling on the top of the world, Dr. Gerhardt walked further along the path, singing, "You and Me Against the World."

Minutes later, he arrived back in the parking area where Mr. O'Reilly stood, leaning back against the car bumper, with a Cuban cigar hanging from his lower lip.

"Come here," said Mr. O'Reilly, greeting him with his arms spread out wide. Both shed tears, embracing in a hug. "What a day," Mr. O'Reilly said, squeezing him even tighter.

Dr. Gerhardt stepped back, exhaling.

"You're an incredible person," said Mr. O'Reilly. "And, so was your mother, grandmother and grandfather." He pinched the tip of his stogie before taking another drag.

"You're not so bad yourself," Dr. Gerhardt said, patting Mr. O'Reilly on the shoulder.

TWENTY NINE

IT WAS A HUMID morning and the sun was on the rise. Thousands of students were tightly seated in narrow rows between white chalked lines on John O'Quinn Field at TDECU Stadium on the University of Houston campus. The stadium seating was completely filled by many who used commencement pamphlets to fan themselves. An American flag waved parallel to one bearing the State of Texas. A bright red colored university banner was tapered against railings beside billboards bearing colorful graphics that read, "Congratulations" and "We are the Future."

"It is with great enthusiasm," the school president announced, "I'd like to welcome, our guest speaker, Dr. Willem Gerhardt."

Dr. Gerhardt waved back to students who stood by portable vinyl padded folding chairs, applauding the renowned doctor who had just been introduced as a *beloved psychologist* and also the U of H valedictorian 20 years ago to the day.

As he looked around the packed stadium, he bowed his head toward students who enveloped the entire synthetic turf field in a resounding standing ovation. Proud family members and friends stood clapping in their respective rows in the more formal stadium seating area. Modestly, Dr. Gerhardt attempted to dampen the cheers by motioning downward with his open palms.

"Thank you," Dr. Gerhardt said, nodding, "Thank you very much."

The thunderous ovation quickly decreased to a lower decibel until complete silence blanketed the complex.

"I have been asked and happily volunteered to speak to you today." His voice resonated from surround sound speakers. "The question of what to say is daunting. I have thought for a long time what I might say on this occasion and am humbled by the honor of trying to find a worthy echo to my voice 20 years ago." He paused for a moment, then said, "7300 days ago, to be exact, on that sultry May 22nd when I commenced."

Dr. Gerhardt unfastened a paperclip and then placed the loose typewritten notes upon the podium. With assistance from university personnel, a microphone piece was attached to the side of his collar before he stepped toward the edge of the platform.

"Don't worry," Dr. Gerhardt said chuckling, "I am not about to jump." After a brief chuckle, he moved to the side. "And no," he said, turning around, "I am not about to do a backflip either, although it is my understanding that the EMS on campus responds quickly."

Beginning amongst the student body and rapidly spreading, chants of his name interrupted his speech. *Doctor Gee! Doctor Gee! Doctor Gee!*

Dr. Gerhardt smiled, then, once again, lowered his palms to encourage silence, particularly waving his arm in the direction of the student section whose chants had grown much more intense.

"Looking for inspiration, I followed U of H principles, both learned and reinforced, of being open to all things. I've read graduation speeches, which are all wonderful resource material for how to live a full, rich and round life—and I urge you to look at or listen to the commencements of others at colleges across the country."

Dr. Gerhardt stepped to the podium and gathered a small stack of notes before returning to the edge of the platform where he proceeded to read.

"It's only a matter of time before you flip your tassels and then soon afterwards, toss your caps. You'll receive diplomas you can frame, verbal praises for your accomplishments and perhaps gifts along the way. These times will be memorable and impossible to forget. But you are still in the beginning stages of your adult life."

Dr. Gerhardt looked out to the silent audience of eager ears. He panned toward the side, narrowing in on Amanda Jensen, who was seated beside her mother, smiling back.

He took a deep breath and said, "You all want to be successful. But, just what is it that defines success?" He paused for a moment and shuffled through papers. After taking another deep breath, he rhetorically asked:

Is it money that drives you?

…Or is it love that defines you?

Is it prestige that you seek?

…Or happiness at the end of each week?

Dr. Gerhardt walked out to the end of the stage. "Listen, folks," he said, smiling, before cupping his hands together. "Ceremony speeches have terrific message content. But they are typically long— so much so that the *terrific message* gets lost." He looked at the student section below him, then lifted his head toward the stadium seating above. "Life is short," he said, pausing for a moment, "… very short." Tucking the packet of papers against his side, he sighed.

"Find joys in the moment. Enjoy what you are doing, now. Most importantly, find pleasure in the journey." He raised his index finger. "Sometimes the journey is more meaningful than the actual destination. Surround yourself with those who raise your spirit. Help others along the way." He nodded and repeated, "Help others along the way…"

Dr. Gerhardt returned to the podium where he placed the stack of papers down before returning to the front of the platform. "Many years ago," he explained, walking with his hands clasped behind his back, "I received a call that interrupted my sleep." His head was dipped as he walked across the stage. "That call was 16 years ago, after two-o'clock in the morning." He nodded and looked out to the student body, then said, "2:25 a.m. to be exact."

Emotional, he cleared this throat before coughing into his clenched fist. He then continued, "As the phone rang, I was awakened with a startle…I pushed the speaker button, trying to catch my bearings."

He paused for a moment, shrugging. "To be perfectly honest, I don't even remember having said, *Hello*."

His voice rose to a higher pitch.

I heard someone say, Oh, Dr. Gerhardt. After she said my name for a third time, I finally said, with whom am I speaking?

She said her name calmly. Today I'll refer to her as Sarah.

You don't know me, she said. But, someone who takes your class said I should give you a call.

At this time? I asked.

Well, no, she mumbled, sounding embarrassed. She then said, I'm sorry, before pausing for what seemed to be an eternity.

Well, are you a student of mine? I asked her.

No, I am not.

Have I ever seen you in my private practice?

No, you have not.

Have we ever actually met?

No, we have not.

The next words I heard her say echoed and will forever echo in my mind. She said, I want to die. Not quite sure what to say and before I could respond, I heard the sound of a gun being cocked. I spoke to her, encouraged her and after a while I asked her to do me just one favor.

Surprised, she paused, then repeated, a favor?

*Please come meet me in my office tomorrow morning at 9:00 a.m. Let
me have the opportunity to meet you face to face, I urged. After that, I
said, it's up to you what you do. Would you at least agree to that, I asked
her. She seemed hesitant, but agreed to it.*

*The next morning, she arrived and sat in my waiting room area until
I invited her to join me in my office. She stepped in, closed the door
behind her, then with rapid speech let me know her thoughts. Sarah did
not even sit down. She said, don't think for a single moment that your
crash course in self-esteem or positive thinking changed my mind for a
moment last night. She then told me, I hope you don't believe that your
ideas of motivation and why life is worth living made any difference
in the way that I feel. If you believe that, she said— then, you're sadly
mistaken. She then stopped pointing her finger at me and calmed some.
Sarah said, I'll tell you what did make the difference.*

*I woke you up at 2:30 in the morning. Instead of saying, look why
don't you call the crisis center? Instead of saying, I'm sorry, you're not
a student of mine—call someone else. Instead of saying, you're not a
patient of mine—why don't you just call another shrink. Instead of even
saying, call my secretary tomorrow, and I'll try to fit you in when I have
time. You could have. But, you didn't. You actually picked up your phone
and you talked to me. You listened to me. You gave me a half hour of
your time. And, you didn't even know me.*

*Sarah stood with her hand still on the door knob, staring at me. Then
explained, if a stranger was willing to talk to me for 30 minutes during
the middle of the night, I might as well give life a second chance.*

*When I spoke to Sarah years later, she told me that she no longer wanted
to end her life and that she was about to be happily married. More recently,
when we spoke, she told me she is happily married with two children.
Sarah is also now pursuing her life dream to become a psychologist.*

Ladies and gentlemen. All it took was 30 minutes. Regardless of the direction you go, and what you choose to do for yourself, keep others in mind and extend yourself along your pathways in life. As much as you do for yourself, try to also do the same for others. There is nothing more satisfying. There is nothing more rewarding.

Nodding, Dr. Gerhardt waved to the student section below.

"Congratulations," he said, "I want to thank you all so very much." He walked across the platform and stepped down the attached portable stairway where he continued to mouth, *Thank you.*

At the bottom of the stairway, Dr. Gerhardt spoke briefly with Ms. Jensen. He then leaned down and kissed Amanda on the top of her head at which time she held her thumb up high.

Dr. Gerhardt glanced for a final time across the stadium and took Ms. Jensen by her hand while placing his other hand on Amanda's shoulder. Together, they walked out of the complex into the busy lot where they awaited their ride.

THIRTY

IN HIS JAIL cell, Mr. Freeman sat on the edge of his cot, listening with attentive ears to a quarrel erupting on the floor below. As someone in the distance shouted, guards rushed to deescalate rising tension in the eating area. Mr. Freeman stepped to the front of his cell to see the commotion.

Over the years, Mr. Freeman had successfully convicted many of his surrounding fellow inmates for murder, armed robbery, weapon possession and rape. Lonely, anxiety-ridden and confused, he started to question his life as he paced in circles. He returned to his cot and stared blankly up at the ceiling, coming to the realization of his new home, at least for now—East Texas State Penitentiary.

He thought to himself, *How did this happen*? Then wondered, *Why?*

THIRTY ONE

AS THE REAR wheels of the airplane lifted off the ground, Dr. Gerhardt and Amanda threw their arms straight up in a hands-free, rollercoaster ride style.

Ms. Jensen chuckled and said, "Okay, I'm in, too." She stretched her arms up high before pressing the button to recline her seat after the initial climb transitioned to cruise altitude.

THIRTEEN HOURS LATER

The plane touched down on the runway at Naples International Airport. A flight attendant made the announcement, "Welcome to Italy," then repeated the same in Italian, "Benvenuto in Italia." Amanda was awakened by a soft kiss that Ms. Jensen planted upon her cheek. Dr. Gerhardt folded a newspaper before stuffing it deeply into the compartment attached to the rear of the seat in front of him.

After gathering their belongings from the baggage terminal, they walked into an open area where they were greeted by Dr. Ballantino as well as his assistant, who stood beside him, leaning against the motorized wheelchair. With a teddy bear in hand, Amanda ran over and kissed Dr. Ballantino while Ms. Jensen greeted his assistant, who nodded back several times from a distance with a courteous smile.

"Alright, Gerhardt," Dr. Ballantino said, "Let's go." He maneuvered his chair toward the nearest exit doorway. Together, they all walked with small duffel bags behind him, wheeling a large cart containing larger sized baggage.

"How long are you staying?" Dr. Ballantino's assistant asked.

"Well, just how long are we welcome?" Ms. Jensen jokingly responded.

"Welcome to Italy!" She said, "Our house is your house."

THIRTY TWO

AMANDA JUMPED UP and down several times before leaping off the vibrating diving board. She then swam to the shallow side where she climbed out of the pool.

"Let me know if you need your goggles," Ms. Jensen called out from her lounge chair. She then continued small chat with Dr. Ballantino's assistant, who lay beside her in a two-piece bikini on an adjustable reclining chair.

"I'm fine, mom," Amanda said, walking over toward the slide.

The in-ground pool extended across the entire rear of the mansion belonging to Dr. Ballantino. Custom built with an infinity edge, a vanishing visual effect created an illusion of water dropping off at the end, further highlighting beautiful distant views.

Chefs cooked various forms of meat at varying degrees of doneness. Wearing a white T-shirt and red Hawaiian floral shorts, Dr. Gerhardt stood by the pool house eating a freshly made burger on a bun. From across the pool, Amanda squealed, "weeeee," as she made her way down the long, open spiral-shaped waterslide.

"Alright," Dr. Gerhardt shouted out before blowing her an air kiss. He reached for a can of soda as he continued to breathe in fresh aromas arising from the open sizzling grills.

Mr. O'Reilly and his wife waved to everyone as they arrived at the party. They engaged other guests as they walked around the pool, socializing while drinking from cocktail glasses filled with Ameretto.

"Let me know if you all need refills," a man called out from behind the bar area.

"We're fine," Mr. O'Reilly said, smiling. He then touched his wife's glass with the glass from which he was drinking, at which time they both simultaneously said, *Salute*, before taking a sip.

Songs from Luciano Pavarotti played one after another on speakers spread across the entire outdoor area. Some couples slow danced by the pool while others stood around in small circles, holding their cocktails of choice while engaging in laughter.

On the side of the property, Dr. Haggerty let out a hearty laugh after noticing that his grandson was balancing himself on a collapsible seat on the inside of a large dunk tank.

"Hey, Santa," his grandson called out, challenging him. "What you got?"

Smirking, Dr. Haggerty scratched his thick white beard and marched over to a tall bucket of baseballs set on the side. After grabbing a ball, he leaned forward in a pitcher-type style, narrowing in on the red circle target. Several misses later, his grandson stuck his tongue out and waved his hands up by his ears. Finally, Dr. Haggerty ran over and punched the lever to the sound of a water plunge. He then made a funny face of his own toward his grandson, who was floating on his back in the shallow water.

"Come here," Dr. Ballantino called out to Amanda. "I have something I want to show you."

In her dripping swimsuit, Amanda sprinted over and hopped onto the back of his motorized chair, placing her hands gently on his shoulders to brace herself. Dr. Ballantino used the tongue-drive system to steer down a path that led to a gorgeous fountain filled with koi fish. Amanda stepped off and looked around at the beautiful assortment of light displays reflecting off different shaped statues that were spewing out water at varying timed sequences, creating an aesthetic design. Slowly, she made her way toward the edge where she squatted near the water, watching the colorful fish rise to the surface to greet her.

"So cool," Amanda said, reaching her hand out as if to pet them.

Dr. Ballantino's assistant appeared from behind, asking if he needed anything.

"Just a massage," he said. She stood above him, gently rubbing his shoulders as he hummed to Pavarotti's, "Nessun Dorma," which played in the distant background.

THIRTY THREE

ONE WEEK LATER

MUSICAL SOUNDS OF waves crashing upon the shore echoed throughout the mansion as the limousine driver pressed on the doorbell. Several soft taps upon the door followed after the final oceanic vibrations had settled.

"He's here," Dr. Gerhardt said, lifting several items of luggage lined up along the foyer wall before opening the door.

"Good evening," the driver said, "I'll take those." He then delivered bags to the stretch limousine, backed into the driveway with the trunk raised high.

Dr. Ballantino's assistant hugged Amanda and then extended one of her arms to pull Ms. Jensen forward to form a three-person, group hug.

"Tino," Ms. Jensen said, turning to face Dr. Ballantino as he drove his chair up to the front door. "Thank you both so much," she said before leaning down and kissing the professor once upon his cheek.

"You're very welcome," Dr. Ballantino said, "Piacere mio."

Amanda skipped over to the professor and planted her cheek against his chest.

"Thank you sweetheart," Dr. Ballantino said, "My sweet girl."

After Dr. Gerhardt helped the driver carry last pieces of luggage to the trunk, he stepped back into the mansion where he exchanged hugs with Dr. Ballantino's assistant. He then stood before his old professor and stared down upon him.

"I really don't know how you do it, Tino," Dr. Gerhardt said, softly touching the professor's limp wrist.

"How I do what?" Dr. Ballantino asked, clearing his throat.

"Your hair!" Dr. Gerhardt blurted out. "It is always so perfect."

They all stood around for a moment, chuckling and discussing the style of the professor's hair, which was, as usual, brushed straight back in a fresh out of the shower look.

"Just so meticulous," Dr. Gerhardt said.

"Squeaky clean," Ms. Jensen said, harmoniously chiming in.

Dr. Ballantino's assistant bowed, basking in the attention for a styling well done. She extended her right foot behind the left, then bent her knees and extended her pinkies as she pinched the edges of her skirt on each side to perform a curtsy. As she gracefully returned to an upright position, she playfully patted down one straggly hair.

"Hold on a moment," Dr. Gerhardt said, smiling, "Not so fast." He folded his arms and stared at the assistant. "You can't take all the credit. I remember this guy from many years ago. He was always meticulous with every single hair perfectly in place." Dr. Gerhardt brought his fingertips up to his puckered lips and made a loud kissing sound as he lifted his fingers away from his mouth. He then leaned down and warmly embraced his old professor before kissing him three times in an alternating, cheek-to-cheek manner.

Along with his assistant, Dr. Ballantino remained at the entry way by the front door, watching the driver remove and then neatly fold his blazer before he hopped into the driver's seat. Amanda excitedly waved goodbye from the rear window as the limousine pulled away.

"Wonderful people," Dr. Ballantino said.

"Lovely," his assistant said, nodding in agreement.

As Dr. Ballantino maneuvered his chair back into the house, his assistant followed and then closed the door behind them.

"What a relief," Dr. Ballantino said, ripping his hands out from the confines of the tight Velcro armrest straps. He stood up, stretched his arms and then shoved the motorized chair to the corner of the room.

"What a week," his assistant said.

"How about some champagne," Dr. Ballantino said, walking toward the kitchen.

"Absolutely," she said, enthusiastically. She then retrieved glasses from the liquor cabinet and grabbed several tea light candles.

"Can you put on our song?" Dr. Ballantino asked.

In the next room, she turned on soft music. Dr. Ballantino walked back into the living room where he poured bubbling champagne into the tall crystal flutes that his assistant had gotten from the wall rack.

"Perfect song," Dr. Ballantino called out. He then said, "Come in here, my love."

As she stepped back into the room, Dr. Ballantino pulled her forward and lifted her off her feet for a moment before gently kissing her lips.

"My Mr. Meticulous," she said as they rubbed noses. They tilted their glasses and drank champagne until their glasses were dry.

In a dark room, illuminated only by flickering candle flames, they slow danced cheek-to-cheek until Dr. Ballantino sang the very last note of, "Endless Love," into her ear.

After blowing out the candles, they walked together, hand-in-hand, up the tall winding flight of stairs.

ABOUT THE AUTHOR

RICHARD S. COHEN is the author of THE LOVE DRUG: MARCHING TO THE BEAT OF ECSTASY. He has published manuscripts in *GLR Worldwide, Explorations in Criminal Psychopathology, Progress in Neuropsychopharmacology* and *Biological Psychiatry*. Subsequently, his publications have been popularly cited in worldwide scientific literature including *European Psychiatry, Behavioral Brain Research, Journal of Forensic Sciences, International Journal of Neuroscience* and *Lancet*.

He is a psychotherapist with his Master's in Psychology and Master's in Social Work.

Made in the USA
Coppell, TX
17 December 2022

89807572R00139